I0603344

THE FALCONER

THE DAWNLAND CHRONICLES. BOOK 2

JENNY BOND

Copyright © 2021 by Jenny Bond

All rights reserved.

No part of this book may be reproduced in any form or by any electronic or mechanical means, including information storage and retrieval systems, without written permission from the author, except for the use of brief quotations in a book review.

Cover design DAMONZA.COM

ISBN 978-0-6484606-6-4

A catalogue record for this book is available from the National Library of Australia

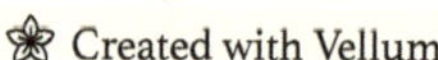

Created with Vellum

PROLOGUE

Tabby was led to her place next to the magistrates' bench. Her seat, an exceedingly uncomfortable straight-backed chair made of pine, was as hard as a ploughman's palm. *Crafted by an ill-skilled carpenter*, she guessed. She half hoped it would not be a lengthy trial for her back would not endure, although in truth she was willing to bear the discomfort for as long as was necessary. Her life was at stake, after all.

She had taken the counsel of friends and worn a simple, pale-green bodice and skirt. Both were borrowed, of course, as were the delicate pins that held her wild red hair in check. Scanning the faces in the courtroom, her gaze fell upon those most familiar, yet their sympathetic expressions did nothing to still the waves of unease ebbing and swelling in her belly.

Dummer and the other magistrates entered wearing their robes of office, their powdered wigs. 'Pomp and circumstance,' her father might have scoffed once. Recalling the sound of his voice as it had been all those years ago was a comfort to her now.

Tabby and the spectators rose at the magistrates' arrival, then sat, following their lead.

She waited as the men shuffled their documents and conferred about various points of interest. It was a torture of sorts, as though being probed and examined by a thousand eyes, a thousand whispers, a thousand suspicions: *Did she do it? A healer? Everyone knows ruddies have fiery tempers. Anything is possible.*

Attempting to inhale a deep, bolstering breath of air, she found herself hampered by the stay she was wearing. She fidgeted in her seat for a moment, twisting her torso left to right as a bear would seeking relief for an itchy back against a tree trunk. No trees here. No bears, either, although she would wager Governor Dummer was just as fierce.

Dummer seemed to be eyeing her with a curious, disapproving stare. She watched as he turned to the onlookers, waiting for them to silence before proceeding.

'Mistress Post, you have been charged with murder.'

A murmur went through the courtroom.

'During this trial, the Crown will present the facts of your crime and your motives for committing such a heinous and unwarranted act. If we can find no circumstances under which your crime was justified then, as you are aware, the penalty is death. You have refused your right to representation, arguing that it is only yourself who can tell your story. Is this correct, Mistress Post?'

She looked at Dummer squarely. 'I believe that is the only way my truth will out, for who knows but me and the dead man precisely what happened on that day?'

Dummer raised an eyebrow. 'A simple "yes" would suffice, Mistress Post.'

A bible rested on the arm of her chair. She had anticipated this moment during the week she spent in prison in the lead up to the trial, and before that as she travelled to Boston from Moosehead Lake. What would she do when called to swear on God's Holy Book? She decided she would not know until the moment was upon her. Now, as fast as a jack rabbit in front of a prairie fire, the moment had arrived. Tabby decided that if there were a God, she would rather have him for her than against. She placed her hand on the book and repeated the oath after Dummer.

Then came the question all present were waiting for.

'How do you plead?' Dummer asked.

A shadow passed across her blue eyes for an instant before she looked directly at the governor.

'Guilty,' she responded.

1

TWO MONTHS EARLIER

MOOSEHEAD LAKE, MAINE

May 1725

As Tabby placed one foot into the canoe, her other sank into the mire of the bank. Tabby eyed Edie, who had already found her usual perch on the bow, expecting the falcon to comment. In Tabby's mind, the bird's wide, inquisitive eyes, tilted head and fractionally open beak often implied the falcon was on the verge of speech, especially after an occurrence such as the one she just witnessed. Tabby imagined Edie quick-witted, with a wry, backhanded sense of humour that would be difficult to rival. Edie looked at things with her entire body, twitching her head this way and that, her yellow cere appearing golden as the sunlight skimmed across its waxy surface.

With a shake of her head and a grin at her own foolishness, Tabby removed her foot from the mud, unlaced the boot and dunked it into the lake water, swishing it from side to side. A thin film of fractured ice skinned the lake, glistening like cut crystal in the mid-morning sun. The thaw was late this year. Tabby watched the mud turn the sky-blue water murky for a moment then clear as the sediment dispersed, drifting to the bottom of the lake. In an instant, her fingertips grew numb. As she looked into the water, a vision became clear in her mind of Augusta, her eventual destination. Tabby had important business to see to there.

Once the boot was clean, Tabby removed the laces and draped them over the seat of the canoe, then cleaved open the neck as far she was able in the hope it would dry quickly. Edie looked at the boot quizzically. It appeared to be gaping at her, tongue exposed insolently.

'Don't fly off with it now,' Tabby said, pointing her finger at Edie. 'Once clean and dry, I'll be able to trade them for something.'

Edie blinked her large black eyes. Tabby removed the other boot from her right foot, sat it next to its sodden mate then rummaged in her back basket for her moccasins. Well-tanned, oiled and supple, her moccasins were all she needed. What's more, if they happened to receive a dunking, the water ran out of them after just one wringing. She placed the boots under the seat, out of sight, annoyed that she had ever accepted them in the first place.

They were a lumberman's boots, received in Hallowell last October, before the lake and the Kennebec River had frozen. The man had been killed as he stood beneath a great white oak. A large branch had fallen to earth, striking the poor lumberman's skull as it did so. Tabby was told by onlookers that he had watched its flight but stood frozen, unable to shift from its path. The distressed witnesses had rushed to him immediately and moved the branch away, but by the time Tabby arrived at his camp, it was too late for healing. Recalling that time, Tabby shunted her sorrow aside and instead praised herself for not having a superstitious bone in her body. There would be no other way she could have accepted the boots of a dead man.

She had sat by the dying lumberman and watched – watched and waited and listened as blood pooled like warm molasses in the leaves beneath his head. In his mother tongue, Alhwin described the Breg, a river he had lived by as a boy, his brother-in-law Per quietly translating the words for Tabby. To her mind, it seemed there was very little difference between the Breg and the Kennebec – water roads connecting people, linking life and death, flowing to the sea.

After Alhwin died, Tabby helped Per lay out the body and stitch the shroud. Tabby had stopped Per from placing the final stitch through Alhwin's nose; there was no doubt that the poor creature was dead. Thinking back, it still saddened Tabby that Alhwin, although only seventeen, had left no widow behind. He had appeared a most respectful and eloquent young man. *Yet a girl alone and penniless would come to no good end*, she reasoned.

Tabby received the boots as payment for her service. It was the first time she had worn boots such as Alhwin's. The leather had seemed unforgiving, so she had packed her moccasins in the canoe as well. Thinking back, she couldn't recall why she accepted the boots as payment. But Per had nothing else to offer and he was so grateful for her services – for her to deny him payment would have only deepened his sorrow.

Before she pushed off from the bank, Tabby closed her eyes and took a deep breath, capturing the piney smell of the spruce trees. May was when the air was sharpest, Tabby believed, when every smell was distinct and pricked her nostrils like needles. In her heart, a sense of immense foreboding took hold. This was always the way when she departed Moosehead Lake. With the surrounding greens of the forest and the jagged mountains looming, it was a refuge, a haven. She always thought twice about leaving, even in the direst emergencies.

The Indians were about by the time Tabby lifted an oar. She raised her hand in farewell to Mongwau, who was walking to the river, tools in hand, children by his side and at his feet.

'Be safe, *Mekwi*,' he called in his own language.

'Always,' Tabby replied. 'Will you watch over my father?'

Mongwau nodded with a certain ease, as though the question need not have been asked.

Four years ago, not long after Tabby had first come to Moosehead, Mongwau had helped her build the canoe she sat in now. He was considered a master builder of the Penobscot people. He had shown her how to shape the bark around cedar frames that had been made soft and pliable by the waters of the lake. Tabby had not realised wood could be so supple, but Mongwau had worked it like toffee. The painting of the seams with warm pine resin was left to Mongwau's children; they were expert at the task. They had slathered it on, thick as butter.

All Hallows' Eve was the last time she had paddled down the Kennebec to Augusta. During the months between, when the snow fell in stinging panels and the river water hardened into dusted marble, Tabby had used snow-shoes to visit those nearby, or borrowed Mongwau's donkey if she needed to travel further. While there had been some consideration of purchasing a sleigh last summer, the sale had fallen over when Tabby had spied a crack in the stan-chions. When the river was neither water nor ice, Tabby chose not to travel at all, unless a person was exceedingly ill or a woman was in travail.

At the end of leaf fall, when Tabby noticed woodpeckers

moving to shared nests for warmth and muskrats digging their burrows deep in the riverbed, she knew it was going to be a harsh, long winter. Why, as late as April 22nd the ice could still support a sleigh bearing the weight of old Thomas Higgins to his burying place in Portland. But it had thawed and now, as she paddled past Sugar Island just before turning into the neck of the river, she let out a low resonant whistle made of three parts with varying tones. A whistled response of a similar length came from the woods.

My father is just an echo, thought Tabby as she passed, *kept barely audible by my fading memories.* It was becoming more difficult to believe that Ephraim Post the man still existed. But he did. He had just whistled proof of it.

The return journey to Augusta would take a month or longer. Her first stop was Winslow. A message had arrived the day before from Henry Farnham. His wife Sarah had the fever and couldn't nurse Henry Junior. Scant on detail, the note that was delivered by the girl who helped Sarah spin flax offered no more information. Tabby suspected broken breast, as she had only delivered Henry Junior on March 12th.

Tabby had instructed the girl to swathe Sarah's breast with a cold tow compress. She was certain that should offer the woman some relief until Tabby could reach her, enough to feed young Henry which was, after all, the best remedy. If the fever became worse, the girl was to rub Sarah's feet vigorously with liquor to draw the heat down from her head. Before leaving the lake, Tabby had topped up the dried rosemary, sorrel and dandelion in her black apothecary case in order to be ready to make a poultice if broken breast was, in fact, the source of the fever.

Other people would call on her services once they heard she was moving down river. Word travelled fast along the

Kennebec, faster, Tabby reckoned, than the water at Cold Stream Falls. With no physicians or surgeons in the region – just quacks and charlatans – Tabby's services were always in demand. No doubt she would be required to tarry for a night or two in some places, tending to those who were too ill to leave, and to ensure her own rest and good health. But patience was a virtue Tabby possessed in abundance.

It was six months since Matthew Hawkins, the town clerk at Hallowell, had told her of an Algonquin Indian named Achak. He'd gleaned that this man knew something of her father's plight. 'Achak' meant 'spirit' and, according to the clerk, he lived up to his name. However, he usually appeared in Augusta at the onset of summer, trading pelts, furs and the like.

During that half year, Tabby's skin had itched with impatience as though she had walked unknowing into a swarm of yellowjackets. But she waited until May, teeth gritted, before commencing her journey. It had been most unbearable at night when there were no distractions. Lying awake, watching the embers of the fire, Tabby would list the questions she hoped to ask Achak when they finally met. It was the only means she had to ease her restlessness. Doing so convinced her that her inactivity was not wasted.

Hawkins had also mentioned a new arrival in Augusta, a landowner and merchant. This man, whose name Hawkins could not recall, had established himself as a banker of sorts in the booming trading town. Hawkins had heard that the Englishman, dealing in lumber, coin, grain, musket balls, furs, pelts and wampum, had already built a reputation as a trustworthy sort.

Tabby eyed the back basket sitting beneath Edie at the bow of the canoe. It housed a bag of coin and wampum that bulged in the same way Mister Hamlin's belly did after consuming a particularly well-cooked batter pudding. She looked to the future.

Tabby was nine and twenty. Although she was a healthy, handsome woman, or so she observed on the rare occasion she examined herself in a looking glass, opportunities for marrying had long passed her by. Yet there was still time to build a proper home with her father, and with it to rebuild the life they had once shared. She had in mind to establish a practice where patients could come to her. She couldn't live in a wigwam forever, after all. Neither would she be able to navigate the Kennebec as she aged and her strength abandoned her.

Then there was Kirkcaldie. Tabby did not include him in her plans – he had no suitable place there – but she liked the salty taste of him and his rough hands on her skin. She would stop in on him on the return journey. She had not seen Kirkcaldie since February, when an unseasonal case of canker rash had afflicted Dolly Weston and Tabby found herself nearby.

She missed him.

Tabby looked at Edie, who was offering the disapproving glare of a school dame. It was as though she was privy to Tabby's thoughts. The falcon did not seem to approve of Tabby's occasional bedmate.

'Oh, Edie ...you've just got to get to know Kirkcaldie. Then you'll like him as much as I do.'

Alerted by the song of a thrush, the falcon's head darted left towards the rocky monolith of Mount Kineo.

It appeared that Edie remained unconvinced.

2

It took Tabby the best part of the day to reach the Farnhams's. When she finally did, the log cabin was in an uproar. Henry Junior mewed in hunger and Sarah groaned and wailed in discomfort. Tabby gleaned that respite only arrived when exhaustion sent the baby into a fitful sleep or Sarah was sent drifting into a delirium by fever.

A blazing fire at the hearth had turned the two-room cabin into a furnace, and the girl who had delivered the note to Tabby had taken it upon herself to cut Sarah's hair back to the scalp. Unlike the soaring temperature in the cabin, the cropping of the hair would do no damage to Sarah's eventual outcome, but it made Tabby seethe when people resorted to unfounded remedies based on superstition.

Within a minute of entering the cabin and taking in the full extent of the chaos, Tabby had scolded Henry Senior for uncountable offences.

'You should have sent for me sooner.'

'Your note did not convey the seriousness of your wife's unease.'

'Why has a nurse not been found to see to the baby? There are any number of newborn babes in Winslow.'

'The fire is too hot!'

When Tabby inquired whether Sarah's feet had been rubbed, the girl, whose name was Hepsy, replied that the only liquor on hand was Mister Farnham's rum and he had forbidden her to use it.

'Do you not want your wife to be well, man?' Tabby had rebuked before violently throwing wide the shutters and the door. Following a final grimace and a glance at the scene before her, Tabby took leave of the mayhem temporarily for, at this point, a minute or two would not make any difference to Sarah or her baby, and she feared she would utter words she could not rescind. Ephraim Post had once been fond of telling people that his daughter's fuse was as 'short as washday grace'.

Edie, who waited on the gatepost, flew to her mistress, descending on Tabby's outstretched forearm. Nuzzling her face into the soft neck feathers of the bird, Tabby took in her nutty scent and immediately regained her composure. Tabby loved everything about Edie – the way her nape feathers bristled in affection, the way she reacted when she heard something, lifting herself taller for a moment and the slight movement of her tail, as sleek and pointed as an arrowhead. But she especially loved the way her eyes searched for and found Tabby's, even when the bird was high in the sky.

'Good girl,' she said to Edie. 'This might take some time. Sarah is exceedingly unwell.' Tabby stroked the ridged feathers of the bird's back. 'It's dusk, do you not see? Time you found some supper.'

As Edie shifted along the muscles of Tabby's arm, Tabby

felt the pinch of the falcon's talons through the leather sleeves of her tunic. She smiled at her friend.

'Ah, but I can tell from the ache in my arm that you are getting fat, my good lady. You may want to watch what you dine on this evening.'

As though sensing Tabby's tone, Edie released a high pitched *chitter* then flew off into the distance. Tabby watched her flight until Edie disappeared over the river and into the glowing pink of the sunset.

BY THREE O'CLOCK in the morning, Sarah's fever had quieted. Her head was cool and she slept peacefully. Henry Junior was nestled in the crook of her arm. Tabby had sent Henry Senior to find a nurse for the baby.

'There are at least seventeen babies that were born in the last year in Winslow,' she had explained. 'And those are just the ones that I had a hand in birthing. I warrant any one of those mothers will nurse your son. Start with the Moodys by Goldfinch Creek.'

In the meantime, she had rubbed Sarah's feet with Henry Senior's rum (taking two or three liberal swigs from the bottle herself) and Hepsy comforted the baby as best she could with a sugar rag that Tabby had instructed her in making. When Henry Senior returned, perhaps three hours later, he entered the cabin in front of a slight, mouse of a girl who held a baby in her arms. Tabby, who recognised most of the residents of the Kennebec settlements, had never seen this girl before. Not much more than a child herself, the girl's complexion was almost grey. The light wood-brown hair that hung to her waist in long, narrow strips gave her the appearance of a ghost. She was wearing little more than a simple shift. Her stockings and shoes were splashed with mud (no doubt from the ride on Henry Senior's horse) and a tattered, crocheted shawl hung around her shoulders. She had a faraway look about her. Uncertain. Neither here nor there.

Tabby tucked Sarah's feet under the covers, replaced the cork in the rum bottle and, setting the bottle on the table, shot Henry Senior a hard look, daring him to touch it. She approached the girl with a smile.

'Thank you for helping this family.'

Tabby wrapped her hand around the girl's scrawny shoulder, doubting such a wispy thing could feed two babes. She led her to the bed.

'My name is Tabby, and this is Sarah. She has been deathly ill, and she is not out of the woods yet. I must get her baby fed or I will have a second patient on my hands.'

The girl nodded in understanding.

'What's your name?'

'Polly Cool,' she said, taking in Tabby's attire.

Her voice was tuneless, as meek as gruel. The surname was unfamiliar to Tabby.

'Where are you from, Polly?'

'Harper's Creek,' she replied.

Tabby squinted, attempting to recall the settlement.

'It's about seven miles from here. Near Vassalboro,' said Polly.

'In my haste, I got lost on the way to Goldfinch Creek,' Henry Senior cut in. 'Came across a settlement in the backwoods,' he said, glancing at the girl. 'Her husband will surely be grateful of the payment.'

Tabby ignored his last remark and turned to the girl again.

'And your baby?' Tabby asked. 'What's her name?'

'Olive.'

'How old is she?'

'She was born in March.'

'She is very beautiful,' Tabby said holding out her arms.

Polly gave her daughter to Tabby. The baby was tightly swaddled in a thick woollen blanket, lightly coated with dew. From the weight of the child in her arms, Tabby could tell that, despite her rake-like appearance, the young mother's milk was plentiful and nourishing. She drew the blanket down to the baby's chin. Olive's cheeks were pink and plump. Tabby cupped her hand over the baby's round head, relishing the sensation of the warm down against her palm. It was almost like fur.

'Polly, please fetch young Henry there,' said Tabby, indicating the bed where Sarah and her son were sleeping. 'While I do not advocate waking a sleeping baby, mind, I fear his sleep is born from lack of sustenance. It is likely his little body is giving up. Be careful when you put him to your tit. He will be hungry.'

Henry Junior woke immediately as Polly leant over him. Her milk had issued liberally during the ride there, almost soaking her shift. The scent sent him into a storm. One-handed, Polly instinctively unlaced the undergarment at the neck and, within just a second or two, Henry Junior – like a hound sniffing out a fox – had discovered the breast and latched on with fierce intent. Polly's eyes shot wide open – the first sign of animation Tabby had seen in the girl – and a sharp pang of regret coursed through Tabby's own breasts.

After indicating a chair where Polly could sit, she quickly removed herself from the scene. With too much still to accomplish before resting, Tabby left the pair and returned to Sarah, taking Olive with her.

Tabby burrowed Polly's child against Sarah's side then

went about examining the ill woman's breasts. Both were swollen. Lumps as hard and smooth as river rocks seemed to jostle for prominence in the left. It was possible Tabby could control the fever for a day or two, but if the swellings were not seen to the fever would return. As she tied Sarah's shift, Tabby considered how to proceed.

'Hepsy,' she began, striding to the corner where she had left her black case. 'Put some water on to boil – not a whole kettleful, mind – then fix Polly some supper. That child will feed all night if I let it, and I intend to, and Polly will need fuel. Then find the girl something to wear – her shift is soaked through, and filthy from the journey. After that, tidy this place up. I won't have Sarah awaken to this mess.'

As Hepsy began on the tasks, Tabby squatted by her bag. She removed a calico pouch that was tied by string at the opening. It was filled with dandelion root that she had ground to a fine powder. Emptying a large quantity into a clay beaker, she then added a quantity of rosemary oil. While waiting for the water to boil, she checked on Polly and Henry Junior. He was still feeding ravenously. Polly gazed at the child through sleepy eyes.

'Your journey must have been a long one,' Tabby murmured looking at the girl. 'But you will be able to rest soon.'

Once the boiled water was added to the beaker, the ground dandelion root quickly transformed into a thick beige paste that Tabby applied directly to Sarah's breasts, painting it on liberally with the back of a wooden spoon. Finally, a tow compress was laid across the woman's chest and the shift retied. Tabby stood over the patient for some time, hands on hips, in contemplation.

'You look worried.'

The voice came from across the room. Tabby turned. It

was Polly. Henry Junior was propped at her shoulder. She was stroking his back in gentle circles. There was more colour to the girl's face now.

'Well, Sarah has a number of worrying swellings.'

Tabby walked slowly to the girl and sat. Polly nodded, slowly.

'She's ailing from broken breast. Some call it milk fever. I don't know why it happens,' she said, sighing, 'but my guess is that the milk in a woman's breast is similar to the water in the Kennebec. The river flows freely if you let it, but if it's dammed, or blocked by rocks or fallen trees after a storm, then the water builds up behind it, creating its own kind of havoc – new channels and waterways, and the like.'

She looked at Polly.

'But milk is not water. If it has no release, it will sour and rot.'

Hepsy went over to Polly and placed a bowl of oatmeal close at hand on the table near her, along with a pot of molasses. Tabby gazed at the steaming bowl as she went on.

'You see Polly, I cannot change the cause of the illness. For when a woman has too much milk, it's like the river when it floods, and I am no match for Mother Nature.'

It helped Tabby to talk through the problem. Sarah's was the worst case of the illness she'd ever seen.

'So, the swellings are milk?' Polly asked, swallowing a heaped spoonful of oatmeal before placing Henry on her other breast. He clamped on with determination. Tabby believed his pale cheeks were becoming pinker by the second.

'Not exactly.' Tabby paused for a moment, considering how to explain an ailment she did not fully comprehend herself. 'The swellings are inflammations.'

Polly frowned.

'A little like boils, but on the inside of the body. That's why midwives and healers apply poultices, same as with a boil – to draw the pus out.'

Polly made a small *huh* of surprise and understanding. She was quiet for a time before speaking again.

'My brother had a boil on his leg, back when he was twelve or so. My father had to cut him with his jackknife and squeeze the pus out. Jonas screamed like a pig half stuck.'

The girl laughed. She was pretty when she laughed.

Tabby smiled. If the poultices did not work, she would have to lance the swellings. Although she had lanced boils and ulcers with a folding pocketknife – a gift from her father when she had fished with him as a young girl – she had never cut a patient in that manner before. Tabby had amputated limbs that had been crushed by a fallen tree or gnarled like a blackthorn by disease, but cutting into living flesh was different, especially a woman's breast. They gave pleasure and nourished life, after all. No, she had never cut through clean healthy skin, even though she carried a knife for the exact purpose in her black case.

Exchanged in Winthrop for three bags of rice, the 'scalpel', as it was known, was made in Sheffield, England. The place of manufacture was engraved into the back of the small wooden box in which the instrument was housed. Although she had never used it, Tabby had often removed her scalpel from its box to study the blade, hoping to gain courage through familiarity. So thin and keen was it that she was sure it would have no trouble splitting a hair. Beauty and violence were contained within the tool in equal measure, like the grace of a bobcat pouncing on its prey.

Yet, despite its artistry, a tool it was – a means of carrying out a particular task. This is what she told herself in her efforts to earn a modicum of ease with the instrument.

Holding the wooden handle between her fingers, she would turn it this way and that. But its elegance never felt comfortable in her large, rough-skinned hand. Then her heart would race, and her mouth would grow as dry as tinder and she would hastily place the instrument back in its box, close the lid and secure the tiny gold clasp. Neither the miner who had hammered into the earth's veins with bone-shattering determination to extract the ore nor the smith who had crafted the instrument with a steady hand and an artist's eye could have imagined that their labours would be wasted.

'Well, hopefully, it won't come to that,' Tabby said, finally responding to Polly. She rose and moved to her patient.

WITH THE AID OF POLLY, who took charge of the infants, and Hepsy, who she found reliable once given adequate instruction, Tabby changed the poultices on Sarah's breast every three hours for the next day and night. When the fever returned around noon, she tirelessly rubbed Sarah's feet with Henry's rum as Hepsy bathed the patient's head with cool clouts. She sent Henry away to do his work. Sarah would be no better off, she told him, if the sheep were not fed and ran afoul in their search for sustenance. Also, Tabby resented the evil eye she was shot each time she reached for the rum.

During these hours, she ate sparingly and slept not at all. By four o'clock the fever had waned and Tabby, still in a trance of urgent focus, lifted the poultice from Sarah's chest to examine the woman's breasts. No longer did Sarah wince when Tabby lay her hands on them, and the swellings seemed to have lessened. Closing her eyes as she pressed fingers into flesh, Tabby struggled to recall the size and firmness of the lumps she had felt only hours before. Were they getting smaller and softer or was she, in her tiredness and desperation, merely imagining it? The scalpel in her case flashed silver before her vision. Tabby opened her eyes with a gasp but, noting Sarah's expression of dismay, restored herself immediately.

'Merely a cramp in my back,' she said, smiling comfortingly at the worried woman. 'I should take some rest.'

TABBY REMOVED herself from the cabin and the gentle honeysuckle breeze immediately brought her back to her senses. Cloudless was the sky Tabby scanned in search of Edie, the violet haze of twilight only just evident in the distance. *What mischief does Edie make when we are apart, what heights does she soar to?* Tabby wondered. When her friend wasn't close by, Tabby felt the loss acutely, as though a small hole in her heart had formed and was left gaping.

All was quiet, as it always seemed to be at this amber hour of dusk, even though all around, from the woodland canopy to the damp litter of the forest floor, life and death were in chorus. For Tabby, stepping into the invisible world of silent hunting and feeding was enlivening. There was a mysterious readiness, a sense of expectation in the air that she drank in after being confined for so many hours, waiting.

Walking some distance from the cabin so as not to disturb the inhabitants within, she pressed her thumb and forefinger into the corners of her mouth and discharged a lusty whistle, cracking for an instance the brittle husk of noiselessness. She rolled down the sleeve of her tunic. Within moments she heard the song of Edie's wings coming towards her over the treetops. First landing with a clatter on the cabin's shingled roof, Edie hopped down to the steps leading into the home then took a gentle flight to her mistress. Tabby smiled when she sensed the bird's talons grip her forearm. Moving up her arm, Edie nuzzled her crown into Tabby's ear, making her laugh.

'Will she come to the sound of any person's whistle?'

Tabby spun around quickly, and Edie flapped the wide expanse of her wings to regain her balance, creating a gust that blew Tabby's ginger hair into her eyes. Pushing it aside, she saw it was Polly. Tabby had left her resting on a pallet by the hearth with Olive. Since her arrival, Hepsy had found her a clean shift and a grey homespun pinafore to wear, as well as a cap that kept her long hair in check. The garments made her appear less shadowy.

'Well, I hope not. She's not meant to. I'd be lost without her.'

'Does she hunt for you? Some Injins use them to hunt.'

Tabby shook her head.

'Edie and I hunt for ourselves.' She looked the bird in the eye. 'Don't we?'

Polly continued. 'I noticed your bow. It's an Injin bow, isn't it?'

Nodding, Tabby stroked Edie's head.

'You dress like an Injin, too.'

'Leggings and a tunic are better suited to my line of work,' Tabby said, winking. 'I haven't worn stays or a skirt for a long time.'

'Can I pet her?' Polly asked, taking a hesitant step towards Tabby.

'Of course.' Tabby held out her arm. 'She likes it best

when you stroke from her head just to the top of her mantle.'

Polly watched closely as Tabby demonstrated the technique. Once given permission, the girl stepped forward confidently and patted Edie, just as she had been shown.

As she was doing so, Tabby asked, 'You know a great deal about Indians.'

'Mister Cool has had some dealings with them. He trades rum for wampum and furs.'

'Mister Cool is your husband?' said Tabby, her interest piqued.

Polly nodded as she studied Edie's slate-coloured feathers.

'Have *you* ever had dealings with Indians?'

Polly moved closer to Tabby, still patting Edie. Then she rubbed her cheek against the soft feathers, closing her eyes in pleasure for a moment. Tabby loved this sensation herself. Smell and touch combined into one glorious moment.

'Mister Cool says trading isn't for women and we should stay inside when the Injins are about in case they get ideas.'

'We?' Tabby asked.

'Me and the children and the other women.'

'How many –'

Tabby's inquiries were interrupted when the door of the cabin opened with a bang and Hepsy ran out onto the porch. Mistress Farnham had woken and asked for food.

'God has chosen to show mercy on the poor woman!' Hepsy cried.

With distance enough between them to go unnoticed, Tabby *tssk*ed and rolled her eyes at Hepsy's proclamation of divine salvation.

Polly looked at her strangely for an instant, not in disapproval, but a with kind of disbelief clouding her complexion.

'You don't hold much with God, do you?'

Shrugging in ambiguity, Tabby had known men whose minds could travel and see into the spirit world of their ancestors. Their souls were lit with a different sort of light.

After rubbing her face against Edie's for an instant, Tabby released the bird. She flew into a nearby maple, ready to join the hushed hunt. As Tabby walked back to the cabin behind Polly, her relief over Sarah's recovery was overshadowed by her interest in the girl and her husband, Mister Cool.

Perhaps she could persuade Polly to talk with her further.

BY THE MORNING, Sarah's swellings had disappeared entirely. Tabby allowed the certainty of her patient's recovery to wash away her fears. The scalpel would not be needed, not this time. Not ever, Tabby hoped, if she could do well enough with her potions, salves, ointments and poultices.

That afternoon, Hepsy returned to her own home. The women in her family were spinning yarn and her mother would miss her help. Tabby was glad to see her go. She was a dull girl who, Tabby had learnt, thought more highly of herself than her actions warranted. Sarah sobbed each time she remembered her fleeced head and ran her palm over its poorly shorn tussocks. The hair would grow back but the tragic recognition on Sarah's face made Tabby want to cry, too.

Tabby remained for a further two days, taking over the household chores until Sarah was well enough to resume her duties. Gradually, Henry Junior returned to Sarah's breast and the balance of everyday life seemed to be restored in the Farnham cabin. Tabby could hear the harmony in the tone of their voices, in the subtle sounds of dough being kneaded and the shovel sliding through soil in the garden. While Tabby gained great satisfaction from healing, it was this that she enjoyed the most: guiding people back to the everyday after illness.

Typically, people relished life and appreciated those around them just a little more after being poorly and Tabby was an avid spectator to their spiritual expansion. Despite Tabby's urgings that she should return to her own family, Polly decided to stay as well, saying her other children would be looked after well enough by the other women.

The 'otherness' disturbed Tabby, although she wasn't sure why. Like an out-of-sight tick bite, it irritated and itched.

Over the course of two days, as they spun wool, washed, sewed and baked, Tabby discovered Polly was not yet nineteen years of age and had, since she married Jeremy Cool five years ago, delivered four children. They ranged in ages from four-year-old Timothy to baby Olive. They had lived all over Maine and Massachusetts, but had settled on a piece of land in the woods beyond Vassalboro last fall, a place Polly called Harper's Creek. Here Mister Cool had founded the Colony of the Fellowship of Universal Believers.

Sharing goods, labour and coin with three other families, the group believed that all God's children would be saved regardless of their good deeds or their sins. And, until God saw fit to do just that on Judgement Day, they decided to shun society. Tabby had heard of such factions before now. The Puritans of the Massachusetts Bay Colony had spread far, but the Dutch and Germans had brought with them a different set of beliefs, spurring the confidence of individuals to break loose in search of freedom, religious or otherwise. Tabby understood this yearning – a longing to tread a singular path in the world.

'Is Mister Cool a minister?' Tabby questioned as they knitted stockings by the hearth one early afternoon. It had been a warm day and the fire burned low but, as Tabby checked the shadows cast in the room, it would not be long before more wood was needed.

Henry Senior had turned the ground in the garden that morning and the fresh scent of dirt drifted through the window. It was the scent of spring and it brightened Tabby's spirit. Sarah was resting with the babies in the other room and Henry Senior had gone into Winslow to buy seeds. Tabby had assured Sarah that she would see to the planting of turnips, carrots and cabbages before she departed.

'I don't think so,' the girl replied. 'Tell the truth, I've never asked him.'

The words were offhand.

Perhaps it was her emboldened spirit or merely the fact that the two had grown extremely familiar over the past few days that prompted Tabby's next query.

'But you have been married for five years?'

Polly shrugged and offered a nervous smile.

Tabby saw that no answer would be forthcoming this day. She returned Polly's smile and the women went on knitting.

SARAH and her baby were in good spirits the following morning. After Tabby completed the planting, it was time for her to leave. Henry Senior was to deliver Polly and Olive to Vassalboro. Tabby's payment – eight skeins of wool – would make a decent blanket or coat come the following winter. Although it wasn't usual to pay girls such as Hepsy or Polly, as it was the custom to help each other gratis in the Kennebec settlements, Tabby knew Mister Cool expected his wife to return with payment. Polly hovered awkwardly in the background as Henry Senior gave Tabby the wool. She seemed impatient as Tabby examined the strands between her fingernails, ensuring their quality. She could see that all the while, worry was etching lines in Polly's pale, freckled brow.

Before they departed, Tabby counted out a generous payment from her bag and into Polly's small, spare hand, a slender white lily. Olive was swaddled in a sling, close to her mother's breast.

'This is for you, Polly. Four shillings. You have done very well. It's almost as much as I receive for delivering a baby.'

Polly stared at the silver in her hand for some time, as though considering its worth. Nearby, Henry Senior was saddling Abram, and Sarah was admiring Tabby's work in the garden, Henry Junior in her arms.

Finally, Polly whispered, 'Thank you for this. Mister Cool would surely be cross if I returned empty handed.'

Her face reddened, seemingly embarrassed by her husband's lack of chivalry. But then she spoke again.

'But I was hoping you might pay me by another means as well.'

Tabby took Polly by the elbow, drawing her away from the cabin.

'I don't understand.'

Polly groaned quietly, gazing gravely at Tabby.

'Speak freely,' Tabby encouraged, sensing the girl's reticence.

'Well, it's just that ... I can't remember a time when I haven't been with child.'

As Polly fingered the coin in her hand, she related a tale that both saddened and angered the listener. Born in the Virginia Colony, Polly was raised on a tobacco farm, just outside Jamestown. When she was fourteen, Mister Cool had stopped at the farm looking for work. Although already in his thirties, he was charming and humorous, and he spun fine stories about the adventures he had in New France while on expedition there. He told Polly that when he returned to the colonies, he embarked on a career as a performer, excelling as a conjurer and exciting audiences with his sleight of hand trickery.

But it was not only his fingers that were fast-moving and nimble. Cool had a dexterous tongue as well and had impressed Polly's father with talk of his plans and prospects. So taken with him was he that he agreed when Mister Cool asked for Polly's hand.

'What was he doing in New France?' Tabby asked, interested.

'He claimed he was on expedition, but I doubt it now that I know him. He is a liar, Mistress. His tongue is as twisted as basket of knotted snakes.'

'Did you love him?' Tabby asked.

'I don't know. I was just a child. Looking back, I don't think so. He made me happy because he amused me with his high-minded tales. But I was happy anyway. If I had a choice, I would not have married him. But before I knew it, we were handfast and leaving Virginia, my family and my home.'

Polly explained that within weeks, Jeremy Cool's true

nature was evident. He had no prospects and no plans. Travelling as far as the Appalachians in the west and Le Coude in the north, the couple survived through theft and deception. Still formally unwed, Polly had attempted to run away one night when Cool was occupied playing cards with a group of woodsmen, but he had found her in the early morning asleep in a hollow, covered with leaves. She thought she would be safe there. But once discovered, Cool had beaten her so viciously, so uncontrollably that he was forced to take Polly to a healer, who was also a midwife. It was then she was told she was with child.

Tabby could sense herself growing warmer. Polly's history was not unusual by any means. It was not uncommon for husbands to beat their wives and keep them bound by hard labour and babies. It was neither acceptable nor moral in Tabby's eyes and, while she wanted to slice the bawbels off the offenders, she knew her role. Although she might appear manly in her leggings, she was undeniably a woman.

Yet she sensed something more about Jeremy Cool. He was a swindler who had cheated Polly's family of a daughter and cheated Polly of a life. Tabby would bet pound to a penny that he was cheating those families he was living with as well.

'And so it has been since. We never married but the children tie me to him. I love them but I cannot have anymore ... not to him.'

She paused for an instant and lowered her head as though ashamed of the admission.

'Mister Cool did not want me to come here when Mister Farnham stumbled upon us and asked for help. It was only the mention of coin that swayed him. But I was glad to get away, if only for a few days. My only reluctance to depart was born from the notion that I could not take my other three children with me ...'

Tears made the soft grey of her eyes misty.

'I've heard women talking about teas and the like, potions to stop it happening,' continued Polly, attempting to compose herself. 'You seem to be a tolerant woman who is not much taken with God, so I was wondering if you might have something that could help me.'

Tabby looked at her thoughtfully for a moment, contemplating all the awfulness contained within such a short life. She nodded. Striding back towards the cabin, she instructed Henry Senior that Polly would be just a few minutes longer. Her black case was waiting for her on the porch. From it she retrieved a small calico pouch. Checking the contents quickly, she halved the amount into a second pouch then retied the string. She rose and turned. Polly was already there behind her.

'These are wild carrot seeds. Queen Anne's Lace is the plant's other name,' she said, shaking the pouch then placing it in Polly's pocket.

'You eat them like any other seed, but take just one immediately after lying together. They may cause a slight oppression in your stomach so drink a cup of water or ale each time.'

Polly nodded in understanding as she felt for the pouch inside the fabric of her pinafore.

'Now remember: you have to eat one immediately after. They are not effective otherwise.' Tabby warned, pointing to the pocket. 'They harvest best at leaf fall. Now I know where you live, I'll call on you on my way back to Moosehead and see if we can find a patch near your settlement.'

Polly let out a huge sigh, as though she had been holding her breath since she left her parents in Virginia.

3

Although Tabby promised Polly she would visit on the return journey to Moosehead, the knowledge that Jeremy Cool was volatile provoked Tabby to follow close behind rather than wait. However, she had been stopped in her tracks only a few miles south of Winslow by a canker sore the size of Fort Western on Martha Winthrop's leg. The woman was in immense distress and had been tending to the sore herself.

Martha was one and eighty. With failing eyesight, she had not ministered to the wound adequately. Her husband had died twelve years before, more than forty years after they had lost their five children to measles. Tabby hated to see people alone. It reminded her of the mare's nest of her father's life and her heart immediately opened. Despite her desire to aid Polly, Tabby could not depart for Vassalboro until she had seen to Martha's ulcer and offered the widow her company, if only for a few days. The widow was exceedingly grateful for the kindness.

Tabby reached Vassalboro five days after she had last seen Polly riding away on the back of Henry Farnham's horse. Nothing more than a tavern, a blacksmith and a modest trading store, it was the kind of town where people knew just about everything about everybody. Yet, when she inquired at the tavern, then at the smith's forge, then in the store, no-one knew – or had even heard of – Jeremy Cool. To the knowledge of all, Harper's Creek did not exist.

Despondent, she returned to the tavern. The owner, Maurice Heathcote, seemed to take pity on her. He wiped down the bar with his sleeve, removing splashes of ale and rum, then rolled out a roughly drawn map of the area. He told Tabby he had sketched it himself earlier in the year. Nothing was to scale, but it gave a fair representation of the whereabouts of local settlers, valleys, landmarks and creeks. Together, they searched the map. There was no Cool and no Harper's Creek to be found.

'That would indicate to me, Mistress,' Heathcote said seriously, 'that if this Cool is indeed a resident of Vassalboro then he is a squatter.'

'And Harper's Creek?'

'I've never heard of the place and I have lived here since 1703. Could be this Cool has named the settlement himself.'

SHE DISCUSSED the matter with Edie later that evening. The falcon's black eyes were questioning, full of doubt; Tabby could easily discern that the bird had no inclination to find Polly Cool.

Although the nights were still cold, Tabby decided to catch her own supper and sleep under a canopy of a million stars while she was in Vassalboro. She had not done so since she had left Moosehead Lake and had found herself missing the sight of the night sky and the freedoms it suggested.

Now a low campfire burned on the bank of the Kennebec and Tabby sat threading trout onto sticks.

'I didn't spot her as a liar, Edie,' Tabby said, reassuringly. *I am a good judge of character, I know it*, thought Tabby. 'There's something not right there, my girl,' she murmured to her friend.

Tabby could sense the bird bristle with agitation and watched as she leapt down from her perch on the canoe.

'You know it, too, don't you?'

Earlier that day, Tabby decided opening a makeshift clinic in the back room of the tavern might draw Polly Cool to her, although Edie hadn't cared for the idea. She had flown away as soon as she heard Tabby discuss it with Heathcote outside the tavern. He watched the falcon's flight into the heavens.

'Is she gone for good?' he asked.

Tabby shook her head.

'It's merely a huff, a show of her displeasure.'

If Tabby was correct and Polly had been telling the truth about Vassalboro and Harper's Creek, then all the residents of the Colony of the Fellowship of Universal Believers had indeed shunned society and never ventured into town. This meant they did not trade with the local community and lived self-sufficiently, trading only with the Indians. By setting up the clinic, surely, she would meet someone who knew where the Cools lived, or Polly might hear word of Tabby's presence and come to town herself. Tabby reasoned the latter was unlikely, but she had to try for Polly's sake. Jeremy Cool had craftily manufactured an environment that kept his wife, and perhaps others, virtual prisoners. He beat Polly and raped her whenever he was desiderate, keeping her with child, knowing her prime instinct – to care for her children and see them safe – would always bind her to him.

On the first day the clinic was open, a steady stream of patients came through the door bedevilled with ailments of the nagging variety. Tabby pulled teeth, removed splinters and unblocked ears. She even fixed a displaced shoulder. Fortunately, the tavern afforded a ready supply of rum for the poor fellow as although the procedure was quick, it was immensely painful. Even with nearly two quarts warming his belly and numbing his limbs, Jeremiah Watson howled like a thousand demons when Tabby gave his arm the final twist and the shoulder popped into place.

With each patient she tended to, Tabby asked a few questions in her efforts to track down the Cools. But the Fellowship of Universal Believers were like spirits – invisible, yet present. Tabby began to wonder if she hadn't imagined Polly.

Eventually, on her third day at the clinic, as she took stock of her herbs and tonics, which had vastly diminished since her arrival in the town, Tabby heard movement in the room. She turned, expecting another patient.

Polly Cool stood in the doorway. Olive was tied in a sling close to the girl's bosom and three more children, two boys and a girl, stood behind her. Tabby brought them all into the room and closed the door, sliding the heavy bolt into the lock as an afterthought.

'Will you look my children over, Mistress?'

Tabby nodded. 'Of course. How did you know I was here?'

'I overheard an Injin tell Mister Cool. He said a healer was in town. He said that by the way she dressed, he'd have sworn she was Injin but she had a "head of flames". I knew he was talking about you.'

Apart from Olive, who was as plump and pink as when Tabby had first met her at the Farnhams's, the children were all scrawny and pale. She squeezed each pair of hands in turn. Despite the heat of the day, they were all cold.

Tabby placed an instrument to their hollow chests, the girl first and then the boys.

'What's that?' Polly asked.

'An ear trumpet,' she replied, holding the device up so Polly could examine it. 'Through it, I am able to hear the beating heart. It was given to me by a widow whose husband had just died. He was as deaf as a door.'

Tabby continued her examination. 'Do you get belly pains?' she asked the children.

Four-year-old Timothy shook his head, then reached his hand behind and into his breeches and gave his backside a thorough scratch. Tabby frowned then pointed to a pail of water and the bar of lye soap standing next to it.

'Wash your hands now, Timothy.' The boy did as he was told.

As Tabby wrote notes in her journal, she considered the best way to proceed. It was clear the children were underfed and suffering from a horrible case of worms. Apart from appearing slightly underfed herself, Polly seemed healthy, despite her circumstances. Tabby could easily give her bolstering tonics, advice on the foods the family should eat and calomel for the worms, but Tabby wanted to see how Polly and the children lived.

Despite every sinew in her body screaming against the notion, she wanted to meet Jeremy Cool.

FOR TWO SPANISH DOLLARS, Tabby negotiated the use of Heathcote's cart and two strong black bay horses. That after-noon, following a dinner at the tavern of potted pork and potatoes for all, she loaded her possessions, four children and Polly into the cart then followed the girl's directions towards the elusive Harper's Creek. Polly and the children had walked into town, so Tabby was surprised when the trip to Cool's property took over an hour. She marvelled at the fortitude of the young mother. Given this, Tabby realised Cool's settlement must only be a short way from Winslow and the Farnham cabin. She marvelled at how Henry Senior got lost so close to home.

During the journey, Tabby's mind wrestled with the hardships of the young woman seated beside her. Noticing the children had fallen asleep, Tabby finally spoke.

'Polly, would you ever consider leaving Mister Cool?' she asked quietly.

She had not spoken to her about Mister Cool until this moment, yet it seemed as though his name had been poised on the tip of her tongue all day.

'I could turn this cart around right now and be in Jamestown by nightfall tomorrow.'

Polly looked at her, frowning. 'Home to my mother and father?'

Tabby nodded.

Polly thought for a moment, turned her head and checked on her slumbering brood in the back of the cart. 'I am a very different girl to the one my parents said goodbye to.'

'That doesn't mean they would not have you back. They have grandchildren now.'

She shook her head. 'He would find me there.'

'Or I could take you to Moosehead Lake,' said Tabby. 'It's where I live. Mister Cool would never –'

'I've made my bed, Mistress,' said Polly, cutting short Tabby's argument.

Comme on fait son lit, on le treuve, the Sisters would repeat. As one makes one's bed, so one finds it. Most often the words were said in frustration or with an instructive tone, aimed to enlighten. On the day Tabby departed the convent at seventeen, Sister Angela had cupped her cheeks in her soft, doughy hands and repeated the dictum once more with an air of such grave concern and bewilderment that it prompted Tabby to doubt her mission. Was it right for her to experience the world that lay beyond the walls of the convent? she had wondered. Since then, experience had taught Tabby the truth contained in the expression, but it seemed to her that Polly had taken no role in the making of her own bed.

Tabby drove the cart as far as she could before the trees grew too dense for her to pass. The last one hundred yards was taken on foot. As they walked through the woods, she became apprehensive of what she might find when they arrived.

Halfway along the track, carrying her back basket, apothecary case and two-year-old Matthew on her hip, Tabby remembered with regret that she had left her bow and quiver in the cart. Her belly immediately twined and twisted like a conger eel.

'Did you tell him you were going into town this morning?' Tabby asked.

Polly shook her head. 'He left at dawn for an Injin camp. Said he'd be back at sunset.'

Tabby looked above her and into the sky; there were a few hours of daylight left. She wondered if Edie was nearby. Tabby trusted in the knowledge that, despite Edie's feelings towards this enterprise, she would be watching.

Then the band arrived at a clearing – a line of four cabins, built with the trees that had been felled, stood before them. The afternoon sun had waned and a pall of thin cloud cast the settlement in a palette of grey. The cabins were slapdash in design and execution – no doors, no shutters, no panes of glass in the window frames. *How do they survive in winter?* Tabby wondered.

She placed Matthew on the ground and he toddled towards one of the homes. The other children followed. In the centre of the clearing was a garden. Near the cabins, a few fat pigs and wild turkeys rooted in the dirt and leaves searching for food. Tabby wagered that with no doors to keep them out, the pigs would happily wander into the homes as well. She walked to the garden and looked over the fence. She was struck by the stench and turned away, aggrieved.

'This is how your children are getting worms, Polly,' Tabby said, attempting to keep her voice calm. It wasn't Polly's actions that angered her. 'You must use animal dung on the garden not your own waste, unless you have turned it with ashes for a number of weeks. I have dosed the children with calomel, but if Mister Cool does not dig a pit for you to use away from here, the worms will persist.'

Polly nodded in understanding and explained how her own father had built an outhouse. It was the first one in Virginia outside of Jamestown. Her mother had even hung curtains on the window. Ashes were dumped on the waste regularly and the pit was cleaned out every three months. It was clear that the young woman had been raised by parents who took pride in their home and cared for their children.

Polly knows better than to live like this, Tabby thought. *She isn't suffering with worms like her children. She must take good care of her own cleanliness, but it would be nigh-on impossible to prevent the children from having contact with the others.* Tabby glanced around the settlement, bewildered and dismayed by its poor condition. *What power does Cool have over this girl?* she wondered.

'Where are the other people who live here?' Tabby asked, suddenly alarmed by their absence.

'Mister Cool doesn't tolerate us leaving our cabins when he is travelling.'

Tabby didn't need to ask the reason for this particular peculiarity because there was no good reason. It was becoming clearer each minute that Mister Cool was a man who fed on control and power.

Accustomed to their father's rules, the children went into the cabin and Polly sat on a low stool by the front door, nursing Olive. She watched her guest closely as Tabby explored the area more thoroughly. Skirting the cabins, Tabby noted that it was practice for chamber pots to be tipped from a window or door, the contents landing only inches from the cabin and providing sustenance for the pigs and turkeys who were now pecking at the earth.

'Do you eat these beasts, Polly?' Tabby called.

Polly nodded. Tabby smiled and waved her hand, not wanting to alarm the girl.

It was a long, securely fixed chain that needed to be broken if the children, and the others, Tabby guessed, were to be free of their affliction. But even if Tabby dosed all the residents with calomel, penned the pigs and the turkeys, and a pit was dug ... She sighed at the enormity of the task. These were just the first steps of many. The garden, crowded with turnips and potatoes, needed more variety – cabbages and spinach, at the very least – to put colour in the children's' cheeks as well as Polly's, who remained sallow and wan despite the hearty meals she was fed at the Farnhams's. However, Tabby couldn't do all this alone in the dwindling hours before sunset. It seemed to her that the project would need Jeremy Cool's consent, and she doubted a man of his peculiar desires and ambitions would find merit in such an undertaking.

Despite everything that was wrong about the place, it was the silence that disturbed Tabby the most. A grim, death-like hush shrouded the remote settlement. From what Polly had told her, the poorly made, rickety mausoleums that Tabby gazed at now housed twelve children in total. Yet the settlement was quiet.

How is it possible, she mused, *for one man to wield such absolute control?*

Walking further into the forest as she mulled over the scope of the problem, Tabby brightened slightly when she discovered a liberal supply of Queen Anne's lace not far from the settlement. All she would need to do was show Polly how to pick the flowers and release the seeds.

As she was making her way back to Polly with the reassuring news of the plant, she heard a voice.

'Who gave you permission to be outside?

While it wasn't threatening by any means, Tabby detected an undertone of menace in the colour of the question. Surmising it was Cool, Tabby broke into a sprint, emerging from the forest to Cool's right. He spun around at the noise, his long, bunched hair whipping his cheek like green rye.

'Your wife was showing me the settlement, Mister Cool,' Tabby remarked as casually as she was able, although she was short of breath and her heart was pounding like a boar. 'I met her at the Farnhams's when she was kind enough to nurse Henry Junior. I thought I would drop by on my way down river to Augusta and check on baby Olive.'

Cool watched her approach across the few yards of earth that separated them. His eyes were as opaque as jade, set in skin pale and translucent as a jellyfish. Tabby returned his narrow gaze with an expression that she hoped displayed self-assurance.

'My name is Tabby Post,' she said, reaching out her hand.

Cool's thin fingers wrapped around her own sturdy digits like vines. Tabby could see Polly from the corner of her eye. She hadn't moved.

'Mistress Post is a midwife and a healer, Mister Cool,' Polly said.

He shot her a cold look.

Noting his displeasure, Tabby added, 'Harper's Creek is a difficult place to find. It's not on any map that I could see. Fortunately, Henry Farnham was able to explain to me its whereabouts. The man has a keen sense of direction.'

A long moment passed before Cool let go of Tabby's hand and smiled, displaying teeth the colour of a rat snake.

'Welcome to the Colony of the Fellowship of Universal Believers, Mistress Post. And how is my daughter?' he inquired breezily. 'Olive is a robust infant, is she not?'

'Indeed. But it is the health of your other children that concerns me, Sir.'

Cool raised an inquiring eyebrow. Tabby took the expression as licence to proceed.

'They are all beset with worms. Fortunately, there is a simple remedy known as "calomel". Everyone here should be dosed. I am afraid prevention is not as effortless, but once a pit is dug and an outhouse constructed ...'

'We see to our own here, Mistress Post.'

Cool's tone remained light but Tabby detected warning in his green eyes. For reasons Tabby could not comprehend, Polly would not leave her husband. Similarly, the idea of Tabby abandoning the girl now was inconceivable. Tabby went on, pressing, attempting to keep the atmosphere sunny.

'I understand, but I warrant that if your children are stricken then others will be, too. Worms spread like gossip after a sewing bee,' she said, laughing feebly. The insincere sound grated like an untuned fiddle.

'As I said, we see to our own. God will provide on Judgement Day.'

'By Judgement Day it will be too late,' Tabby explained. The edge she had struggled to keep from her voice reared its head, resonating in Tabby's ears.

Polly rose and took the baby inside. She reappeared instantly.

'For the sake of your children, Mister Cool, will you at least permit me to leave the calomel along with instructions regarding its use and the dose? Your wife is familiar with the digging of a pit and the maintenance of it. I am certain she would be glad to supervise the labour.'

At this he scoffed and glanced Polly's way in annoyance. Tabby suddenly feared she was doing more harm than good. Cool examined her face closely. The sun was fast fading and an icy breeze had sprung from the south, yet Tabby felt sweat trickling like hot tears down her spine. She refused to look away. Tabby detected a slim sliver of appeal in Cool's countenance. He had been attractive once, she could tell, years ago when his eyes were clear and before his complexion had become mottled by drink and time. His straggly hair was receding as well, she noticed, ebbing like the tide.

Tabby held her breath, fearing the putrid rush of air from Cool's mouth.

'Your wife told me you were in New France with an

expedition,' Tabby said, attempting to distract him. 'May I ask which one?'

Cool was silent, examining Tabby's expression with a new interest.

'Why do you ask?' His voice was as thin and reedy as a lone mosquito.

'My father and uncle travelled to New France with the forces of General John Hill,' she said, her heart pounding once more. It took all of Tabby's might to hold Cool's gaze. 'I was wondering if you might be acquainted with them.'

Cool's eyes flashed for a second in recognition. A connection was made, Tabby was certain, but he hesitated before responding.

'No ... I do not know a general by that name, nor any Post apart from yourself,' he replied.

'Is this *your* land, Mister Cool?' Tabby hazarded to ask.

'Oh, yes. Yet the governor has other ideas. He dispatched a surveying crew on Friday last.' Cool reached into his pocket and drew out a leather case.

Tabby watched as Cool's thin, spidery fingers clasped the object. It was Kirkcaldie's compass. Tabby recognised the leather case, embossed with a 'K'.

'I sent them packing, tails between their legs like cowering dogs,' said Cool, his eyes on her face.

She took a deep breath, struggling to contain her rage and concern.

'I trust no-one came to any harm?'

Cool smiled. 'I am not a violent man, Mistress Post.'

Tabby's eyes flashed to Polly for an instant then back to Cool.

'This compass was given to me in compensation for the distress the trespassers brought into the hearts of my family and brethren. They were heartily ashamed of their actions.'

Tabby knew Kirkcaldie would never give over his compass willingly. It was a surveyor's most vital tool.

'Mistress Post, you should be on your way now. It will be dark soon and the woods grow quite perilous at night.'

'From my experience, Sir, the woods are quite perilous no matter what the hour.'

Cool's mouth twitched, part grimace, part smile.

'I would advise you to leave now, Mistress Post,' he said, clutching her arm suddenly.

Tabby's heart seized.

'I will oblige you with an escort through the woods back to the Vassalboro road. The sky will be starry within the half hour.'

If she was able to break away from Cool, Tabby knew she could run swiftly through the forest, away from the odious man. But it would be dark within minutes and without a lantern or torch she feared she would lose her way, or trip or both. But to allow Cool to lead her alone into the woods was unthinkable.

As she weighed up her options, Tabby heard the familiar sweep of wings through air and, in an instant, Edie alighted on a fence post in the vegetable garden behind Cool. He turned. Tabby took the opportunity to wrench her arm from his pincer-like grasp and move swiftly to the bird. She stroked her soft mantle. Edie released a loud, fierce screech that Tabby knew to be a cry of warning.

Confidence restored, Tabby spoke. 'My friend here will escort me to the road.' Then, without seeking approval from Cool, she moved hastily towards Polly.

'A dense cluster of Queen Anne's lace lies behind your cabin, about fifty yards into the woods. It has white flowers and nestles between two fat oaks,' she whispered quickly.

Polly nodded. 'All that is required is to shake the seeds from the flower heads.'

The girl smiled weakly, her heart's staccato beat visible through the light fabric of her gown. Reluctant to leave, but with no other choice, Tabby turned and walked away from her. She passed Mister Cool, then turned back for a moment.

'I've explained to your wife the dose of calomel required. It is up to you to decide about the pit.'

Cool made no comment.

Tabby turned back to the path and began to walk. All she longed for at that moment was the safety of the woods. Aiding Polly any further would have to wait.

Edie flew from tree to tree, guiding Tabby back to the road.

'Thank you, my friend,' said Tabby as they moved quickly away from the settlement.

4

'Do you not think it is unusual, Mistress Post, to grow so close to a bird?' Dummer questioned, glancing at his notes.

Tabby rolled the question in her mind for a moment like a shiny stone.

'Not at all. Why should humans not have attachments to animals just as they would to another person? Is a bird somehow lesser and not deserving of my kindness and affection? Governor Dummer, are you a God-fearing man?'

The governor looked at Tabby over his spectacles then nodded warily.

'Then would you not agree we are all God's creatures? If it is true that God gave man – and *woman* – kind dominion over all creation then surely that means we all should find glory in it?'

He gazed on her doubtfully.

'Perhaps, Sir, if you knew how Edie and I came to be partnered ...'

Dummer, while mildly exasperated, indicated with a

nod of his large, square head that Tabby was permitted to proceed.

'It was high summer and my friend Mongwau, knowing I was in need, had told me of a plentiful supply of wild ginger he had come across in the forest. I set out at daybreak the next morning to find it, following the map he had sketched for me in the dirt with a stick by way of explanation. By noontide, when the sun was high in the sky, I felt that Mongwau had sent me on a fool's errand. I had trod the same piece of forest for hours, head down, scanning the ground for the unmistakable heart-shaped leaf of wild ginger. How could I have read Mongwau's directions so poorly? I asked myself in my frustration. I sat down to rest against a fallen branch and drank deeply from my water skin.'

Tabby paused for a moment and licked her lips. Just thinking of the moment made her thirsty.

'Wild ginger helps with physical ailments as disparate as dysentery and earache. In my profession, it is always prudent to have a ready supply. Although I was determined to keep on with the search, the dappled sunlight filtering through the branches of the tree above me made me drowsy. The pungent blend of damp earth and fallen leaves always seems to have a relaxing effect on me and –'

'Mistress Post,' Dummer interjected. 'I believe you have established the setting very well. Would you mind moving on?'

Tabby raised an eyebrow, unwilling to hasten her testimony. She cleared her throat.

'I'm unsure how long I was asleep, but I was awoken suddenly by a sharp, ear-piercing cry. It took me a few seconds to remember my whereabouts. Then I looked above me. Two falcons, clearly in great distress, were swooping at something on the ground. I rose and walked to the patch of earth expecting to find a milk snake threatening the birds' nest. However, what I found was a mottled egg, hardly bigger than a goose's, cradled in the foliage of a wild ginger plant. The egg must have fallen from the nest, landing in the cushion of the thick, dense leaves.

'Mongwau would have stepped over the egg without a moment's hesitation. He would have counselled me to let nature find its own way. However, the sorrow I felt for the parents and youngling stung my heart. I knew that if I touched the egg the mother or father would destroy it, killing the chick,' Tabby said.

A number of gasps coursed from the gallery. Dummer turned his head in that direction, an expression of disapproval etched on his stony countenance.

'You should be a storyteller, Mistress Post,' he remarked sarcastically as he turned back to her. 'Everyone is quite enthralled. Continue.'

Undeterred by Dummer's mocking tone, Tabby did just that.

'Yet there was no way for the mother and father to take the egg back to the nest that, I assumed, lay in the high branches of the tall cedar that I stood beneath. Neither would the egg survive unprotected on the forest floor.

'I picked up the egg and placed it quickly in the leather pocket I wore when collecting herbs. My hands were trembling and I feared that, in my nervousness, I would smash the fragile, buff-coloured shell. Anxious the parents would dive for me yet mindful of my original purpose, I hastily clawed some of the wild ginger from the ground. Then, cupping the egg against my thigh, I ran into the forest, far away from the grieving parents. They did not swoop or try to harm me. Perhaps they realised my actions were born from kindness.'

A small *harumph* issued from Dummer. Tabby ignored him.

'Once I was back at my canoe, my nerves finally settled and I was able to take stock. I doubted the chick would survive. Nevertheless, I made a makeshift nest for it in my pocket, swaddled it in the foliage of the wild ginger plant, then rowed back across the lake to my home.

'I did not tell Mongwau about the egg. I knew he would think me foolish and sentimental. So I made a nest of straw and leaves for Edie in my wigwam. I kept careful watch as I knew the chick was still alive. You see, at night I would hold a candle to the egg and through the glassy shell I could see her moving like a shadow puppet.

'It took Edie another ten days to hatch. When she did, I killed wood mice and finches and tore strips of their flesh away from their bones for her sustenance. When Mongwau discovered what I had done, he merely shook his head. I'm sure he thought nothing good would come of it.'

Tabby paused for a moment, lost in the memory of those early days. Then she turned to Dummer.

'But he was wrong. Only good has ever come from Edie.'

5

Tabby knew that for now, there was nothing more she could do to help Polly and delaying her departure from Vassalboro only placed the girl in more danger. So, at dawn the following morning, Tabby departed for Augusta, less than fifteen miles downriver. However, it was not a speedy journey. Once word travelled that she was about, her schedule was thrust into the hands of the ailing and afflicted, or those in travail. Still she never lost sight of the purpose of her journey: finding Achak.

She had no knowledge of the man's appearance. However, she pictured him as tall and proud, perhaps wearing a grand headdress, like some of the men in Mongwai's tribe. She imagined – hoped – that Achak would be the kind of Indian who would help her.

Many Indians had been killed in the wars. Many others had been forced to flee west, or captured then indentured or sold as slaves. But those who knew how to get along with the English – who traded with them, accepted and exploited their presence – often engaged in an adequate, if not contented, existence. Yet whether Negro, Indian or English,

Tabby often ruminated, who among mankind was ever content? There was always something just out of reach. For Tabby, that something was discovering the answer to her father's troubles.

It was the thirteenth day of June when Tabby arrived at the town. Once an important trading port, the English had all but abandoned Augusta during the Indian uprisings. Now, with Governor Dummer's forces at the advantage and a treaty imminent, settlers were returning, building homes and mills, doing business.

She was worried she might be too late, having been delayed by her stop in Vassalboro, or, perhaps, too early for Achak. Hawkins had indicated the beginning of summer and, as a rule, Indians, despite the lack of a timepiece, were more punctual than Englishmen. *Does thirteen days into a month still denote the beginning?* Tabby worried as she paddled towards the bank.

Edie alighted onto the glossy pebbles of the shoreline as Tabby dragged the canoe onto the bank. She had departed Pittston, a town nearly eight miles further south, at dawn. She'd heard news a young mother was in travail and experiencing some difficulty. While it vexed Tabby that the stop meant tracking back to Augusta the next day, what choice did she have? The sight of Pollard, the ten-pound baby boy whom she brought into the world after a twelve-hour labour, proved a potent salve for her irritation.

Standing tall for the first time since departing, Tabby twisted her shoulders this way and that as though wringing out her waist. Mimicking her mistress, the bird stretched, too, expanding one glorious, glistening blue-grey wing to its full extent while lengthening the opposite leg. The movement was repeated on the opposing side. Tabby laughed and a flock of loons huddling on the shoreline took flight, skimming across the lake. Her father had always considered the energy contained within his daughter's laughter worthy of commendation, often boasting to others that it was as irresistible as a roundelay. That was, at least, before his current troubles.

'You did none of the rowing, Edie,' she said. 'There's no good reason that you should be aching all over.'

The water lapped against their feet. Tabby stepped back but Edie lowered her beak for refreshment. This time, it was Tabby who followed suit, crouching and cooling her face, lapping river water as she did so and taking in its sweet, simple taste. The water dripped onto her tunic and she wiped her face with a sleeve. It was hot and the heat had a noise to it, a deep pulsating throb.

'Where do you think we should start looking for him, Edie?' Tabby asked, placing her hands on her hips and surveying the town.

Augusta was busier than she'd ever seen it. Water traffic, foot traffic and the movement of horses and donkeys leading carts caught her attention. Like the water road that separated the eastern and western shores of the town, the man-made road that ran parallel to the shoreline spoke of errands, engagement and occupation.

'A tavern,' Tabby concluded eventually, 'is where we should begin.'

Patrons hushed and all eyes turned her way when Tabby entered the Green Dragon Tavern. She pushed back her hat so it hung down her back, giving her hair free rein. During her journey from Pittston, it had mostly come loose from the braid and now curled like coppered ivy around her neck and shoulders. Tabby was not known in Augusta, so the image of her with her blazing red hair, fringed leggings and beaded tunic astonished the male clientele.

It took a moment for her eyes to adjust to the darkness of the establishment so she could find her bearings. She stood in the doorway for a time, allowing the mutterings and sniggers to drift towards her through the feeble light and mist of smoke, the sole marker in the gloom that the tavern was indeed inhabited. Tabby was well acquainted with this reaction. She gave the patrons time to reconcile the sight of her with their personal, preconceived pictures of womanhood before walking to the bar.

As she passed by a table, a man poked her in the rump with a finger as though seeking proof of her reality. Tabby stopped. The man, who was slightly addled by ale, turned to his companions and laughed, pleased with his gesture. Tightening her fist around the hickory limb of her bow, Tabby glanced at him in disdain, thought better of a confrontation, then continued on her way.

An Oriental, who Tabby guessed was the owner of the establishment judging from the tavern's name, was serving a customer a large mug of ale. On sighting her, he moved in her direction, offering Tabby a stunted smile and a brief nod as he approached.

'How may I help you, Mistress?' he asked, his voice gentle. He was about her own age, Tabby judged, with skin pale but aureate, as though tinged with gold.

Tabby had only seen a few Orientals in her life. She had tended to one near Sewell, a member of a felling crew she had come across. The man's ripsaw had slipped and sliced his finger to the point of no repair. It was hanging by a thread when Tabby found the man wailing. She snipped the digit off with a pair of cast iron scissors just below the knuckle then stitched the wound with twine. The Sisters at the convent had often despaired at Tabby's lack of prowess with a needle and thread when she hemmed her skirts but when it came to stitching up human flesh, she was exceedingly skilled.

'I am looking for an Indian, an Algonquin,' she said in answer to his query.

'I meant by way of refreshment.' There was humour in his wide brown eyes.

Irritated at the diversion, Tabby glanced around the tavern, considering the choices on offer.

'Rum will do nicely.'

'My name is Riyogi,' he said, bowing then filling a cup for her.

She considered the formal gesture overly courtly for a tavern owner.

'Tabby Post,' she replied, reaching across the counter to offer Riyogi her hand.

Instead of shaking it, he turned it over and examined her palm, bringing it close to his face in the dim light. Tabby tried to pull away but he tightened his grip around her fingers. Riyogi appraised the calloused, hardened skin.

'You're the midwife, the healer with the falcon.'

She nodded, removing her hand from his grasp. 'You knew that from looking at my hand? Do you read palms?'

Riyogi smiled. 'There are many stories about you, Mistress – about your bravery, the risks you take to care for the sick. I heard from a journeyman just last week that you once travelled five miles through a snowstorm to tend to a child suffering with measles. The child survived because of your care. You are the stuff of legends.'

Tabby frowned at the description. She certainly did not feel like a great hero or a goddess or a mighty beast, towering above man in both birth and deed. Sweating and aching to the bone, loaded to capacity with her back basket, bow, quiver and apothecary case, she felt decidedly mortal. *I resemble a pack mule*, she thought.

'Do not believe everything you hear, Riyogi. It was only four miles and the child was not afflicted badly. She would have survived had I been there or not.'

'There are other stories. You live among Indians, do you not? Do you shun white society?

'I do not. It is in white society where I make my living curing the sick'

'You are bridging a gap then, Mistress Post.'

'I am merely answering my calling in the best way I know how.'

'A calling from God?'

'No. From myself.'

The landlord smiled at this, revealing a full set of clean white teeth strung together in his mouth like pearls, a novelty around the Kennebec settlements. *Riyogi ate his greens as a boy*, thought Tabby, sipping her rum.

'I brush them, too,' he said, noticing Tabby's gaze. 'With a pig bristle brush and eggshells.'

It appeared to her that the Oriental must be a mind reader as well.

'Egg shells?' she inquired. Baking powder, alum and brimstone were common tooth powders known to Tabby. She had even heard of Indians using ground seashells. Mongwau had shown her how to grind animal bones to a fine powder for use in this regard, but she had never considered eggshells.

'It is a safer substance to place in one's mouth than gunpowder,' he added, referring to another common tooth powder used among woodsmen.

At this, Tabby laughed. The sound was so joyful that the ill-mannered patrons of the Green Dragon turned their heads once more in her direction in wonder.

The easy banter with Riyogi had distracted her. She grew serious as she remembered her business. She lowered her voice.

'I am looking for a man named Achak'

Riyogi hesitated. 'Is he unwell?'

'Then you know him?' Tabby asked eagerly.

Riyogi nodded.

'I hope he is in very good health for I must speak to him. I believe he has knowledge of a great wrong done to my father.'

Tabby watched as the Oriental's face darkened with suspicion and concern. His eyes became shadowed with doubt; none of the mirth that had brightened them only minutes before was now discernible. Achak must be a friend, she realised. She had said too much. Her honesty was a flaw, her father had often cautioned; Tabby knew she had no aptitude for dissembling.

'I wish Achak no harm.' Leaning across the counter, she gripped Riyogi's hand, hoping to convey the weight of her request through gesture alone. 'All I seek is information.'

The Oriental's face began to soften but she could see he was torn, unwilling to betray the trust of a friend. *Riyogi must be an exceedingly virtuous man*, she thought.

'Is there some place we might talk? Perhaps if you knew why I wish to see him ...'

Riyogi hesitated then nodded. He turned, indicating she should follow. Tabby allowed Riyogi, padding lightly over the ground in black canvas moccasins, to lead her to a room behind the bar. As she did, Tabby noticed that his tweed breeches and linen shirt ill-fitted his slight, compact frame.

The room, stacked with crates, was a storeroom of sorts but it also housed a straw pallet where, she assumed, the Oriental slept. A small window at the back of the room was covered in a thin but neatly hemmed length of calico that served as a curtain. The space was redolent with a rich, sweet fragrance, almost creamy to her nose, like fresh cow's milk. Next to the pallet sat a hyacinth-coloured vase painted with strange and colourful birds and bold orange flowers. Here, joss sticks of vibrant red burned slowly, the source of the scent that hung heavily like a snow cloud in the small room. Tabby noted that the room was spotless, with no dust or signs of rodents; as she did, a cat, mottled ginger and black, emerged from behind a crate with a musical trill. Riyogi lifted the animal into his arms and whispered into a black-tipped ear words that Tabby could not hear.

'What is the smell?' Tabby asked. She had only been in the room a moment but already felt light-headed and languid. After removing her back basket and placing her belongings on the floor, she sat down heavily on a crate.

'Sandalwood,' Riyogi replied. 'It helps me relax during meditation.' He placed the cat on the ground gently then removed a number of sticks from a box and handed them to Tabby. 'They can also be used medicinally, for headaches and stomach pains, even toothache.'

Tabby drew the incense sticks slowly beneath her nostrils and inhaled deeply.

'Thank you.'

Riyogi bowed again then removed his moccasins, crossed his feet at the ankles and lowered himself to the floor. Sitting cross-legged in front of her, he said no more, clearly waiting for Tabby to begin. Having never voiced the tale of her father's plight in its entirety, she found herself nervous as she attempted to order the events. She swallowed. Her mouth was dry but when she looked down into Riyogi's earnest brown eyes, her agitation instantly wafted away like the light-grey smoke from the joss sticks.

She began with her father's time in New France. The listener knew something of the mercenary nature of the expeditions undertaken in the area, a relief for Tabby, who could not shake the burden of her father's choice to be party to the plunder of the colony. She felt the shame more strongly now than she had ten years ago when she was just nineteen. Now, at nine and twenty, she had seen men die violently at the hands of others; it sickened her to know that, at one time, death had been her father's calling.

'Ephraim Post had been a dead shot,' said Tabby. She had witnessed her father's skill numerous times in the early days, when they had been hunting together. He could catch a wolf between the eyes at fifty yards if it threatened the flock, a 'gift' he had passed onto his daughter. While Tabby refused to raise a gun at either man or beast, her accuracy with a bow and arrow had, in recent years, become much talked of among the Penobscot, who had observed neither a squaw nor a white woman with such an eye. Tabby wagered they had never witnessed a man with equal skill either.

'He enlisted as a sharpshooter in the expeditionary force under the command of General John Hill. After many months in New France, he awoke one morning in chains, fettered to an oak tree. Guards stood by him with muskets raised and pointed at his head. The guards told him he had killed a man – his own brother Ebenezer. Eb's cold, bloodied body lay at my father's feet, apparent evidence of his crime.' Tabby took a deep breath then exhaled, as if to rid herself of the image. 'The battalion had been drinking the night before and my father, stewed beyond all hope, had no recollection of the events that had passed.'

'He killed his brother?' Riyogi asked, astonished.

Tabby nodded, distressed to hear another say it so plainly, but thankful for the brief respite it offered her. She steadied herself before continuing.

'Originally, my father and Uncle Eb had joined the force with the hope of saving Eb from debtor's prison,' she explained. 'They were both farmers, but Eb made poor choices, often against or in spite of my father's advice. My uncle owed more than he and my father could repay in a year. By joining the force, my father hoped he could use his skill to earn enough coin to free his brother of debt. But he also wanted to protect Eb from failure; you see, my uncle had been a wantwit since childhood.'

Tabby rose and wandered to the window. She pushed the calico aside and looked towards the sky. Her father's tale was more difficult to articulate than she realised.

Unable to see Edie, Tabby faced Riyogi and continued her tale.

'According to Hill, there had been witnesses – other mercenaries at the camp – who saw the brothers fight. Eb had, in his drunkenness, acted the fool and stolen up on my slumbering father, cuffing him about the head as a bear might and growling all the while to enhance the drama. Still drunk himself, Ephraim awoke and, fearful that a bear had entered the camp, went for his gun, rose and fired.'

'How did you learn of this?' asked Riyogi when Tabby finished.

'I was working as a maid and midwife in Wallingford at the time. I heard news of my father's return to Maine from one of the other girls in service on Long High Way. She had spied him in the woods while she was gathering chickweed. When she called his name, he turned on her and raised his rifle then fled like a dusky cloud.

'Later I uncovered more of the story after asking in town, putting snippets of gossip together. It was a story I could scarcely believe, knowing my father's honourable character and, despite everything, his affection for his brother. But all my inquiries met with dead ends. Covert as the expedition was, there were no documents recording the names of the complete battalion, no documents pertaining to the 'witnesses'. And I couldn't find any soldier who was in Quebec at the same time as my father, or under General Hill.

'Eventually, I wrote to Hill himself. Kindly in his relation of events, his letter informed me that he had released my father, whose skill and character he respected, out of pity. He wrote that my father's conscience would be the "arbiter of his crime" and would punish him more severely than the sternest judge or jury.

'But there was an element of the general's account of the tragedy which struck me as strange. He said my uncle was shot in the back – twice in his legs and once between his shoulders.'

Riyogi raised an eyebrow. Tabby paused for a moment, ensuring the tale did not run away from her.

'Yet if my father thought a bear was close by to him, he would aim for the head. And, even as busky as he might have been, he would have hit the mark, first time.'

Riyogi carefully considered the conclusions Tabby had reached.

'You suspect foul play?'

She nodded, frowning.

'After some time, four years in fact, I tracked my father down at Moosehead Lake. He was living on Sugar Island alone, as though he could tolerate the human race no longer. When I found him, he refused to recognise me, refused to acknowledge my presence. I saw shame and self-loathing written all over his face.

'I know his actions were intended to push me away but, despite my respect for him as my father, I refused to leave. I reminded him of our life together, both before and after my mother had died. I spoke of how he'd taught me to hunt and fish and swim, and of my mother's gentle way in all things. It was then that I saw a light in his eyes. I'd ignited something. I thought he was lost to himself, but that small spark convinced me he could be saved.'

Riyogi leant forward slightly, clearly gripped by the tale and the teller.

'What did he say to you by way of explanation?'

'Nothing. He hasn't uttered a word since the shooting.'

The Oriental frowned, not quite understanding. Tabby attempted to clarify her meaning.

'He doesn't speak. He appears to be stone deaf and dumb, or so he would like me to believe. After that first instance of recognition, he most often looks at me as though I were a stranger. It's as though he has locked the door on his previous existence. I believe he would poke his eyes out if he might harness the courage. On the rare occasions he must impart a message to me, he whistles as a shepherd might and I reply in kind.' Tabby smiled ruefully. 'At least it proves that he can hear me.'

Tabby paused for a moment, considering how the events have affected her life so completely.

'The general was right. My father has placed himself in a gaol of his own devising. And Riyogi, I believe Achak is the key.'

Riyogi raised his eyebrows again. Tabby went on to detail the contents of her long-ago discussion with Matthew Hawkins.

'He said Achak had been the guide for the expedition. Hawkins described him as privy to things normal men were not. Seeing as has no ties to the British, perhaps Achak might be willing to speak to me? I am certain it is guilt and remorse that shackle my father so completely. If I can discover what really happened that night, I believe I can help my father return to himself.'

After just a moment's thought, Riyogi rose.

'I will take you to him,' he said, bowing once more.

6

Leah missed the peace of Cape Cod, of Eastham and most recently Wellfleet. When Palgrave had brought her to the Augusta plot he had purchased in the fall before last, she had insisted the house he planned to build would be too near the town. Her opposition to his scheme only seemed to ignite Palgrave's determination and he set about the project with all the over-whelming confidence he had brought back with him from New Providence, brushing away her concerns as if they were a plaguey midge.

Yet, on every day except the Sabbath, there was noise emanating from the town from sunrise to sunset. Someone was always splitting a shingle, or hammering a nail into the latest new dwelling, barn or storefront. And when the wind was blowing from the east, even the rhythmic thump of the smith's hammer in his forge was audible to Leah's ear, the ringing reverberating from her head to her toes. Although it was something she had once appreciated and cherished – the sound of her husband at work – in this setting, it made her querulous and eggy.

She missed her little house. She had found peace there.

She missed the ocean, too, the fresh, biting smell of it, its quicksilver nature and the possibilities it seemed to offer. It had taken her husband from her for nearly a year, but it had also returned him. Hopefully, it had been as merciful to his friend and fellow seafarer Samuel Bellamy. Where he was she knew not, but her sister's hope of Bellamy's eventual homecoming had not ebbed one drop in eight years.

Now, as Leah stretched her eyes to the horizon, all that was visible was Augusta, stone and wood, rising from the ground as haughtily as the Devil. Palgrave would remind her of the Kennebec's 'multifariousness', of its 'diverse and interesting nature' and how, from their windows, they could track its course, read its currents and eddies and find calm in the stillness of its glides. But to Leah, the stench of it, the drab, miry colour of it, like milky coffee, made her want to wretch. Rising from the earth, she wiped her brow with the back of her hand. The heat closed in around her like a beast, panting foul-smelling, wet breath.

Her small garden was in full sun, no longer in the shadow of the house. She went to cast her gaze critically over the dwelling, but the white-washed shingles glinted violently in the noontide sun, seeming to sear her eyes in their sockets. Instead, she considered her little patch of green, so at odds with the home Palgrave had built. Poring over pattern books that had come from England, he had researched architectural styles and fashions relentlessly for a year before the first stone was laid. With the help of Elizabeth, who had inherited her aunt's knack for art, and Joseph, who had acquired his father's natural inclination for mathematics, they had drawn up copious plans. Nothing was perfect to Palgrave's eye, as though his dreams were impossible to capture with a human hand.

What he eventually conceded to reached far beyond the

scope of Leah's paltry imagination – two storeys, an attic space, five bedrooms, a roof with dormer windows and a great hearth at each end of the house. Palgrave embellished the structure with a balustrade with ornamental trim and decorative pediments over the windows and around the entrance. Occasionally, she recalled the modest home they first shared in Eastham, the dwelling her father once described as 'middling'. *It would be considered a hovel in comparison to this edifice*, she thought now, *yet Palgrave had built them both*. She marvelled at how his dreams had expanded in that time. Or perhaps it was not the dreams that had grown bigger, merely his capacity to realise them.

Recalling that 'middling' place, the house where her five children were born, always sparked a sharp pang of regret. Palgrave had built that house for Anne, his first wife. It was for Leah who Palgrave had built the second. The irony was not lost on her.

Now her baby kicked, jolting her from her daydreams. This one was a mule, she was certain. Feisty when in the mood for play, but when he was not, a stubborn foal who refused to budge an inch and allow his mother rest.

Leah laid down her shovel then circled her hands over the impressive girth of her belly. From the size of her, she knew Palgrave feared she was carrying twins again. Anticipating a birth as difficult as that of Joshua and Sarah thirteen years ago, she had noticed that his gaze often turned to her, so clearly frightened and perturbed that she could almost taste his brackish fear. Abby, who safely delivered the twins, had tried to comfort him, from 'It is your sixth child, he is bound to weigh at least twelve pounds,' to 'I saw her safe through one set, I'll see her safe through another,' but Palgrave would not be comforted by platitudes.

Resuming her work, she placed her foot on the shovel

and drove it into the ground through the thick, protecting mantle of winter and into the fertile soil below, soft and spongy to the touch, fresh and sweet to the nose. Palgrave had counselled her to wait, that the townsfolk had warned him that the weather was still unreliable. This was typical of an Augusta spring they said; a sudden rise in temperature that roused the senses then, just as sudden, snow again. But Leah could not wait. Cabbages, beans, squash and carrots needed to be planted before the baby came. Abby called it 'nesting'.

Palgrave did not approve of her tending the garden, 'working like a field hand', especially now that she was with child. He had not stopped her when she was with child in Eastham, she argued. In truth, since they had come to Augusta, Leah seemed to need the earth around her more and more. The blackening of her fingernails and the grit on her tongue when she inadvertently wiped her hand across her mouth sustained her.

The baby kicked again and she stopped her work, panting, so easily out of breath. For a youngling so large, his current home was cramped. Leah closed her eyes, envisioning the child as he attempted to stretch and make some room for himself.

'You must have long legs like your father,' she said quietly. 'He has the same problem. I remember him in meeting, trying to accommodate those legs in between the narrow church pews, twisting and shifting until he discovered a position that might be tolerable for the tiresome duration of the day's sermon. Then, as soon as the final 'amen' was uttered, he would rise like a jack-in-the-box, uncoiling finally. He was always the first one out of the door, striding across the green.' She paused for a moment, smiling in thought. 'It was one of the reasons why I fell in love with him ... his discipline, his mastery over a body so determined to be unbound ...' The words trailed off as she considered how he had altered since that time.

When she told Palgrave she was with child, she noticed a lightning streak of fury blaze across his pale-blue eyes. It was just for an instant, but she saw it, clear as a comet in the night sky. She had wondered at the time if he realised she had designed it, and that she had been willing to bear his anger.

She rested the shovel against the fence that surrounded her garden. It was built by Joseph to deter the chickens and goats that Leah let roam free around the property. Resting on a bench that her husband had placed nearby for just that purpose, Leah, in the full bloom of her pregnancy, recalled the night she had planned nine months ago.

She had undressed Palgrave meticulously, gently, caressing his bare skin softly as she did so, sensing him shiver. Flattering him, lauding over the scars that defiled his body. Knowing the pride he took in them, she had kissed them one by one, anointing each pocked and ridged piece of flesh with her lips. She had blessed even the monstrous wound on his belly, the taut, pink skin glassy in the flickering candlelight.

As she read those markings like an ancient scroll, she created a truth for herself. Leah discerned long ago that Palgrave had not been honest about his experiences at sea or in Nassau, where he had spent many months. A mere silversmith would never receive such wounds.

Like a feather-stroke, her lips and fingers had incited moans of longing, yet she had been patient until she recognised a frantic edge to his sighs. He could bear the excruciating wait no more. Whispering praises of his great daring and courage in his ear, she had finally spurred him into rapture towards the brink of a fast-flowing waterfall. Then they had fallen together like a plummet into the spume, sweating and panting like beasts at the plough.

Despite the ruse, Leah had gained pleasure from the liberties she had taken with his body, taking control, bearing her sights on a thin point in the distance. Afterwards, as he lay beside her, Palgrave was quiet, weighing and assessing the possible consequences, she assumed. Since the twins came so harshly into the world, he had fought against another child, fearing the outcome. When Caleb, her youngest son, was born three years after the twins, she had called him 'God's holy miracle', and comforted Palgrave's concern. But God had played no part in the creation of the child growing in her belly now. This was her will. It was her body. And she was prepared to pay the price.

7
___

Tabby continued to turn heads as she strode business-like alongside Riyogi through the streets of Augusta. At least a head taller than her guide, she was aware that the sight of a red-haired woman dressed like an Indian walking with a diminutive Oriental might raise an eyebrow or two. Unfazed, she walked on, disregarding the stares and mutter-ings of disapproval, her heart pounding as she struggled to recall all that she needed to say to Achak, all the questions she needed to ask. *But what will I do if he can provide no answers?* she wondered. Shoving the thought from her mind, she walked on.

'From which part of the Orient do you hail?' Tabby asked as a means of distraction.

Riyogi smiled. 'You are the only European I have met who is aware that "the Orient" encompasses a rich and varied number of nations and races. I am impressed.'

'I have been educated, Sir.'

'In my experience, Mistress, knowledge makes little difference to understanding.'

Tabby nodded, weighing the meaning of her escort's comment.

'For the record,' she added, 'I consider myself *American*.'

Riyogi tilted his head in acknowledgement before finally answering her question.

'Japan,' he responded as they entered the blacksmith's stable.

Tabby knew little of Japan. She recalled being informed by her mother that it was a closed country. The topic had arisen once when Mistress Post had been called a 'Papist' by Betsy Pitts, the milliner. Mistress Pitts had considered Tabby's mother's choice of violet thread somehow indicative of her faith. At the age of six, Tabby did not recognise the word, but the woman's tone of spite and revulsion was unmistakable; it was mordacious. Her mother thought it necessary to explain the biting intonation with which the woman had coloured the word, which was already a slight.

'Since the Reformation, we have been persecuted by tyrants and the small-minded,' she had said, then went on to detail numerous examples of similar oppression. The one that had wedged firm in young Tabby's mind was of the Japanese who, some time ago, had massacred thousands of Catholic Christians. She had asked her mother why. 'Difference makes people scared, Tabby. For them, so immense was their fear of outsiders, violence was their only solution to the unknown.'

Clearly Riyogi did not share this fear for he had established his life in Augusta, thousands of miles, Tabby figured, from the place of his birth. Tabby's thoughts were interrupted when they reached the blacksmith's stables.

Horses awaiting shoeing were housed in the stalls. The beasts took scant notice of the mismatched pair as they headed towards the final stall in the row, seemingly preferring the sight of their feed buckets to that of two strangers. Despite the sun outside, the stable was dim and the air was thick with the smell of manure. Tabby breathed deeply anyway, attempting to calm herself.

'Achak,' Riyogi called quietly when they reached their destination.

A rustle of straw and a reply came from the corner of the stall, out of the darkness. 'Riyogi.' Although it was just one word, to Tabby's ear the accent sounded neither English nor Indian.

Then the man rose and stepped forward. Tabby judged he stood at more than six foot. A coarsely woven blanket was wrapped around his broad shoulders and his black eyes were doubtful, rippling mistrust like flowing waters in the wind.

'This is Tabby Post,' Riyogi began.

Achak nodded in recognition, casting his eye over her form, evaluating.

'She would like to speak with you.'

The Indian frowned.

'You can trust her,' said Riyogi gently.

Achak's concern seemed to ease at these words and his expression softened. He moved closer.

Having registered his temperament, Tabby blunted her keenest instinct to ask the Indian the scores of questions that had catalogued in her mind since the time she had be told of his existence.

'I appreciate you speaking to me,' she said, extending her hand. 'You cannot believe my relief at having found you.'

His expression was blank. He did not take her hand.

'I have questions about the time when you were scout for General John Hill's expeditionary force.'

Achak emitted a low *humph* then brushed past her so hastily that his blanket whipped her arm. Tabby looked to Riyogi for counsel.

'Come. Follow me.'

Outside, in the heat of the day, Achak had dropped his blanket. Wearing only a breechcloth and leggings, his burnished skin glistened in the sun and his hair, a cascade of glossy ink down his back, shimmered radiantly, firing off sparks of light as he moved and turned. The taut lines of his muscled arms and chest flexed and quivered like the string of her bow readied with an arrow; she wagered they would be just as deadly.

Tabby decided he was very beautiful. Gazing at him, she noted the authority in his movement and presence. He was formidable; a disgruntled monarch who saw no good reason to conceal his moods.

The blacksmith, who hammered away in his forge to the right of the yard, glanced at the Indian with an expression of disinterest. He was obviously well-versed in the strains of Achak's tempers.

'Why is he so angry?' Tabby asked her companion.

Riyogi sighed. 'He feels I have betrayed him.'

Tabby took her eyes off Achak and gave Riyogi a questioning look.

'Achak's preference is for a solitary existence,' he explained.

She frowned 'Then how did you become such close acquaintances?'

'It is a long story for another day,' Riyogi responded in a low voice, adding a short bow of apology.

Tabby bit her lip, wondered how to proceed. Glistening in the sun, Achak seemed god-like to her. She wondered which of the great Algonquian spirits inhabited him in this moment: *Gitche Manitou* or the evil *Matchi Manitou*? Tabby hoped it was not the latter.

She took a step forward and Riyogi reached for her. She shook his hand from her arm. Then, walking slowly towards Achak across the yard, steadily and carefully as she might on the frozen Kennebec, she attempted to convince herself she was not frightened of this man. Because a *man* he was. Furthermore, he had no weapon that she could see. *What's the worse that could happen?* she asked herself, sensing the sweat trickle between her breasts. Then she stopped, alerted by a hoarse, screaming *kee-eeee-arr*.

Edie alighted on the domed, wooden roof of the smithy's forge wagon. Instantly, Tabby was reassured.

Edie's cry had also halted Achak, who now stared at the bird quizzically. Edie returned his gaze with equal incredulity. A stillness now settled over the yard, as though time itself had stopped, yet Tabby continued forward. When she reached Achak, she placed her hand softly on his arm. The immense heat of his bare flesh radiated through her own body making her flush. He turned and looked at her. She removed her hand.

'I mean you no harm, Achak,' Tabby said. 'I merely ask for your help.'

He turned back to Edie, moving towards her. She remained perched on the wagon, stately as a queen. Inching his hand towards her, Achak fondly stroked the feathers of her mantle.

'Falcons are the totem of my clan,' he said quietly.

To Tabby's eye, it was as though a thousand memories flickered over his face, colouring his expression in a single moment.

'I will help you. But not now and not here. I will come to the tavern after dark.'

~

TABBY FINGERED ASIDE the calico that covered the small window in Riyogi's storeroom. To her mind, it was as though the sun was refusing to set. It hung annoyingly low in the sky, a great, stubborn vermillion orb. Now she was so close to knowing the truth, her patience had deserted her. She sighed as she let the fabric fall, crossed her arms and sat, waiting. As she did so, Riyogi entered with a tray of food. His cat, whose name Tabby learnt was Minstrel, slipped through the room's opening and between Riyogi's legs like a stream of quicksilver. A bubble of noise from the tavern also entered with the pair, popping as Riyogi closed the door. Placing the tray on a crate, he invited her to sit and eat with a swift and elegant movement of his hand.

Tabby hadn't eaten since she had broken her fast at five that morning, after delivering Pollard Franklin at half four. Mouth-watering drifts of steam rose from the tray reminding Tabby of her hunger. In an instant, she was seated, shovelling the food, a rich and fragrant vegetable pottage, ravenously, gracelessly into her mouth. Riyogi watched her, a slight smile forming on his lips. After a few minutes she wiped her mouth on the folded napkin he had also placed on the tray.

As she continued to eat, her host related the events of Achak's life. He believed it wise to share his friend's story; he wanted Tabby to be aware that Achak was not like other Indians, that he was, in a sense, lost, trapped between two worlds.

'Achak was born in the Quebec area, into a tribe called "Atikamekw". They were nomads, if you like, hunters and traders who travelled the region, only settling for short periods in one place. Achak was the sachem's eldest son, well-liked, intelligent, handsome and, from a young age, a skilled hunter. He could track a deer for days without sleep or sustenance, without the animal knowing. Although the position of leader or chief was not hereditary in his tribe, all considered that Achak would be bestowed the title when he became a man.'

Riyogi paused for a moment, considering his next words.

'Then the French came, followed by the British. To preserve his tribe, Achak's father realised he would have to ally with one of them. He chose the French. All was well for a time then, when Achak was fourteen, a Jesuit missionary, Philippe de Mazarin, convinced the sachem that it would be wise to educate his son in French and English, and in the politics of these great nations. With such knowledge, Achak could safeguard the future of the tribe. Of course, both Achak and his father were aware of de Mazarin's true motive. He hoped Achak would return to the Attikamekw a Christian, an Indian who could help him in his mission.

'So Achak was taken to study in Paris. First at an *académie* where he was instructed in horseback riding, fencing, marksmanship and war, as well as all the social skills that young noblemen might need to succeed at court: languages, dance, music, writing, arithmetic, drawing. Achak exceeded De Mazarin's expectations. Despite his alienation by the other students, Achak dedicated himself to his studies, always aware of his purpose, his people. But he was also an excellent mimic, so he excelled at French, Italian and English. Even his tutors could not fault his speech.'

Tabby laid down her spoon, finally recognising Achak's accent. It was French, just like her mother's.

'After two years at the *academie* he moved on to the University of Paris with the intention of studying theology. In order to do so, he was required to become Catholic, which he did willingly. You see, to Achak, beliefs are rooted in more than ritual and ceremony. He studied the Bible in the same way he would any other text: he stole the knowledge and nothing more.

'When he finally returned to Quebec in his twenty-first year, he discovered his entire clan had been decimated by smallpox in his absence. He had left his tribe in order to save them; he could not but feel the painful sting of bitterness. Yet, although he had lost his family, Achak still possessed the vast learnings he had acquired while in Paris. He offered it to other clans, then to other tribes. But in obtaining new languages and manners, he had lost the nuances of his own and was rejected by his people.'

Tabby thought of the Indians at Moosehead. They had been accepting of her father when he found his way to Sugar Island and then, of course, they had accepted her as well. It seems that the grief and loss the Penobscot recognised in them rendered the father and daughter benign. But would they be tolerant of one of their own who they viewed as a traitor? Tabby wasn't certain.

'Where was he to go?' Riyogi continued. 'The colour of his skin barred him from European society. But they would, at least, pay him for his skills and knowledge. Since then, Achak has used his innate talents, along with those he acquired abroad, to aid the British and the French – whoever will pay his fee. Although he does not think it so, his possesses an extraordinary gift, one armies pay handsomely for.'

'That is how he became a scout for General Hill,' said Tabby, finding another piece of her father's puzzle.

Riyogi nodded.

Tabby considered Achak's history as she finished her meal, but she soon pushed the tray away, suddenly filled with a sadness and injustice she could not articulate. As her eyes began to sting, she rose and faced away from Riyogi, towards a wall lined with racks of bottles, struggling to compose herself. She did not want to appear weak and emotional before one who had faced real sorrow and suffering. Riyogi squeezed her shoulder then lit the lamp.

Within moments there was a soft knock on the storeroom door. Tabby drew her palms across her eyes and turned.

ACHAK ENTERED the room and immediately filled the space. Aware of his overwhelming presence in the cramped storeroom, he lowered himself onto a crate. Tabby considered him; *equanimous and temperamental all at once*, she concluded, *as though behind his eyes sleeps a water snake waiting to uncoil*. Dressed in the same garb he wore earlier, Achak fixed his large hands on his knees and secured those black eyes on Tabby.

'How can I help you, Tabby Post?' he asked. She detected a mild note of mockery in the query. Why would she want to live like an Indian? Tabby suspected was the question colouring his expression. But Tabby had not chosen this life, it had somehow found her.

'Mister Matthew Hawkins, the town clerk at Hallowell believes you might be acquainted with my father, Ephraim Post. He was General Hill's sharpshooter.' She watched as Achak frowned in concentration. 'He has hair the same colour as mine,' she added, hoping the detail would jog his memory.

Achak remained silent.

'He was accused of killing his brother, Ebenezer Post. It

was said that, thick-witted with liquor, he mistook my uncle for a bear and shot him three times. Let me be clear – he does not remember this. It is what he was told, what he was led to believe and what he still believes.'

Tabby went on to convey her suspicions and describe her father's altered humour since the incident.

'The thing is, my father wouldn't need three shots to kill a bear. Anyone who knew him would know that.'

'Yes,' said Achak, titling his head in acknowledgement of Tabby's words.

Tabby rose, the breath catching in her throat. 'You knew my father?

'We spent much time together,' he said in a deep, polished voice. 'I would hunt the targets and lead your father within range. Then he would lie there, often for hours, waiting. I've never known a man so stocked with patience, cold patience, waiting for the perfect shot. He was quick with the reload, too.'

Tabby remembered. It took her father less than twenty seconds to reload a rifle.

'He could fell three men before the third was able to raise his weapon. Ephraim explained to me that he was able to foresee the kill before he pulled the trigger. I never saw him miss.'

She walked the short length of the room and stood before him, tears welling in her eyes from relief.

'Then you must know he did not commit this crime. You know he did not kill his brother.'

Achak nodded.

Tabby's eye's widened. 'Did you see who did kill Eb?'

'Is this a blood debt, Mistress Post?'

Tabby was taken aback. She hadn't even considered the possibility. She thought for a moment. *Do I want to take a man's life to avenge another's?* she wondered. *Just what am I planning?*

'No,' she replied firmly. 'It's not revenge I am seeking but justice. General Hill saw fit, for his own reasons, not to charge my father with the crime. My father is a free man. He has neither a price on his head nor the stain of past imprisonment besmirching his present. So that is a blessing, I suppose, if you consider what my father has endured Heaven sent.

'But he needs to know he did not pull that trigger and I need to see the killer come to justice. It was not just Eb's life that was lost that morning. Ephraim Post lost his, too. I only want to reclaim it for him.'

Achak stood then, looking down upon Tabby in consideration. Switching his gaze to Riyogi, he sighed quietly then walked the length of the room, just four paces.

Tabby and Riyogi both moved aside, taking seats against the wall.

'Please tell me what you saw that night.' Tabby's appeal was made with both dignity and emotion.

Raking his fingers through his hair, the Indian came to a decision. Then he began.

'Hill's mission had been covert, sanctioned by the governor but with no official record written. As a result, Hill did as he pleased. Raiding French settlements, he would steal their goods and weapons and sell them to the Indians or the English. The following morning, disguised, he would attack the Indians to whom he had sold the weapons. All the while Hill was stockpiling goods, cash and wampum. It was a lucrative business.

'On the company's final night in New France, we were camped within a few miles of a settlement near Hull, only a day's ride from the border. Earlier in the day, there was news of a troupe of performers who had arrived in the settlement. Bolstered by full pockets, and likely sheer relief at having endured the campaign, I saw your Uncle Eb readying to go to Hull that evening with our comrades. Your father attempted to dissuade him, fearful he would be fooled into debt again. I watched as Ephraim followed Eb into town; all the while, he tried to persuade him to turn back. But Eb would not listen.

'I found out later that once in town, they had fought. Nothing but words were thrown between them, but the confrontation garnered a slew of witnesses. In his disappointment over Eb, Ephraim returned to camp to drown his sorrows.

'I had no interest in going to Hull. I was at the camp when he returned. It was then that I spoke with him. I watched him keening with distress. He told me that his grief was not only for his brother, but for what he himself had forsaken *for* Eb – a daughter and a home in New Haven.'

'He told you about me?' Tabby said, her voice shaking momentarily.

'Yes. And with much pride.' He looked Tabby in the eye. 'That is what convinced me to tell you my story now.'

Tabby recalled her father's anguish on the day he departed for New France. Although he had been stoic, Tabby could see he was cast down by the situation. He did not want to leave his daughter. He did not want to leave the farm. Tabby could see that sending her to Wallingford to live as a servant pained him immensely. Concerned he would never return, she had embraced him tightly in an attempt to reassure him of her wellbeing. 'I raised you to be nobody's servant, Tabby', he'd said as they held on to each other.

Achak continued his story. 'Ephraim fell into a liquor-fuelled sleep. I left him and retreated to the woods. He was not long unconscious when his brother returned. I was alerted by Eb's puffing, as though he had been running. I rose and moved closer. He was being followed.

'I could not discern the features of the man that pursued him but saw that he was tall – taller than me – and thin, reedy, like the shadow of a hair. Toting a rifle, he also carried a pistol in the waistband of his breeches. The man called and your uncle turned. Words were exchanged. I could not fully hear, but I gathered they had been involved in a game of chance.'

Tabby slapped her hand against the wall and released a low grumble of frustration. Aware of her uncle's weakness for gambling and meagre skill in even the most rudimentary of card games, she buried her face in her hands.

As Achak continued, her back gradually straightened. He told her how Eb had crept towards his slumbering brother, then ransacked his possessions until a bag of coin was found – her father's earnings from the expedition.

'Eb handed the bag to the man. "What will you tell your brother in the morning?" the stranger asked. Eb simply shrugged and turned back towards the camp. The thin man began to walk away but then turned and drew his pistol, firing three shots. Your uncle fell to the ground, dead. His killer, cool as a November twilight, placed the pistol in Ephraim's hand then stalked off into the woods.'

Tabby rose, indignant. 'Did you not attempt to hold this man?'

'Apart from my knife, I had no weapon,' he replied without emotion. 'To throw my knife would mean stepping into the clearing where no trees or low branches impeded its flight. He had a rifle that he had not fired. I assumed it was fully loaded.'

Tabby realised that his inaction was not born from cowardice but pragmatism. Nevertheless, her anger clouded her reason.

'But surely,' her voice rising, 'surely you could have done something! Spoken out in some way after the fact!'

Achak was silent, his expression incomprehensible in its stillness.

'Tabby,' Riyogi went to her, stroking her with his gentle tone. 'He is an Indian, and, as such, powerless. There is nothing Achak could have done to improve upon that situation. And there were a score of onlookers who had witnessed the brothers fighting earlier. Nothing anyone could have said would have swayed General Hill.'

She stared hard at Riyogi, reeling. He simply waited for her fury to ebb. *Achak had been well tutored by his European masters to serve himself*, she thought. Yet perhaps Riyogi was right; as an Indian, Achak had no other choice. She could see that he walked the finest of lines between two civilisations, always watchful, forever wary.

By way of apology for her outburst, Tabby touched Achak's arm. His flesh was still hot. A fire raged somewhere deep inside. In turn, he placed his hand on hers, patting it like a forgiving father.

'And the tale of the bear?' Tabby asked, confused.

'I cannot tell you why or by whom that myth was invented.'

Tabby thought for a time. 'Would you recognise this man if you saw him again, Achak?' she asked

'Perhaps.' He paused, as if more words were poised on his lips. A moment later he spoke.

'He bore a tattoo on his neck. I saw it flash in the moonlight as he turned and walked away.'

'Can you describe it?' Tabby pressed.

'It was a likeness of the King of Spades.'

BEFORE THE TRIO PARTED, it was agreed that Achak would journey to Moosehead Lake immediately and tell her father the truth about the murder. It would ease his conscience, he explained. Tabby would travel in the opposite direction, further south. She was to carry out some business with the banker; she could think further on the matter then. But there was a feeling simmering inside her, as potent and as unpleasant as an overcooked stew. There was something just out of reach that she couldn't place, something pertaining to the King of Spades.

Born from utter exhaustion, anguish or the scent of Riyogi's joss sticks, Tabby fell into a fathomless sleep once her head hit the pillow. In her dreams, her father came to her across a springtime meadow awash with the honeyed fragrances of the season. His red hair flashed against the clear, blue sky. In the distance, against the crisp line of the horizon, she saw their cabin. White linens, freshly washed, hung from the line to the side of the dwelling, billowing and rippling like sails in the breeze.

When her father reached her, his rough and calloused hand enveloped hers in a protective and tender cocoon. They walked across the meadow, through birdsong and butterflies and the bracing tang of fresh-mown hay, to their cabin. But as they approached the door, Tabby looked up at her father and he had transformed. The King of Spades stood beside her with his crown, golden curls and fur-trimmed robe, glowering at the child next to him.

Tabby woke with a start. Breathing hard, it took her a few seconds to remember where she lay – on Riyogi's thin straw pallet in the storeroom of the Green Dragon. Gaining her bearings in the dark, her breathing gradually calmed and she turned her head to view the sleeping man on the floor beside her. Riyogi lay on his back, his arms to his sides slightly akimbo, his face entirely serene.

She stood, careful not to wake Minstrel who was huddled like a loaf between her legs, purring a low refrain. Walking silently in bare feet, Tabby slipped through the door, through the deserted tavern and to the outside where the chill of the night awakened her fully. She raised her face to the sky, staring into the blackness and the shimmering stars, then released a shrill whistle. Within seconds, Edie soared out of the dark like a seraph, landing gently on Tabby's outstretched arm. Tabby guessed Edie weighed no more than a bag of corn but the weight of her on her forearm was still surprising.

'I've been neglecting you,' she said to the falcon. 'So much has happened since we last met in the blacksmith's yard.' Tabby recalled Edie's presence and her effect on Achak. 'And it is all exceedingly confounding.'

Tabby scratched the bird's speckled chest then stroked her tail feathers, soft and sharp all at once, interleaving secret, buried colours of grey and green. Tabby imagined them fanning out in flight.

She was not sorry that Eb had been killed. Perhaps, without knowing it, the tattooed man – the 'King of Spades' – had done her family a good service, no matter how heartless the act. *It had relieved us of the great burden of Ebenezer Post's debt*, she thought.

'Is that wrong of me not to mourn for my uncle, Edie?' She stroked Edie's feathers again. 'I'm growing cruel, I think. The Sisters would certainly chastise me for my heartlessness.'

She walked further on, to the road, admiring Edie's colouring. Her slate-coloured feathers, iridescent, flared almost azure in the moonlight.

She'd spoken the truth to Achak. *I do not seek revenge,* she thought. *I don't need to see my uncle's killer hanging from a gibbet. I seek only justice.*

She looked again at her friend.

'Who is the tattooed man?' she asked.

Edie gave no response.

If Uncle Eb had been playing a game of chance, surely the man was a card sharp. His tattoo would suggest as much. He must have been travelling with the entertainers, Tabby thought.

'The King of Spades…' she mused. The falcon blinked, tilted her head as though concerned.

Sighing, Tabby gazed into Edie's black eyes.

'I wish you could speak, Edie. You'd possess the answers to my questions. You are far wiser than me.'

8

———

Dummer eyed her quizzically, tilting his head as though he had never seen anything like her before.

'You are a midwife, Madam; a healer, not a physician. You have never been made to swear an oath on nonmaleficence as physicians have.'

Tabby nodded. 'You are correct. I took no oath, Sir. Like all midwives and healers, I have no formal education in the field. Instead, I learnt from other healers and midwives, and the Indians, of course. However, I have a physician friend. Although he has not had my experience in the field, he is an extremely gifted doctor. He described to me the oath he made to Hippocrates, how he affirmed his "dedication to the ancient gods of healing".'

Tabby gave a short *humph* of frustration. Dummer raised an eyebrow.

'But to my thinking, as many physicians are quacks, it makes no difference whether they swear an oath or not. There's no point in proclaiming your dedication to healing if you don't know the tonsils from the testes.'

The spectators laughed, looked at one another in

surprise and delight. She clearly had the support of the audience, probably most of Boston. Dummer frowned, exasperated.

'Mistress Post, I must advise you to curb your turn of phrase.'

'I apologise, Sir.' She lowered her gaze to the floor in brief deference then lifted her eyes to Dummer's once more.

'But do you understand my meaning? I swore no oath to any god, but in my heart I vow to each patient that I will do my best to help them. Whether they suffer from a bunion or from beaver fever, I give that promise to them. An oath is just words on a page and easily broken. What matters is the practise.'

She took a deep breath in an attempt to ease her agitation.

'Sir, my friends have gathered more than a dozen witnesses who will testify, who will swear on the Holy Book, that I have healed them. Healing is my vocation. I have only ever wanted to help people.'

'If that is the case, how do you account for your actions on July 16th of this year?'

The spectators hushed, waiting on Tabby's response. It was as though not a soul present in the courtroom drew breath in the time it took Tabby to answer Dummer's question. Knowing the importance of her reply, Tabby's breath stilled, too, as she ordered then reordered the words in her mind.

'I cannot account for my actions on that day. The same question plagues me from morning 'til night. How could I so easily have taken a human life when it has been my purpose to only do good?'

'Well, Mistress Post, what is the answer?

'Sir, in all truth, I don't have one.'

9

Tabby rode the barge across the river. The water was flowing quickly that morning; she reckoned the warm weather had prompted a large snowmelt somewhere in the mountains. She did not possess the energy to fight the current in her canoe. Her dreams had provoked a restless slumber. While heartening, Achak's revelations had also left her with a sense of unease. The Indian's disclosure would surely remedy the guilt that ran through her father's veins like a disease, but Tabby was not satisfied. The King of Spades, General Hill ... *Just what was their role in the murder?* she wondered.

These were her thoughts as she trod the cypress-lined gravel drive that led to the grand white house on the hill. Carrying her bag, back basket, quiver and bow, Tabby was sweating like a porous pitcher. She stopped, removed her hat and fanned herself in the shade of a cypress.

Edie hovered and soared high above, gliding then diving, clearly enjoying the sport as well as the sustenance. On one pass, Tabby observed an ill-fortuned meadow mouse gripped in Edie's talons. She'd typically hunt mice and voles on the ground, but Tabby could see the falcon was also relishing the game. She had witnessed Edie's skill as a hunter develop, from chick to fully fledged adult. Edie was clever, adaptable and it didn't take her long to realise speed wasn't always enough to catch a wood pigeon or ptarmigan in flight.

Without parents to learn from, Edie had studied other falcons who nested in the trees or mountains around Moosehead Lake, sitting for hours on a high tree top or huddled in the crag of a rocky cliff face. She was too young to cause the other birds alarm, so there she would sit, undisturbed. It was in these hours, Tabby believed, that Edie had learnt to manoeuvre and alter her speed, to stoop low and approach her prey from below or tack from the side. Edie took her time to herd her prey, ensuring the other bird tired. Tabby still stood awestruck at the sight of her in flight, on the hunt: a pinprick of black among the scalloped-edged clouds becoming a comet shooting towards the ground, wings tucked, the teardrop-shaped body perfectly created for its purpose.

Many would credit God with the design. But Tabby believed Edie was just another of nature's miracles. Tabby's heart welled at the sight of her, at the privilege she felt from having Edie in her life. Although they often did not see eye to eye on matters, Edie was her family, her bosom friend.

Tabby watched as Edie disappeared into the distance, figuring the bird had probably caught sight of something tastier than meadow mice. Then she lowered her gaze slightly and took in the view over Augusta: the river, the burgeoning township and the fields beyond. *I would never tire of this vista*, she thought, allowing the breeze to cool her. She was always satisfied when she saw man and nature working in harmony. The river fed the township in more

ways than one. The plentiful waters of the Kennebec nourished the crops; likewise, all those timber bones of homes
and buildings were evidence of the river's valuable function.
It fuelled the mills and transported the timber. Without it,
Augusta would be lifeless.

She hoped people never took it for granted. She had
witnessed too often the way men would treat each other
with disdain; why, her own uncle was gunned down for no
clear reason. *What's to stop a man from treating a waterway
with equal contempt?* she asked herself. Tabby feared for the
Indians, too. Tribes had been pushed north and west, away
from their traditional homelands and burial grounds. Tabby
understood the rancour of Indians like Achak who had been
treated so callously by both races. She knew she was lucky
to be able to move between both worlds. She had chosen to
create an identity that was neither Indian nor European,
and it suited her. *I like my life*, she thought as she reached
the house.

Before Tabby knocked on the door, she stood back and
examined the pillars framing the entrance. *Even the houses in
Wallingford are paltry in comparison to this residence*, she
mused as she raised her fist to the wood. But before it
touched the oak, she heard women's voices and the heartening *thump* of a hoe hitting the earth. She turned, guzzling
the panorama a final time before being drawn towards the
noise.

At the side of the house, towards the rear, three women
worked in a garden fenced by white pickets. Two were
planting busily and, as they did so, they conversed and
laughed, seemingly enjoying one another's company as
much as the toil. By the colour of her skin, one appeared
Indian, but her familiar tone and air of authority suggested
to Tabby she was not a slave. The other woman had a soft

musical voice and her braided gold hair roped down her spine to her buttocks. The third, whose back was to Tabby, rested on a bench, pointing to this spot and that, clearly giving instruction. Her honey-coloured hair was tied in a scarf.

The scene reminded Tabby of the years she had worked as a maid to the Ives family. She had taken great pleasure in the company of the other girls who worked in the houses on Wallingford's Long High Way. Despite their different ages and backgrounds, for some were indentured and others, like Tabby, were in service by choice or hardship, a camaraderie had developed between them that made the daily struggles bearable. Now, as she contemplated the lives of these three before her, Tabby suddenly felt bereft. Connections she had formed then had been instantly severed when her father had returned from New France and she had left in search of him. She hadn't been back to Wallingford since.

The seated woman remained where she was while the other two laid down their implements and left the garden, making their way to the summer kitchen. It was a stone structure with a wooden door and a stout chimney. Tabby stepped into the shadow of the house so as to go unnoticed, such was her pleasure in watching this moment. Alone, the woman with the honeyed hair surveyed the work the trio had achieved, her head turning and her neck reaching and stretching so she could view the furthest spots in the garden without standing. Then she rose and, laying her knuckles against the small of her back, arced towards the sky as far as she was able. Tabby knew immediately from the gesture that she was with child.

Tabby moved closer. 'Good morning,' she called.

The woman turned. She *was* with child, possibly more than one. She was bursting like a bean pod.

'Good day,' the woman responded, moving towards the gate. The effort from standing and walking just a few steps rendered her breathless and red-faced.

'How can I help you?'

'My name is Tabby Post.' She extended her hand.

The pregnant woman wiped hers on her apron before gripping Tabby's. It was a strong hand, a labourer's hand, which made Tabby wonder whether this woman could be the mistress of such a fine home.

'You should sit in the cool, take a little water.'

'Thank you,' said Tabby. She gazed at the woman's belly. 'The baby has dropped, I can see. When are you due?'

'I think the time has come and gone. This child is hanging on for dear life,' she said.

Even the small exertion of a smile forced her to wince in unease. Then she stared at Tabby, confused, considering the young woman before her in her entirety. Tabby could detect no judgement in her intelligent blue eyes.

'Why are you here?' she asked.

'To see the banker.' Tabby jiggled her shoulders so that the coin and wampum in her back basket rang out in a series of *clinks* and *jingles*.

The woman raised an eyebrow. 'You must mean my husband, Palgrave Williams. Come inside. You look like you would appreciate something cool.'

THE TWO OTHER women from the garden already sat drinking cider at a large oak table in the summer kitchen. Branches of sage and rosemary hung from the rafters and more herbs were drying on a rack in the corner. It was sweet-smelling and peaceful there. A place where everything, from the iron pots that hung from hooks on the wall to the wooden washing barrel in the corner, seemed to gleam. The summer sun that surged through two immense windows, hitting the lime-washed walls, added to this effect.

Leah made the introductions while her sister, Maria, collected a cup for Tabby. Placing it on the table, she brushed against the guest as she passed, their hands grazing lightly. Her skin seemed charged. Tabby flinched and Maria glanced at the newcomer. The fleeting look transformed into a long gaze of intense interest as though the woman was privy to a secret, as though she could see more than other people. Her blue eyes were as round and perfect as stars and, while her staring was odd, Tabby felt no unease. In fact, the force of Maria's gaze passed through Tabby then was gone as though she had woken from a fever.

Relieving herself of her hat and her load, Tabby sat. The cider was tart, tongue-numbing, but refreshing. The conversation which ensued was energetic and generous. Tabby learnt that Abby was a friend of many years standing who was visiting from Wellfleet until the baby was born. She explained that although she had once been a slave, she was now a free woman who lived in a house by the ocean and practiced her skills as a midwife throughout Cape Cod.

'However, Mistress Post,' Abby concluded, 'unlike you, I travel by horse and gig.'

A young boy named Caleb, who seemed about ten years of age, sat with the women. He had inherited his aunt's golden hair and it sat in a thick fall across his brow, almost concealing one eye. He had been silent until then but was struck by Abby's final statement. He laughed, knowingly.

'Ha! The Indian travels in a gig while the white woman travels in an Indian canoe,' he declared.

His mother raised a cautionary eyebrow in his direction. Ignoring Leah's silent warning he turned to Tabby.

'Why do you dress like a savage when the savage at the table dresses like an English woman?' the boy inquired eagerly, clearly attempting to be provocative. 'It is a *conundrum*, is it not? Even your names are similar – "Abby" and "Tabby". What can we make of that?'

Leah and Abby exchanged testy glances.

'As you know, Caleb Williams, "Abby" was not the name I was born with. "Alsoomse" is the name my parents gave me.'

'And "Tabby" is a shortening of "Tabitha",' put in Tabby, amiably. 'So really, our names are not alike at all.'

'My children have a tutor, Mistress Post, which in equal parts is a blessing and a curse. While Caleb's mind is expanding, sometimes its reach is perplexing. He truly believes he possesses the wisdom of Solomon, the artistic ability of Leonardo da Vinci and the curiosity of Galileo. So,' Leah continued calmly, 'in attempting to be *all* men he is being *no* man at all.'

Tabby smiled and glanced at Caleb. He was frowning as he attempted to untangle the 'conundrum' concealed in his mother's statement. Then Leah sent him on his way as the tutor was expected.

ONCE SHE HAD FINISHED her cider, Tabby was led through a wide corridor and along the polished mahogany floors of the main house. Tabby could tell from Leah's slow, careful waddle how uncomfortable she was. She visualised the infant's round head pressing hard against the neck of the womb as Leah pushed open a door at the end of the hall.

Tabby was shown into a sitting room with long sash windows that framed the view Tabby had earlier admired. A man – tall and lean – rose from a writing desk that featured a hutch. It contained many small drawers with brass handles and nooks, many crammed with scrolled paper.

'I watched you coming along the drive,' he said, moving towards her. There was a small amount of wonder in his light-blue eyes. 'I observed your bird, too. Quite astounding, the pair of you.' Remembering himself, he extended his hand. His fingers were long and slender.

'Palgrave Williams.'

His hair was the colour of river sand which, Tabby considered, was probably a more remarkable shade ten years ago before it became flecked with grey. Clean-shaven, he wore brown serge breeches and waistcoat with a white cotton shirt. Round wire-rimmed spectacles were perched precariously on the end of his narrow nose.

'Leah,' he said. His wife still hung in the doorway. He drew her to him with a gentle opening and closing of his fingers, 'this is the midwife Ben spoke of.'

Palgrave took Leah's hand and aided her gently as she lowered herself into an elaborately carved armchair by the window. He continued to recount all this Ben had said in a slow and measured voice, ensuring the accuracy of each utterance.

As he did so, Tabby looked about her – at the books that lined one wall, the braided rug of red and cream that she stood upon and the grouse mounted on a stand above the desk. The room was more a library or a study, she supposed, than a sitting room, a space for a man. She glanced at Leah. The summer kitchen was her space, Tabby reasoned. Less a kitchen and more a space for women.

Ben Shute was a doctor, Tabby learnt, recently returned

from Utrecht where he had studied at Leiden. The description was wasted on Tabby who knew neither where Utrecht lay on the vast surface of the globe nor what Leiden was. Likewise, she hadn't a clue about Doctor William Douglass, the young doctor's mentor. Tabby said as much to Williams in a tone in which she hoped he'd find no offence.

The truth was she had no interest in Benjamin Shute. Everyone knew that men who called themselves doctors possessed scant knowledge, no experience, charged like a French dragoon and went to the knife too readily. All she wanted was to see her business finalised quickly then be back on her way to Moosehead. Of course, a short detour to visit Kirkcaldie had been factored into her timing, a detour of which she was in much need. This final point was not mentioned to Williams and his wife.

'Will you not stay with us for a day, or possibly two?' Williams asked, flicking his wife a glance. She nodded. 'Ben will be joining us for supper this evening. I'm certain your opinion will alter once you meet him.'

When he noticed the resolute expression on Tabby's face, he continued.

'What's more, we expect Leah will deliver soon, very soon, in fact, and it would ease my mind to have you at hand.' His brow furrowed. 'Your skills are widely spoken of, Mistress Post. It would calm me to have a midwife of your experience close by.'

'Who a woman has at her side when in travail should be her decision, Sir,' Tabby put in. 'You speak so highly of Doctor Shute that I assumed he would be at hand when the time came. And is Abby not a midwife?'

Husband and wife exchanged glances. Tabby could not decipher the complex message that shot between them in such a fleeting glimpse. Many years of history and shared experience coloured the intricate weave of their marriage, Tabby figured. Williams turned to his guest then nodded slowly, shamefaced.

'I would like you to stay, Mistress Post,' Leah said finally. 'From my sense of such things, I believe this baby will come soon. Abby and my aunt delivered my other children, and the birth of the twins was difficult.'

'Extremely,' Palgrave put in sombrely.

'But I worry Abby no longer possesses the ...' Tabby waited as Leah searched for the appropriate word, '*detachment* needed under such circumstances. As for Doctor Shute ... I'm certain he has been well taught and there is no doubt that he means well, but I would rather a midwife at my side during the birth.'

Tabby liked Leah already. She possessed a great intelligence, a calm knowing that Tabby had seen in the faces of wise women. She seemed out of place in this great house in her apron and homespun. This place was too small for her.

'It is settled then?' Williams asked.

'I will stay until the baby is born,' Tabby agreed, slightly vexed that her plans had been delayed further. 'But you will address me as Tabby.'

Once Leah departed the room, Williams explained how he planned to 'invest' Tabby's savings, a procedure Tabby was unfamiliar with.

'Now the Indians have gone, Augusta is a town rich with new settlers, many of whom are wealthy. But there are others who are not so fortunate. I offer services to both. It is a simple process,' said Palgrave, 'where I act as an intermediary.'

Tabby nodded. Palgrave's explanation was clear and direct, but she wondered if he was a man she could trust. She listened intently as he continued.

'Land in outlying regions is being surveyed each day and more plots are opening for purchase from the Crown via Governor Dummer's officials. As a member of the Committee for the Sale of Eastern Lands of the Colonies, I can assure you that within a year all these tracts of forest that you see,' he said, pointing to the window, 'will be home to hundreds of settlers, eager to build a future.'

Tabby's thoughts flew immediately to Jeremy Cool. 'And the squatters?'

Palgrave nodded. 'Squatters will be given an option to purchase the land they have settled. Otherwise they will be required to leave, bringing hardship for some in the short term, unfortunately. However, were they to borrow money and buy the land, in the future these families will be rewarded with stability, security and certainty.'

Tabby considered Palgrave's words. She wagered Cool would not depart compliantly. Neither would his warped sense of justice allow him to pay for the land that he had settled, if one could call the wretched pit where Cool lived a settlement. While she had no sympathy for the likes of Cool, she wondered how Polly and the children would fare, most likely driven by the barrel of a Redcoat's musket from their home.

'Many with excess funds, such as yourself, entrust their money to me,' Williams went on. 'On their behalf, I lend money to those in need of finance to build a home, for instance, or to purchase seeds or livestock. These funds, including a nominal amount of interest, are then repaid over a period of time. Interest earnt is split in equal proportion between myself and the customer.'

'What do you consider nominal?' Tabby had asked. She had seen families undone by money lenders and she had no plans to be anyone's undoing.

'Just four cents on the dollar.'

Williams looked at Tabby's concerned face then, very softly, sighed.

'I am not a usurer, Tabby. I operate a bank. My ambitions go far beyond the lining of my own pockets. I hope to see this community thrive and, in the process, ensure the future prosperity of not only my family, but all the families on the Kennebec. In that, I believe, our goals are aligned.'

Finally reassured, she poured the contents of her money

bag onto his desk. Williams's eyes opened wide. Silver and gold, wampum included, coated the surface of the table.

'Where to begin ...' he murmured to himself, ruminatively, tapping the arm of his spectacles against his teeth.

Placing his spectacles back on the end of his nose, he rolled up his shirtsleeves and started to separate the coins into their different currencies. He seemed completely transfixed by the task and Tabby could sense there was no place for conversation. So she sat in the armchair Leah had vacated and watched him work. Very soon, she found herself drifting away in a trance of her own, induced by the gentle ring of coin and the steady cadence of Williams's movements.

She stared for a time at a portrait on the wall. While she recognised Williams, his wife and Caleb in the rendering, there were two other children who appeared to be in adolescence and a slightly younger girl and boy who so resembled one another that she took them to be the twins who had been so troublesome to birth. It was an unusual interpretation of the group; none of their imperfections had been glossed over as they might when an artist is commissioned to produce a likeness. While pretty, the elder girl had been replicated with a remarkably conceited air, and Williams's nose seemed as long and thin as a cat's elbow, much more so than in reality. Likewise, the arrogance of the boy from the kitchen, Caleb, had been captured to perfection –Tabby could almost hear his scornful taunts. Maria did not feature in the representation.

When the currencies were at last divided, Palgrave placed each one in a canvas purse. Then, leaning back in his chair for a moment, he cracked each knuckle purposefully before proceeding to tip out the contents of each purse that he had just filled and counted it. He did this quickly, with his forefinger darting left and right, moving coin across the smooth plane of the table. Once counted, a number was recorded in a fresh, dark leather-bound ledger with an elegant quill, which Tabby guessed to be goose feather.

Williams then turned his attention to the wampum, some of which was Indian-made, the other Dutch. In a similar fashion, he slid the beads with his forefinger around the surface of his desk to group them, made his silent calculations then recorded the numbers in the ledger.

'Are you only paid in coin and wampum?' he asked as he wrote.

She shook her head then answered matter-of-factly, 'I've been paid in everything from shingles to snuff.'

'And, when you are paid in kind, where do you store it?'

'If I cannot use it then I usually trade it for something I need. A pair of lumberman's boots, for instance, I traded in Pittston for six yards of clean linen.'

'I can invest such items for you as well, in a fashion ... if you are interested. On your behalf, I would sell them for cash, if that is the currency with which you are most comfortable. I am, at present, having a storehouse built. My barn is crammed with corn and tobacco and it makes my wife tetchy.'

Finally, he rose from the table.

'You are a wealthy woman, Mistress Post. You have stockpiled a considerable sum.'

'I suppose I have. You see, in my current situation, I don't have much need for money. But in the future, I plan to build a house for my father and me. Not a grand house like yours, Mister Williams, but a property with acreage enough for my father to have a flock as he once did, and where I might operate a practice,' she explained as she rose and moved to the window. 'I do appreciate your view, however. A house overlooking the river would be lovely.'

Palgrave was reminded of his wife's dislike of the river. Although he would never admit his preference to her, he too was fonder of the sea, albeit for reasons that differed to Leah's.

'You have enough money for that now, Tabby.'

'I do?' She turned from the window, a look of surprise lighting her face.

'In coin alone.'

Although it had been a part of her purpose in coming to Augusta, she had never considered that she would be in possession of such a large amount. She watched Williams thoughtfully as he returned the coin and wampum to the purses and waited for her direction.

What would happen, she wondered, *if the township didn't prosper, if all Mister Williams's investments failed or if he turned out as duplicitous as Jeremy Cool?* Tabby looked at the portrait and considered the family and all their imperfections. Finally, she decided that she would trust Palgrave Williams and his wife, and hope for the best.

'Then you'll have to keep it safe for me until I'm ready. "Invest" it, as you said, Mister Williams.' She paused for a moment, considering her next words.

'There are matters I must see to first. Matters that you might be able to help me with.'

He removed his spectacles and raised his eyebrows, an indication she should continue. As briefly as she was able, Tabby told Palgrave her father's story and the information she had gleaned from Achak. Palgrave sat listening, nodding occasionally in understanding or frowning in distress.

'I was wondering, Mister Williams, if, in your dealings, you have ever crossed paths with a man matching Achak's description of my uncle's killer? Or, indeed, with General John Hill? Although Hill's correspondence was sympathetic, I have a notion that he knows more that he was letting on in his letter. And based on what Achak revealed to me, I now believe the general's dealings in New France were not aboveboard.'

'I have known a good many men in my time, Tabby, who have sported tattoos but none that bore the King of Spades. However,' he rose and walked swiftly to his writing table and searched the contents of his hutch, eventually withdrawing a small slip of parchment, 'I do know the whereabouts of General John Hill.'

TABBY'S back basket was exceedingly less burdensome as she followed Maria up the staircase to the room where she would stay. In addition, she felt a modicum lighter for being one step closer to finding General Hill thanks to Palgrave Williams. He had revealed that Hill was a fellow member of the land sale Committee and, coincidentally, a patient of their soon-to-be guest, Doctor Benjamin Shute. She thought that dinner might well be more interesting than she had anticipated.

The staircase was an imposing structure, not like the boxed variety that Tabby was familiar with, a single flight of steep, narrow steps that was virtually no more than a ladder. To Tabby's eye, this staircase was impressive; sitting to the right-hand side of the entranceway, it consisted of wide stairs enclosed by white serpentine balusters and an elaborately turned newel. It led up to a landing where Tabby stopped for a moment as this particular architectural detail was a novelty to her. From the landing, the staircase turned and continued to the second storey.

After some toing and froing as to where she would sleep – Tabby refused to dislodge anyone from their chamber and Leah refused to allow her to sleep in the barn or under the stars – it was decided she would share Maria's room for the duration of her stay. It was Maria who had voiced the option as though it was the only conceivable one.

The room lay at the front of the house, overlooking the river and the town. Tabby was glad of that. Although, waking in the morning was never a misfortune for Tabby, she would make certain to especially relish the act while residing here.

Near the window of the white-walled room, where a writing table would usually be, stood an easel with an unfinished painting of the sea resting on it. Tabby observed rolling, foaming waves in colours of deep crimson and sapphire, dotted with splashes of rich, buttery cream. As she looked, she realised that Maria must be responsible for the portrait in Mister Williams's study.

Adjacent to the easel was a hearth. Beside the hearth, standing like an altar at the end of the room, lay a spectacular cupboard. *Maria Hallett* was emblazoned upon its frontispiece in brilliant blue lettering. The name was surrounded by images of stars, roses, vines of flowers, insects and flourishes of emblems of love and fertility – love hearts, rabbits and the like. Beneath the frontispiece lay three long drawers, embellished in colours of similar intensity. Tabby had never seen the like of it before; it was a simple cloth cupboard made bold.

She was immediately drawn to the piece, possessed with

a strong desire to touch it. *How unusual for a woman (or a man for that matter) to brand their name into a piece of furniture*, she mused. *What was the purpose?*

'I planned the composition of the motifs and mixed the colours myself,' Maria explained, proudly, noticing Tabby's interest. 'This colour,' Maria pointed at a square of striking amber, 'is called "Naples Yellow". The pigments arrived by post, from London. The cupboard itself was made in Hadley. My sister bought it for me to house my supplies. And other things.' Maria pulled open one of the long drawers. In it, standing like sentinels, were rows of phials, corked at the top. They looked like the bottles Tabby used for her own tinctures and treatments.

'Are you a healer?' Tabby asked eagerly, moving closer, always keen to trade remedies and experiences. She examined the contents of the drawer. *In another person's possession this would be filled with table linens and sheets*, she thought.

'Not exactly.' Maria smiled peculiarly then closed the drawer.

Apart from the cupboard the only other piece of furniture was a high, wide bed surrounded by four carved posts. These posts were seemingly hemmed in on all sides by a short piece of lace that hung from the top. Rising to her toes, Tabby examined it closely. The texture was fine to the touch, but the flowers embroidered into it were pronounced, lending it a deceptive weight.

'It is *Brussels* lace,' Maria said as Tabby fingered the edging. Naples Yellow, Brussels lace; Maria took obvious delight in voicing the names. Tabby could not discern whether this stemmed from pride or weariness.

Tabby had heard mention of Brussels lace among the ladies in Wallingford. From the exclamations that it garnered, Tabby was sure it was tremendously expensive and superior to all other lace.

'Palgrave brought it with him when he returned from his *adventures*,' Maria added.

'Adventures' was a curious word to use. Tabby wondered what adventures such a staid and steady man as Palgrave Williams might have embarked upon.

Unsolicited, Maria went on.

'At the time, my sister did not know how to use the lace and it was boxed away for many years.' Maria smiled at the memory. 'When we moved to Augusta, Palgrave discovered it and urged Leah to use it at last. Leah made a pair of elbow ruffles for herself following Palgrave's precise instructions. She pinned them to the sleeves of her finest dress. Well, the dress *was* fine by Eastham standards once, long ago, but perhaps it had grown shabby in the intervening years.

'She and I laughed at the spectacle before Leah said, "To adorn a sleeve so is utter folly." Leah sees no value in that which is not useful. She has always been this way.'

'What did she do with it then?' asked Tabby, unexpectedly transfixed by Maria's story.

'Leah removed the pins and fashioned the ruffles into petticoats for Sarah's favourite doll. Up until the present, Mistress Post, we led a very simple life. It is not in our natures to adorn our bodices, aprons and caps with lace as many women do. Yet Leah did not want to hurt Palgrave's feelings. She adorned our beds with the remainder of the fine fabric instead.'

Tabby could see that Maria treasured her room and its contents. It was her private space. She wondered why Maria had insisted she share it with her.

'I think it's very beautiful,' said Leah's unusual sister as she touched the edges of the delicate handwork. 'When the moonlight filters through the lattice in the night, I *believe* I am in Heaven.'

Tabby stood for a moment, transfixed. Conscious that she was staring, she turned to take in the whole room, examining all its varied elements again. As she did so, she realised Maria was looking at her strangely, in the same way she had in the summer kitchen. Then she moved closer, seeming to explore Tabby entirely, inside and out, an expression of extreme concentration fixed on her lovely face. Maria's dark blue eyes floated over her like a shimmering veil until her skin tingled. It was as though streams of liquid fire ran through her veins. Although Maria did not touch her, Tabby sensed the enlivening, tender strokes of countless feathery fingers. Goosebumps rose like prickles on her body. All that existed at that moment was Maria's probing gaze.

An exasperated cry from outside in the yard tore open the intimate cocoon that had been spun around the women in the few short minutes they'd spent together. Tabby whirled towards the window.

'Fiona has gotten to Leah's seedlings again,' Maria said calmly, still standing close.

'Fiona?'

'Our goat. You should rest now until dinner.' She walked towards the door then turned and smiled.

'I shall enjoy sharing a room with you, Tabby Post,' said Maria, before departing.

DOCTOR BENJAMIN SHUTE arrived promptly at four toting a fresh, keen face with lively amber eyes. He removed his hat as he entered the parlour where the family and Tabby stood, waiting as though on display. Except for Leah, who sat; by the afternoon she found it difficult to bear her own weight. The windows had been opened wide to allow a cool breeze entry into the parlour.

Gazing outside for a moment, Tabby wondered where Edie was. She had not seen her since her flight this morning. Tabby looked down at her gown. *I hope she does not see me in this*, she thought. *She will barely recognise me.* While she had been resting, Leah and Maria had found a shift, skirt and bodice for Tabby to wear.

'I think the green will set off your pretty hair, Tabby,' Leah had said as she lay the garments on the bed. 'Abby will bring hot water for the basin shortly.'

Then she walked towards the door. Turning around, she went on. 'All people have their eccentricities. Please believe me when I tell you that I am accepting of all quirks of character. Unfortunately, I fear Ben Shute will likely die of shock if he is confronted with a woman's bare legs. He is only twenty-two and I do not want this meal to be his last.'

Tabby smiled as Leah left the room. Aware her choice of attire was unusual and shocking to those with limited perspective, Tabby decided to oblige, so had examined the skirt and bodice, rubbing the soft fabric between her fingers. Besides, she reasoned, she was a guest of Leah Williams and her husband and, although she may look like a savage, as young Caleb had so bluntly declared, the Sisters and her mother before them had branded her with their mark: respect. Tabby believed Leah Williams was worthy of that.

Now her attention was drawn to the young doctor who wore breeches and a jacket made of homespun cloth, the elbows of which had been mended and patched. Ben Shute was attractive, Tabby judged, with light brown hair bunched together with a leather thong. He had a prominent square jaw that she expected would garner much admiration once it was more thoroughly whiskered.

As Palgrave made the introductions, Abby and Maria served punch into silver canns engraved with the initials *PW* and *LH*. The punch bowl was deep and wide and sat nestled in small chunks of ice in an even wider silver bowl, elegantly engraved on one side with poppies, stars and a crescent moon, and on the other with morning glories and butterflies. *What a whimsical touch*, Tabby thought as she examined the bowl, poking a finger at the ice in wonder.

'Where did you find ice at this time of year?' Tabby said, inadvertently interrupting the greetings. The river around Augusta had thawed completely a month ago.

Palgrave spun around. 'I have built an icehouse, Tabby.'

'An icehouse?'

Leah rose then and made her way to Tabby, slowly.

'I had never heard of such a thing either until a short time ago when my husband began digging a great hole in the ground next to the summer kitchen. What came of the hole was something similar to a basement, kept cold by the surrounding earth. When the river is frozen, we cut large slabs of ice to store there so that, in the summer months, we can have luxuries such as cold rum punch and flavoured ices.'

Leah winked at her guest. Although she had met Leah Williams only hours before, Tabby knew her well enough to realise that unseasonal ice would be considered a *folly* as well.

In a kinder tone, Leah went on to tell her that Palgrave had made the punch bowl and canns himself, a gift for the anniversary of their marriage.

'He was a silversmith once, in another life,' she whispered. Before she continued, she took a deep breath. 'But we have forgotten the poor doctor,' said Leah, speaking at volume. 'Tabby Post, this is our friend, Doctor Benjamin Shute.'

The doctor took Tabby's fingers in his hand and offered her a slight bow.

11

―――――

After supper, Tabby felt a fit of gripe coming on. She had not eaten such a feast ever, she reasoned – roasted venison, buttered onions, cabbage farce, ramequins of cheese then, finally, tea creams – and her belly ballooned uncomfortably, rumbling in discontent. When she was travelling, Tabby ate only when her body indicated it was in need of sustenance. Sometimes Tabby could last three days without a square meal, subduing her hunger with berries from the forest. But now she needed to stand and walk after so many hours at the table.

Making her way to the front of the house, she stepped outside. Moosehead Lake called out to her and such was her urgency to answer, she jogged partway down the gravel drive. She longed to feast her senses on its space, air and solitude, and to cure her spirit that had so waned under the weight of supper and the conversation.

She'd see to Leah's babe being born and call on Kirkcaldie. After that she would respond to its call. Feeding on the familiar scents, sights and sounds of nature. Taking in the gentle lap of its water against the bank, its hidden inlets and bays, the bite of it on her tongue and Mount Kineo rising like an inhalation from its satiny breast – the burdens of each day would seem weightless. Moosehead was an elixir. It was her haven.

The confines of the Williamses' house (not to mention the stay Leah had lent her), the constant questions from Mister Williams and Doctor Shute, and the generous servings of rum punch she'd imbibed this evening had combined to make her realise what she had lost – a tolerance for civilisation.

The eldest son and daughter, Joseph and Elizabeth, had joined them for dinner. At eighteen, Joseph was a young man made in the image of his father. He was destined for Harvard University in the fall, but Tabby noted by his direct conversation and homely ways that the life of a scholar would not suit him. Sixteen-year-old Elizabeth was very beautiful, possessing her mother's treacle-coloured hair and her aunt's generous features. Tabby wondered if the doctor's sights were set on her. They would make a handsome couple and, in Tabby's experience, make handsome babies.

Then there were the twins, Joshua and Sarah, cut from each other's image but not temperament. The boy was outgoing and eager to join the discourse of the adults. He would likely become the scholar, Tabby judged. His twin, Sarah, appeared a shy, studious girl who also took an avid interest in the conversation of the adults but didn't dare comment. Unlike her sister, Sarah resembled her father in appearance. At only thirteen years old, she possessed a mature, regal quality. However, Tabby could see by the blush of her pale cheeks each time the attractive doctor spoke to her, or even glanced her way, that Sarah's affections were still of the girlish variety.

Tabby groaned. Flushed and uncomfortable, she pulled

at the neckline of her bodice, allowing the cool air to seep between her breasts. Unconvincing bursts of cloud muted the radiance of the violet sky at sunset as she gazed above her, searching for Edie. Then she released a whistle, high-pitched, shrill and insistent. Almost instantly, the sky ruptured and through the fissure shot Edie, like a meteor, towards her. In a moment, the falcon's talons were wrapped comfortingly around her hand but then quickly tightened.

Tabby winced. 'I know. You do not approve of my altered appearance.'

Tabby spoke to Edie softly and quickly the bird's spirits returned to normal.

'Have you had a good day, my girl?'

She stroked the bird's crown as Edie offered her a low chirrup of pleasure.

'To be truthful, I'm at sixes and sevens.' Now that she knew where General Hill was, she wanted to act. But having given her word that she would assist in delivery of Leah's baby when it comes, Tabby felt she had to stay. She never reneged on a promise.

Doctor Shute had not spoken of Hill in glowing terms. 'Self-seeking' was how Mister Williams described the man. *Then again, most men are*, thought Tabby. And from what the men had discussed at dinner, it appeared that the governor's committee was also on shaky ground.

'Too many men with interests at odds with each other, my girl,' she said to Edie. 'Mister Williams seems intent on moving slowly, preserving tracts of forest and relations with the Indians. But Hill is determined to drive the Indians far away from the river and forests that are their birthright.

'The committee's conflict over land stokes my concern for Kirkcaldie, too.'

The bird twitched her head sharply. Tabby laughed.

'No matter your opinion, he is a good man. I do not want to see him undone by bankers or government officials and the like.'

Tabby decided she would form her own opinion of the general. She would call on him after the baby was born, on her way to Kirkcaldie.

Tabby stroked the falcon's feathers once more.

'At least we know where Hill can be found. The news gives me hope, Edie.'

'I must confess, Mistress Post, to be quite terrified of wild animals.'

Tabby turned. She had been so deeply lost in her thoughts that she hadn't heard the doctor's tread on the loose gravel.

'Edie is quite civilised, I can assure you, Doctor,' said Tabby. 'Perhaps more civilised than me,' she added. 'Why, did you know that falcons are so refined as to pluck their kills before they eat them?'

'I did not know that,' replied the doctor.

'And they can talk to us, in a fashion,' she added. Tabby enjoyed educating people about Edie, adopting the role of teacher. 'I always know what Edie is feeling by the sounds she makes, and I'm certain she can discern my humour.' Tabby laughed as the bird's beak got tangled in her hair. 'See what she's doing now?'

The doctor nodded.

'She's searching for lice and the like, taking care of me.'

'Is she likely to discover any?'

'I hope not,' Tabby replied, the echo of her laughter piercing the still evening. She watched as Doctor Benjamin Shute gave Edie a wary look. 'You have nothing to be frightened of,' she said, beckoning him closer.

During supper, Tabby had watched the doctor as he earnestly discussed medicine. Ben Shute had studied at Leiden University in Holland. According to Shute, the institution received only the most promising students of medicine. After university, he worked briefly at the hospital in Utrecht. Yet, while surely impressive to some, the six-month duration of his studies and short period of practical experience seemed inadequate to Tabby who, after almost a decade serving as midwife in Wallingford and on the Kennebec, still faced new and peculiar challenges every day. None of her learning came from a book. But Tabby kept her misgivings to herself. Sensing the disparity in their experience, Shute had directed a volley of questions at Tabby, seeking her wisdom. Mister Williams had joined in the assault; he seemed to have some medical knowledge of his own, but from where it had been gained, he chose not to reveal.

It had been difficult to explain her work. So much of her way of healing boiled down to instinct, she realised. Reading the expression of a fevered child; listening to the breaths of a labouring mother; staring into the eyes of a dying man, eventually giving him silent permission to die ... Much of it was guess work, intuition and blind hope – nothing that could be written in a medical tome.

'Come closer, Doctor,' Tabby said. 'You may pet her. Edie enjoys the firm touch of a man's caress.'

Shute shot her a look. Blushing, he moved towards the pair slowly.

'Stroke her back and then her chest. Can you note the difference in her feathers?'

Shute stood close to Tabby now, petting Edie gingerly. She examined his face and features as he did so. As far as she could see, his teeth were white and all accounted for and his skin wore none of the pockmarks and scars of disease.

'I can indeed,' he remarked. 'The feathers about her neck and on her chest are as soft and downy as a chick's.'

Tabby smiled in agreement.

'Ouch!' he cried suddenly, when Edie nibbled at his nose.

'Don't be alarmed, Doctor Shute. She is kissing you.'

'Good heavens,' he exclaimed. 'That is her idea of a kiss?'

'If Edie meant to harm you, your nose would be torn through and hanging from your face. Fortunately, she likes you.'

'And you, Mistress Post?' The doctor's amber eyes looked into hers. 'Do you like me?'

Tabby was taken aback by the query. Perhaps it was merely the lingering effects of the rum punch but Tabby could swear she heard a tinge of affection in his tone. Her heart began to race, and she immediately thought it would not be such a great hardship to kiss this young doctor herself.

'What does it matter?' she asked nonchalantly, attempting to regain control of herself.

'I know you are sceptical of doctors. I can read it all over your face. You are a gifted healer, Mistress Post, but your skills are lacking in the art of concealment.'

Tabby felt a flush rise in her cheeks. The doctor took a moment to clear his throat.

'However, I earnestly believe that medicine is my calling, as stentorian as your own, and I hope someday to earn your trust and equal you in skill. You are quite renowned, Mistress Post, for your talents and your compassion in equal measure. I believe there is much I could learn from you and, perchance, there are procedures that I know of that you might gain insight from. If we were to form a bond, an alliance or partnership of mutual learning and the sharing of knowledge, perhaps we could join forces when it was required ...'

Edie flapped her wings and the doctor leapt back in surprise. He looked at Tabby. There was amusement in her eyes.

'What is Edie telling you now?'

Tabby laughed. 'Edie suggests that I sleep on it.'

12

'My father spoke about sheep a great deal. Endlessly. He knew more about sheep than he did about shooting. Papa knew that the weight of a just-born lamb was nigh the same as a just-born babe. He knew that a mother sheep would sometimes attack her baby, although he did not know why. He told me that a sheep's cough sounded exactly the same as that of a human. He knew their fleece would grow forever if it was not shorn and he knew that sheep could see behind them without having to turn their head.'

'That is extremely interesting, Mistress Post,' Dummer said, drily. 'What is the point you are travelling very slowly towards in your homily?'

'There is no direct point, Sir, but I believe it is useful for you and the other magistrates to gain a full and clear portrait of Ephraim Post. He was a mercenary for only a small fragment of his life. He had been a good and simple man, a shepherd from the time he was a boy. If his story is coloured by the blot of his months in New France, then I am concerned mine will be tainted also.'

Impatient at the level of detail the stubborn woman insisted on providing, Dummer nevertheless nodded. 'Go on'.

'He had a dog named Gus, a rough-coated, bob-tailed butcher's dog, who he trained to respond to his whistle. Gus knew sheep, too, almost as well as my father, and it was a sight to see Gus herd the flock, running right and left, in front and behind, in response to my father's calls. Papa loved Gus and, when that old dog died, I saw my father weep for the first time. Gus left him not very long after my mother. He had not cried when my mother died. Had I witnessed his tears, my small, fragile world would have unravelled in that instant. I know now that tears must be shed when a loved one dies. Bottling them, holding them in will come to no good end in the long run. But then I was grateful not to see them shed by him. He was the bedrock of my world.

'Papa met my mother when he travelled to Quebec to purchase a ram that was well-known among sheep farmers in the north east for its siring abilities. Bacchus was his name, a fitting moniker for a beast of his talents. Bacchus was worth a king's ransom, but Papa was young, just four and twenty, and ambitious. He believed that his future prosperity was contained solely in Bacchus's loins.'

Tabby paused a moment when she heard sniggers from her audience. She saw the governor's face tighten.

'Governor Dummer, this tale does not begin in the most romantic of ways but, I can assure you, the ending is worthy of Shakespeare.' Tabby turned back to her audience, who, despite Dummer's scorn, were waiting for her to continue.

'My father was travelling with his younger brother, whose eventual demise sparked my current circumstances. I can tell you, good people, that the irony of this unfortunate situation has not been lost on me. In a sense, my father's story begins and ends in Quebec saving his brother, and this is where my account begins, too.

'A few miles from the farm where Bacchus would be found, the brothers were attacked by a band of Cree. My uncle was wounded in his shoulder by an arrow. Their horses and supplies were made off with. My father never spoke against these Indians – he knew that he and Eb had been crossing Cree lands.

'As good luck would have it, for it *was* good luck from my point of view, they were also just a short distance from the convent where my mother was a novice. Her name was Sister Margaret, although her true name was Marie.

'It was Sister Margaret who tended to my uncle's wounds. My father recalled she was gentle and quiet and that her touch was as soft and as warm as sun-kissed clover. I believe both brothers fell in love with her, explaining my uncle's oft peppery demeanour with my father. However, it was my father she chose, over Eb and over God.

Tabby paused. 'In truth, if Sister Margaret had chosen God she would, most likely, be living today. But she did not.

'When my mother dedicated her life to her faith, she sacrificed all she had known before. She vowed to live in chastity, poverty and complete obedience. It is only now that I realise how difficult it must have been for her to leave the convent. What did she read in my father's eyes, his words, his touch that had awakened something more powerful than the love of God in her?'

Dummer eyed her irritably, waiting for her to conclude.

'I will never know. But it must have been something deep and profound for she did love God and I can attest to that. And I can attest in equal faith that, regardless of my father's actions, he was a good man – good enough to be worthy of a woman such as my mother.'

13

———

Leah lay on her back in her bed, staring at the huge bulge before her. She could barely draw breath, trapped under such a mountain. She had once heard that suspected witches were pressed under a boulder. Leah now knew their suffering. Occasionally, she dreamt of her own child, a small babe still wearing a clout, pressing a pillow over her mouth or holding her head under water, his face straining, the tiny muscles prominent in his arms. Dreams of an expectant mother were always absurd. *Absurd to the point of bizarre*, she concluded.

Lifting her bulk then lowering it to the ground, she walked to the window and flung it wide open. The panes rattled with the force. The fine muslin curtains billowed gently in the breeze and Leah, resting her hands against the window frame, breathed in as deeply as the child would allow. Indistinct voices carried to her on the wind and she craned her neck to view the speakers. Tabby and Ben. The falcon was present as well. The young doctor stood close to Tabby; the unusual woman's startling red hair was lit by the moon. Leah raised an eyebrow, wondering.

Making her way back to bed, she propped her pillows against the bedhead and sat upright, a trick she had learnt to relieve the pressure on her chest. Closing her eyes, she took in the music of the voices from outside and, as she waited for sleep to arrive, she mused over Tabby Post. What an extraordinary creature she was. Strikingly beautiful, she had chosen to remain unmarried and live like an Indian. Why, she even carried a bow and quiver. Judging from the long lines of her arms and her precise movements, Leah wagered she would be a good shot. Leah envied her freedom. She had not felt free since Wellfleet, yet, at the same time, she was certain a woman of Tabby's passions would long for a mate. Leah knew those passions, too.

When Palgrave had returned from Nassau, there was a long period of harmony. Bellamy had been lost but, while very much saddened by his friend's death, Palgrave seemed to take greater delight in his family. He seemed to want for nothing more than he had at his fingertips: Leah and his children. He opened a small smith's store, she grew what they ate and, between them, Maria and Abby schooled the children.

The saddlebags – 'our future' as he had called them on his arrival in Wellfleet – rested for many years in the bottom of a chest in their chamber, covered by linens, untouched. She had never looked inside and, having never discovered the linens disturbed, she assumed neither had he. It seemed to Leah the saddlebags and their contents had been forgotten and with them, the time they were apart. It seemed to her that the ten months he had spent at sea had been erased.

Palgrave never spoke of his time away, of Bellamy or of what became of his friend. Although Leah could not conceal the scars on her back where she had been whipped for 'tarrying with the Devil', she had never spoken to Palgrave of Silas Dent's bastard child. That midnight in her father's field, when she lay the tiny babe in an unmarked grave haunted her still; for Maria, it was as though she had never given birth at all. Likewise, she and Abby never returned to the night in Reverend Dent's chamber. And so, memories of that trying period – all she had suffered, the crimes she had committed – dispersed and drifted far away like fire sparks.

She had supposed that during that time that she and Palgrave were getting to know each other again, each of them changed by the events of those months. Somehow, perhaps in silent recognition that the events were immense, they each reconciled their past with their present. What came between was of no concern. Homelife was not perfect. It was not the same as it had once been. But the family had seemed to rebuild.

It was only after, when Palgrave designed the grand house and insisted on the move to Augusta, did she realise the depth of his overwhelming hunger to be a man of status and means. His decision to found Augusta's first bank struck her like a thunderbolt. She realised at that moment that he had always been ashamed of his honest and humble livelihood. She could not fathom his insatiable desire for change, to be reborn. Her relief at Palgrave's return had blinded her to that need – the same desire that had attracted him to Bellamy, and led him to leave her for the sea.

Tabby's sweet laughter bounded through the window. Leah opened her eyes. Tabby had enthralled them all at supper with tales of the people she had helped and of her calling, 'a loud and constant call to arms' to attend those suffering. She was brave and forthright and spoke plainly of her deeds, unaware of the courage it took to complete them. Leah smiled to herself, recalling their exchange in Maria's chamber before supper.

'I would like to examine you tomorrow, Goody Williams, but I have an inkling that the child is long overdue,' Tabby had said as Leah placed the garments she'd selected for her on the bed.

'If there was something I could do to bring on its arrival ...'

'Well, there are many methods – some more reliable than others.'

Leah smiled as she remembered the mischievous tone in Tabby's voice.

'Such as?' Leah ventured.

Tabby tilted her head slightly and her mouth curled.

'There are herbs I could give you, and long walks help gravity play its part, but the surest way ...' Tabby paused for an instant, taking in Leah's grave expression. 'Just imagine a woodpecker going at a soft, young pine. It takes no time at all for them to ... *prick* the bark and release the sap.'

Leah hadn't gleaned her meaning for a moment, but as the image of the woodpecker formed in her mind, she felt her face redden.

'You mean ...'

'Lie with your husband, Goody Williams. It is the surest way.'

Leah had never heard a woman speak in such a coarse manner, yet she wasn't offended. The vulgarity of the actual words was tempered by the speaker's gentle, kind tone. Leah was embarrassed by her own naivety and lack of acuity.

Perhaps Tabby had not yet met the man who possessed the self-assurance needed to be her partner, who could match her and not be perturbed by her daring and independence. *She would make most men feel insubstantial*, Leah thought. *Was Ben Shute the one?* she wondered and quickly doubted the notion. Too young, too uncertain. He was not her equal. Yet he reminded Leah in many ways of Samuel Bellamy. Ben was not as handsome or as bold, and certainly not as cock-sure, but he was ambitious and optimistic.

She had noticed Ben's effect on Palgrave was similar to that of Bellamy's. She could see her husband was moved by Ben's dreams and ideas for the future, just as he had been when Bellamy arrived in Eastham nine years ago. It troubled her that his eye could turn so resolutely and, if she was completely honest, she was jealous.

Palgrave had first met Ben in Wellfleet. The doctor had required a set of blades for surgery. He had travelled from Boston, taking it on good word that Palgrave was the finest silversmith in the east. Following the illustrations in a medical book the doctor had provided, Palgrave had crafted four keen blades of various sizes and weights that glinted in the light. The spark had been lit and Leah was unable to douse it. Within weeks, Palgrave was discussing the notion of funding a practice for the doctor in Augusta. Not long after, he began petitioning to move the family there, too.

Then one evening she entered their chamber. The chest was open and her clean linens had been thrown on the floor. The saddlebags were gone.

That was two years ago. Now the children had tutors, Elizabeth wanted for silk dresses and ribbons and Joseph (who always hoped to be a silversmith like his father) was bound for Cambridge, Massachusetts and Harvard University. Now she and Palgrave seemed to tiptoe around each other like strangers. Sometimes they would sit in excruciating silence, neither of them wanting to raise the ire of the

other with an ill-timed remark that would surely be miscon-
strued. There were truths that needed to be told, truths with
the power to break down walls, but neither had the courage
to voice them. They still came together often, in the dark. It
was in bed that the gulf between them could be bridged. No
words were needed, just longing and touch and fierce intent.

While she could see the value in Palgrave's business
ventures and the security they provided, she longed for the
time when they had nothing, although she would never
express that to him. Those times had been the most difficult
for Palgrave, when he felt he could not provide for his
family. It is true that those times had been difficult for her as
well, but in a different way. Now, they were what she longed
for. It seemed that for so many years her purpose had been
survival. With that assured, what was she living for?

THERE WAS a soft rap on the door of the study. Palgrave knew
it was Ben; he had heard him and Tabby enter the house
and say goodnight. Then he'd heard the midwife's quick
footsteps up the stairs to her chamber. There was laughter
in their parting words, a lightness and ease that wounded
Palgrave with a sharp dart of sorrow. It reminded him of the
early days with Leah. When they came to Augusta, he
realised their ambitions had always been in conflict, from
the very first. When they had met, she had been determined
to save him, despite his stubbornness. She had, to an extent.
Now, almost twenty years on, he could not fathom how to
fuse their forked dreams. Instead, he stared down at the
neat columns of figures on the page and soon felt restored.
There was order and predictability in the digits; he understood them.

He had watched his young friend at supper. Ben was surely smitten by Tabby. He hung on her every word, punctuating her tales with compliments and queries. Despite her unpretentious ways, she was his equal in intelligence. Palgrave wondered if she had been schooled. She wrote in a very fine hand.

It had been the same between Bellamy and Maria. His friend had never concealed his feelings for her. Perhaps if he had been more discreet ... Palgrave shook his head, keen to put thoughts of his friend aside.

'Come in, Ben,' Palgrave called from his desk. The doctor entered and then sat in the armchair without waiting for an invitation. Palgrave liked the familiarity that had developed between them over the past year. Although just two and twenty, Ben had become a close friend as the pair had nutted out their ideas for the practice. For a young man, he had grand vision, a quality Palgrave respected. There were too few people in the world, it seemed to Palgrave, who dreamt large. Content to suffer their lot, too many were incapable of even imagining a more fruitful, contented existence. In fact, it seemed to Palgrave that many people shunned the notion of working harder, taking risks and stepping outside 'their lot'. Ben was not one of these people.

Benjamin Shute came from a merchant family of great wealth. The family had accrued immense riches on the back of slaves, sugar and rum as the colonies expanded, and his father, Samuel Shute, had been the governor of the Province of Massachusetts Bay until two years before. But Palgrave knew Samuel Shute as the man responsible for sending the survivors of the *Whydah* – his friends – to the gallows.

Palgrave recalled that day in the Boston courthouse eight years ago. Boston was known as a hanging town and, if the nine men being tried that morning were found guilty, they would be strung from a gibbet overlooking the river before the week was out. During his journey from Wellfleet, a weight like a cannonball had come to rest in his belly. If one of the nine prisoners turned out to be Bellamy, Palgrave was determined to free him.

But Bellamy was not among them.

Palgrave had been disappointed. It was then that Palgrave had been forced to accept his friend's death. Bellamy would never be saved.

Knowing Ben's family background led Palgrave to often wonder whether he and Bellamy had ever captured one of the Shute family's ships. If so, Palgrave was gladdened. He had witnessed the mockery of a trial orchestrated by Governor Shute that resulted in the executions of his friends and comrades. *What a mischievous world it was,* Palgrave thought now, *that united me with the current generation of that family.*

Samuel Shute, Massachusetts's eventual leader, was not destined to become a merchant like Ben's grandfather. Instead, he joined the English army. His bravery and cunning in battle earnt him the rank of Lieutenant Colonel and, later, the position of governor of the most powerful and prosperous of the thirteen colonies. So it was in Boston where young Ben spent his formative years living a life of great privilege, being spoilt and pampered by his mother and five sisters. It was assumed by all that Ben, as the only son, would follow his father into the military. But Ben had other ideas.

His interest in medicine was ignited by the death of his beloved sister, Patience. When he was fifteen, his younger sister had succumbed to an illness that had not only eaten away at her body but gnawed viciously at her mind as well. None of the practitioners, the 'experts' and 'specialists', his father had procured from Europe were able to diagnose Patience's illness. Ben had sat by uselessly as foreign doctors had poked her and bled her. He had listened to her screams as they burned her and bored holes in her skull. He had cried with her when they dosed her with opium. Eventually, after many agonising months, she had died, a mere shadow of the young woman she once was.

From that point on, Ben felt medicine was his destiny. When it was time to enter the army, he refused, explaining to his father that military life was not the one chosen for him. Yet despite Ben's appeals, his father would not soften in his rigid stance. Ben was aware he had disappointed his father, but the dying figure of Patience clouded his every thought. He knew he could do better, be more compassionate than the plethora of surgeons who had visited his sister's bedside.

Unable to sway his father, Ben fled the colonies, stowing away on a ship bound for Holland (this was the part of the story Palgrave enjoyed the most) then paid for his tuition at Leiden University by serving the undergraduates' meals. This was a novel experience for a young man who had spent his life being served. He suffered his exclusion and the jibes of his classmates with good humour, comforted by the knowledge that he would be able to help those in need when he graduated.

Now Ben fiddled with the button on his coat and looked, to Palgrave, as uncertain as he must have appeared when he snuck upon the frigate bound for Holland.

'She is an unusual woman,' Ben said.

'"Unique" is probably a more apt term,' suggested Palgrave.

Ben nodded thoughtfully. 'And the bird ...'

'Hmmm,' Palgrave offered.

'Mistress Post is vastly knowledgeable,' said the doctor, pausing as he moved to the window. He gazed into the night. 'I suggested we work together, if the opportunity ever occurred. She would be an immense asset to the practice.'

Palgrave nodded. Tabby had shown him what a good healer was capable of earning. He had invested more than one hundred pounds in Ben's practice; now he was confident of a handsome return.

'Tabby would be an asset under many circumstances, I imagine.'

Ben turned then. A smile appeared on his lips. 'You read my thoughts.'

'It is not difficult.'

Ben gave a quiet *huh* of acknowledgement. 'She is a good deal older than me.'

'There are twelve years between Leah and myself. Years make no difference if you are on the same journey.'

Ben sat on the windowsill, staring at his hands as he rubbed them together in contemplation.

'Is she already spoken for, do you know?' Ben said hastily, looking up.

'I do not. I would guess not.'

After a minute of waiting, listening to the doctor's thoughts turn over in his mind, Palgrave asked, 'What is it exactly that concerns you so?'

Ben sighed. 'I tell myself I am different from my father, that I do not see wealth or status or rank but ...'

Palgrave walked to him and took him by the shoulder. 'Get to know Tabby and you will see beyond her Indian trappings and the bird.'

'You're right, of course, as always.' Ben rose, seemingly restored. 'I will tackle the problem after a good night's sleep.'

'This isn't a problem, my friend. It is a gift.'

Ben closed the door softly behind him and Palgrave returned to his figures. After a minute, he removed his spectacles and rubbed his eyes.

If only I had given more thorough counsel to Bellamy, he thought.

14

Tabby remained with the family for four more days waiting for the baby to arrive. It was certainly a stubborn child and Tabby found herself musing on just how long the babe could hold out. Ben was often present at the house, usually working with Palgrave in the study until late into the evening making plans for the opening of his practice. However, he always made a point of seeking her out, sometimes with a medical question or simply to inquire about her day.

On the morning the baby decided to arrive, Tabby, attired in her usual garments – tunic, leggings and moccasins – worked in Leah's garden, and Leah toiled in the summer kitchen. Refusing to rest, she insisted on getting the bread baked before the dinner. Tabby sensed the baby would come today. An unwanted, inexplicable urgency overcame most women within hours of labour beginning.

Doctor Shute had stayed the night, on a pallet in the stable, and was now seated in the shade of a pine alongside Palgrave. They seemed to be discussing matters of some importance. As the older man spoke, he held his place in a book with a finger. Their voices, low grumbles as though they were at matins, drifted to her across the yard. Tabby could sense Shute's eyes on her as she tended to the seedlings and hauled water from the well. Tabby did not mind the attentions he was paying her. Men gazed at her often with hunger in their eyes but the young doctor's expression was different – thoughtful, as though contemplating the future. She liked him. He still viewed hardships as challenges, and he displayed a fierce longing to learn. This kind of desire, in her experience, was a rare commodity. But she was also certain that if, in fact, he harboured affection for her then nothing could arise from his feelings. She did not long for a husband and it was clear that Shute was of the husband mindset.

It would have been no later than ten when Leah cried out from the kitchen. When Tabby made her way inside, she found Leah leaning against the table, flour covering her hands and a puddle of water at her feet. Abby was already gathering cloths and basins.

'Apart from the twins, her babies have come fast,' Abby said. 'We need to get her inside.'

Tabby nodded in agreement.

Palgrave was already by Leah's side. Shute stood on her other side, ready to offer assistance. Tabby wondered for an instant where Maria might be but there was no time to find her.

'Your suggestion seems to have worked,' Leah said. Her words tapered into a low guttural groan as the first pains began. She clutched at her husband, leaning on him so heavily that he stumbled backwards a few steps.

'Sure as eggs in April,' Tabby replied as she made her way to Leah. Palgrave shot her a confused glance but before he could raise a query, Tabby began issuing orders. From the tone of Leah's cries, Abby was correct and they may only have minutes.

Abby, take Leah to her chamber and make her comfortable.

Gather straw from the stable, Doctor Shute. Enough to cover the floor of the chamber.

'Tabby.' Palgrave clasped her arm as soon as Abby had ushered his wife from the kitchen. There was anguish in his expression. All of a sudden, he appeared at least a decade older. 'Promise to take care of her. The birth of the twins was so difficult ...'

She noticed tears forming in his light blue eyes. Just how difficult nobody seemed capable off articulating, not even Abby.

'Of course,' Tabby replied, smiling kindly, attempting to dispel his fear, even though she knew it was useless.

She could read in his pained countenance that it was a fear long harboured and not likely to be erased with a few kindly words. Nevertheless, she had to utter them.

'I promise.'

Tabby herself collected a bucket of water and a mug (women in travail acquired an unquenchable thirst), a few more cloths (thrown over a shoulder), a freshly baked loaf for sustenance (tucked under an arm) then she stopped and took a deep breath. She stilled herself for a moment, readying herself for what might come. Then she made her way into the house.

DOCTOR SHUTE ASKED to watch the birth. Leah agreed. Tabby was thankful; his practice was to open in just one month's time and Shute had never witnessed the birth of a human child, let alone had a hand in delivering the child himself. Reasoning it was for the good of the community, Tabby viewed it as her responsibility to teach this young doctor as much as possible. She considered knowledge of childbirth essential for any healer. As a doctor, it would likely be Ben's bread and butter.

As the pain came in waves, Leah clutched at the bedpost, breathing slowly and deeply. Tabby could see she was well-versed in the desperate melodies of childbirth. Abby rubbed her back and sang softly to her, a song Tabby recognised by its chant-like rhythm as Indian, Algonquian probably. But it had a mournful tone (or perhaps it was just in the rendering) that tainted the atmosphere in the room. When the pains eased, Leah took a seat on her bed.

'You're doing very well,' Tabby said. 'I think you must have done this before.'

Leah smiled wanly. She was sweating, already exhausted. Tabby wiped Leah's brow with a cool, damp cloth.

As she did so, Tabby sensed a distinct atmosphere of foreboding in the chamber. She could feel it pulsating like heat on a high summer's day. It came from below them, where Palgrave sat in his study, and from beside her, where Abby hovered in her nervousness. Such an air was of no use to herself or the mother, so she sent Abby to distract Palgrave and the children.

Leah lay on the bed in her shift. Tabby lifted it to her knees and Leah instinctively bent her legs. Tabby gazed seriously between them for a moment.

'Look here, Doctor,' she said. Ben was standing far away from the bed. Tabby beckoned him closer. 'The neck of the womb has already expanded. It is going to be quick.'

Shute inched slightly towards the bed. When he was within her reach, Tabby yanked him to her side.

'Look,' she demanded. Tabby watched his expression as it altered from distaste to wonder.

'My goodness ... Is that the infant's head?' He leant in for a more thorough examination of the small circle of the crown he could detect. It was the size of a penny.

'Yes, Sir,' Tabby said delighted. 'Wash up. There's nothing quite like the feel of a warm, slick babe in your hands.'

The doctor looked at her in horror.

'I want to stand,' Leah said. Tabby offered her arm and guided Leah to the area in front of the hearth where Ben had spread the straw.

'Get ready, Doctor,' Tabby advised. 'I warrant nothing more than catching will be required of you, but you should be vigilant.' Then she addressed Leah. 'When the pains come again, I want you to push.'

Leah nodded.

'It's time,' said Tabby, then helped Leah lower herself onto the straw where she had placed a stool. Leah leant her elbows against it.

'I thought ...' Ben began.

'For a woman in travail there is nothing more unnatural than lying flat on her back. Do you know how gravity works, Doctor?'

He nodded.

'Standing or squatting is the best position, but this one,' she pointed at Leah, 'gives the midwife greater vantage. Babe doesn't end up with a head as flat as a beaten coin either.'

Tabby was speaking quickly. Aware that the baby's entrance into the world was only minutes away, she hoped to instil in the doctor as much knowledge as was possible in such a short time.

Tabby continued to give the doctor guidance, telling him where he should position himself behind Leah and where he should place his hands.

'Typically, the head pops out like a cork from a bottle of cider ...'

'Stop your prattling, Tabby!' Leah shouted.

'Women in travail can chew fire. Do not take it to heart,' Tabby murmured to Ben. He nodded, taking in her words as seriously as gospel.

At that moment Leah released a loud, growly moan of complete exertion and the baby's head appeared with a liquid *schlip*, glistening with blood and mucus.

'I will support the head, Doctor,' Tabby instructed, 'while you get your fingers around the shoulders. One more push, Leah.'

After a few second's rest, Leah pushed again. The doctor felt for the shoulders and eased them through the passage. Once free, the little girl slid comfortably into Shute's large, safe hands.

15

———

After a brief discussion between mother and father, the child was named Patience. Judging from the grave expressions on their faces as they conversed, Tabby took it to be a name of some significance for the couple. It seemed a fitting name for a baby that had displayed such restraint in her desire to be born.

Once the child was suckling, Tabby left the chamber. Aware her supplies of stinging nettle were dwindling, she made her way back to Maria's chamber and attached her leather pocket around her waist, wondering again about Maria's whereabouts. She was gone from the bed when Tabby had awoken that morning, and she had not seen her since.

As she was heading towards the staircase, Ben came from Leah's chamber. Tabby could almost see his skin tingling in his exhilaration.

'Where are you going, Mistress Post?'

Tabby smiled. 'You shall call me Tabby and I shall address you as Ben. Agreed?'

He nodded.

'I am heading to the woods to gather stinging nettle. It is a ready tonic for women after childbirth,' she explained as she took the stairs to the landing. Shute followed. 'It strengthens their blood as well as their constitution. And at ten pounds, Patience will be hungry, always. Leah will need all the assistance on offer.'

'May I join you? I know little about natural remedies.'

Thinking fresh air and exercise might do the doctor good, she agreed. *Besides*, thought Tabby, *armed with greater knowledge of the remedies supplied by nature, he might be less willing to turn to the knife.*

Occasionally, in the early days of her life as a healer, Tabby was so energised by high spirits following a birth that she would take to the forest at a run, leaping fallen branches and hurtling over streams and brooks like a deer, her feet barely touching the ground. Even now, Tabby still felt a charge as she held a new life only seconds old in her hands, although the sensation had grown briefer over the years, a momentary buzz that quickly faded during the mundane chores that followed the birth. But she remembered what it was to feel powerful and god-like.

She glanced at Ben now as they walked together across the yard towards the woods. His cheeks were flushed and he was grinning. She glimpsed what he might have looked like as a child and she grinned, too.

'I feel rather intoxicated,' he began. 'I cannot stop my hands from shaking and my heart ...' he stopped suddenly and clutched at her hand and held it to his breast. She felt his heat through the fabric of his shirt.

'It is what we experience when we are frightened or angry, or excited,' Tabby explained, his heart beating against her palm. 'It is as though our bodies are not vessel enough to contain all the emotions bubbling inside and occasionally, under provocation, they spill out. Do not let your feelings be of concern. They are entirely normal, I assure you.' Tabby removed her hand promptly and kept walking.

The pair were silent for a time as they walked through the cool, dappled woods, but Tabby could hear the doctor's breath as he trailed her. It distracted her from her task. Turning her head fleetingly, she noticed he was at least five paces behind, yet she would have sworn she felt his warm breath on her neck.

'Palgrave was quite stunned,' Ben called, breaking the silence.

Tabby stopped and waited for him to reach her. 'In regard to ...?'

'He was expecting twins. When I told him his daughter had been born, he replied, "Merely one? Are you certain there isn't another waiting in the wings?"'

Tabby continued on, smiling, musing on the untamed power of fear. Palgrave's fear, born from past experience, had convinced him Leah was carrying twins and, consequently, the birth would be a savage trial for his wife, possibly resulting in her death. Tabby pondered how such a powerful emotion might be conquered. *Perhaps the safe delivery of this child will help*, she thought.

A flutter of birds in the treetops seized her thoughts and she looked above, hoping it was Edie who had caused the disturbance. It was not. Tabby and Ben were alone.

She thought Ben would make a fine doctor, eventually, with more experience. He seemed to have good instincts and had shown gentleness and warmth during Patience's birth. What's more, he realised his limitations and seemed an eager conduit for knowledge.

'Why did you not choose to close the loin?' he asked, interrupting her contemplations. From his question, Tabby realised he had been revisiting the events of the morning as they walked. 'To stem the bleeding, I mean.'

Tabby had never heard of the term 'close the loin' but an image came into her mind – a woman wrapped tightly in a strict girdle of bandages from belly to thigh.

'The mother usually bleeds for a number of days after the birth. A few thick clouts laid under her and changed regularly is enough.'

'I see.'

They walked on a minute or so before he continued. 'But if the air is allowed entrance to the womb, will this not cause inflammation and fever?'

'Not to my knowledge. The best course is to allow the body to purge the womb of everything – the afterbirth, the blood and the like – so it does not fester and rot.'

'But one would not leave a wound open ...'

She stopped and turned on him. 'A woman is not *wounded* after childbirth, Ben.'

As he considered her words, he gazed at her with such sincerity, an acknowledgement of his own shortcomings as a doctor, that she felt her heart well with emotion.

'I see,' he said again. 'I was touched they named the baby for my sister.'

'Oh?'

'Patience was my closest sibling. Her death ignited my passion to be a doctor.'

'That is often the case.' Tabby remarked gently, hoping it might offer him comfort. Her own reasons for becoming a healer were not dissimilar. She briefly wondered if she should share them with Ben but decided against such a conversation. Their acquaintance had been, as yet, too brief.

They walked on side by side. Occasionally, as they moved though the damp leaves, stepping over roots and rocks, she cast a glance sideways. He still had the birth on his mind, she could tell. *How strange it is to be discussing loins, afterbirth and bleeding with a man*, she thought. Yet she felt no embarrassment. Ben's earnest queries were couched in such genuine curiosity that she could do nought but answer him frankly.

Finally, Tabby came to a thick bush of nettle. Ben stood next to her and reached for the leaf. She gripped his wrist before he could touch the plant.

'It is not called stinging nettle for nothing, Ben,' she laughed, producing a pair of leather gloves from her pocket and plucking a leaf from the bush.

'Brewed into tea it can do only good,' she held the leaf up to the light. 'But see those tiny hairs?'

He nodded.

'They are like needles dipped in poison. If you let them touch your skin, you will be burning like hate for days at best. At worst, breathing becomes difficult, like a boulder has been laid to rest on your chest.'

'What relieves it?' he asked, examining the leaf closely.

'Nature is very clever,' Tabby went on, looking around her at the forest floor as she did so. 'Usually, quite near a stinging nettle bush will lie a dock plant.'

She moved a few steps to her right.

'Here,' she said, pulling at the wide, lush leaves of the dock. She crushed them in her hand and immediately a tangy smell like sour green apple filled her nose. She rubbed the sap on Ben's hand. 'This relieves it.'

'It's cold,' he commented, shivering.

She laughed again, freely, the noise made more joyous by the silence around it, like church bells on a Sunday morn.

'That is the most beautiful sound I've ever heard,' murmured Ben in wonder.

Startled, Tabby raised her eyes to his. In their amber depths such longing was contained that she was momentarily lost for words. He took her silence as license to proceed and leant in and kissed her, their hands still touching. When she did not resist his advances, his kisses became more ardent. She felt the press of his hands through her tunic and she wished there was no barrier between them. His grip tightened and, with her passion now ignited, she imagined laying down with him in the damp leaves, feeling the weight of him, feeling him inside her. She took his hand and placed it on her breast. But in doing so, she dropped the dock leaves she had been holding and the piquant scent of the sap jerked her violently from the dream. She instantly pulled away.

'Tabby?' he asked, surprised.

She turned and ran into the woods. Within moments, she was lost to him.

SHE RAN until she could no longer hear his cries then stopped and walked in circles for a time as her breathing calmed. *I allowed him to distract me*, she thought. She had banked her money and birthed Leah's baby – she should find Hill then return to Moosehead Lake immediately. And of course, there was Kirkcaldie. No promises had been made between them but Ben's kiss, that had only minutes before tasted so sweet, now tasted bitter with betrayal.

Tabby ran her hands through her hair, realising she had lost her hat in the flight. She groaned at her own impulsiveness. Then, from afar, she heard a song, a woman's voice alone. It was a call, pure and sweet as the harmonies of spring, drawing her closer.

Just a few yards away Tabby came to a clearing, a small, pretty glade smelling of violets and buttercups. Bowl-shaped, the space seemed to capture the sunlight that funnelled through the opening in the canopy of trees, shining with such intensity that the grass shimmered gold.

In the middle of the glade, Maria sat in a circle of stones. They were all of similar size – eight in total – and flashed like jewels in the afternoon light. By the way the sun glinted off their smoothness, Tabby guessed they were river rocks, polished sleek by the running water. She wondered how long it had taken Maria to haul each stone from the Kennebec, at least a mile away. Tabby took a step sideways behind a tree so she could remain unobserved. With her face lifted skywards, Maria seemed to be praying, revering nature – perhaps the universe – as her God.

Soon she rose and began to move, her body seemingly honouring all around her. When the sun's rays lit Maria from behind, the shape of her figure, clothed only in a fine shift, glowed. While it was no dance Tabby had ever seen, there was freedom in the rhythm of it. She watched as the woman's graceful body ribboned around the stones.

A moment later, Maria bent to pick up a shallow bowl, then continued her movement around the circle, dabbing each one with a fingertip dipped into the vessel she held in her palm. Her flowing, golden hair seemed to sway in perfect time with her body. Her movements and the elements around her seemed in exacting harmony, creating a pulsing cadence that Tabby could almost hear. It had been at least twelve years since Tabby had stepped foot inside a church, but there was a familiar type of magnificence to the scene she was witnessing now.

After a few minutes, Maria stopped, put down the bowl and knelt among the stones, rounding her back and flattening her shoulders to the ground, assuming the shape of the rocks around her. Then she lifted her head and looked towards Tabby who, in her fascination, had emerged from behind the tree that had concealed her.

'Tabby.'

She stepped out of the woods with a smile. 'I am sorry. I did not want to interrupt.'

Maria rose. 'You have delivered the baby safely.'

Tabby sensed it was not a question. She nodded. Maria drew closer to her and took her hands.

'Thank you.'

Tabby could see Maria's milky complexion was flushed pink by her exertions. When their skin touched, she felt the spark ignite between them once more.

They were flint and steel.

Maria's eyes searched Tabby's. 'There is a power to you, Tabby Post, I can sense it. There is a fire burning around you like the setting sun.'

Then Maria embraced her. The warmth of their bodies merged. Unexpectedly comforted by the gesture, Tabby slowly put her arms around her and returned the embrace.

'There is something between us,' Maria whispered as they held each other. 'Our paths are joined, although I am not certain why.'

TABBY LEFT Maria in the glade. Maria said she would not return to the house until after midnight. It was the summer solstice. She explained to Tabby that each year, on the longest day when the elements were at their most powerful, she asked them for her beloved's return. Tabby learnt that in Wellfleet, Maria's preferred spot had been on a clifftop, beneath which the currents of the sea converged in a gyre that plunged to the ocean floor. As the sea had taken him from her, Maria had said, so she believed the sea would bring her beloved home.

When the family had moved to Augusta, she had discovered the glade. She told Tabby that she considered the fierce surge of sunlight between the treetops even more powerful than the surging sea. Its strength had renewed her hope for the return of the man she had loved and waited for these past eight years. His name was Samuel Bellamy.

It was the most Tabby had learnt of Maria's life in the entire time she'd been at the house.

Tabby walked through the woods in the direction of the house slowly, almost creeping towards the spot where she had fled from Ben. No words had formed in her mind that would adequately express her feelings if, in fact, she were able to identify them. *What had provoked me to kiss him with such passion? He is so green, probably still a youngling*, she thought. While this, Tabby confessed to herself, had a certain appeal, she did not believe that the attraction lay there.

When she reached the stinging nettle bush, she found only the crushed dock leaves where they had fallen on the earth. She picked them up, held them to her nose and breathed deeply. She wagered that some would say she was growing more wild every day, falling on her basest instincts with blatant disregard of others. No-one she knew, settler or Indian, acted with such carelessness.

When Tabby returned to the house, Ben was waiting at the top of the drive. He was seated on the ground in the shade of the house, holding her hat in his hands. As she approached, he stood and wiped the dirt from his breeches.

He offered her a courtly bow when she drew near.

'Please accept my apology. I was too forward. There are no excuses for my actions, and my shame at offending you – someone whom I admire and hold in such deep regard – is at best, overwhelming.'

How many times had she been grabbed and groped by strangers, returning their unwanted affection with a cuff to the head or a knee to the tarrywags? How many times had she been kissed by men without invitation? Yet never had she received an apology. And the truth was, Ben's actions had not offended her. In the moment, she had welcomed them.

She touched his arm and looked into his tender eyes.

'I enjoyed your kiss and answered that kiss with mustard enough to warrant the heat of your reply. It has been almost five months since I have felt a man against me and I let my nature overrule my reason. If I have misled you, I am truly sorry, for there is nothing that can come of us in *that* regard.'

'A more forthright woman I have never met,' he said fondly with a smile of wonder. 'Are you spoken for?'

Tabby paused. 'No, I am not.'

'Then ...'

'You are so young,' she said gently. 'In the forest, as we searched for the stinging nettle, you needed a release for the emotions you encountered so unexpectedly after the birth. It is a natural urge. I will not hold that against you,' she said with a soft laugh. 'To my mind, Elizabeth is a more suitable and lasting match for you.'

'Elizabeth is a child,' said Ben, affronted. A frown appeared on his smooth, tanned brow. 'I will willingly take your instruction on medicine, Tabby, but please do not instruct me in matters of my own heart.'

Tabby was taken aback. 'I ...'

'My feelings for you are quite profound and it offends me that you dismiss them as an "urge". Yes, I kissed you, Tabby, but not on impulse. I kissed you because I have wanted to kiss you since we first met. In truth, my feelings for you go beyond affection.' He paused for a moment, taking in her expression.

'I believe I may love you.'

16

'Excuse me for saying so, Sir, but you are ill informed.'

Dummer rolled his eyes to the heavens, sighing.

'How so, Mistress Post? Please enlighten me.'

'You wonder why Mongwau and his people welcomed me rather than scalped me when I arrived at Moosehead Lake. The Indians weren't born a hostile people. They learnt their ways from the Europeans. They were forced to take arms.' Tabby paused, thinking. 'Just imagine, if you will, a knock one night on the glossy oak door of your Beacon Hill home ...'

'How do you know where I live?' Dummer said, alarmed.

She smiled. 'I merely assumed ...'

'Very well. Continue.'

'You tiptoe downstairs to receive your midnight caller – perhaps a Red Coat, perhaps a messenger boy with an urgent missive from King George – in your banyan and cap.'

Dummer heard the gallery snigger at the image. He shot his steely gaze towards them. Silence.

'You open the door and before you stand a band of armed militants, forcing you and your family to surrender your home. Not only that, they take the lovely house you dwell in and, along with it, all your wealth and possessions. In a heartbeat, you're dispossessed.

'So, tell me, Governor Dummer, what action would you take?'

He was quiet for a moment, struck by the nature of the question.

'I am not the one standing trial, Mistress Post.'

'Of course, you're not, Sir, but it is a simple question with an exceedingly simple answer. Like any person – man or woman – you would fight back, defend your home, possessions and family. For it is neither just nor ethical to steal. All here would agree to that. I am certain you're familiar with the Eighth Commandment, Sir.'

He nodded. 'Like all godly men.'

'Indians may not believe in your god but they are men just like you. And they have only done what they must to defend their lands and their homes. When I arrived at Moosehead Lake searching for my father, Mongwau's people could easily see my coming had not been spurred by any malice. I was a lost soul, a woman alone, searching for my father ... They showed me charity and kindness, the same as any godly people would do.'

17

———

The morning after Patience was born, Tabby fled the Williamses' home as quickly as she could, like a leaf in a gale, inventing an excuse about an outbreak of measles at Merrymeeting Bay. She hoped that setting her sights on General Hill would be a comfort to her and dispel the confusion with which Benjamin Shute's actions had clouded her usually clear mind.

She had felt compelled to leave the Williamses' house the moment Ben declared his love, unsure how to counter such a revelation. It was the first time a man had ever said those words to her and she wished she might have uttered the same in reply. But to do so would have been a falsehood. Ben had gazed at her with such genuine, unambiguous emotion – love, admiration, bewilderment – that she had not known how to reply, stammering and blundering like a girl. *But how could he love me?* she asked herself. *He's known me for less than a week.* Then Tabby remembered that it had taken less time for her father to declare his feelings for her mother, and his love had proved true.

Now that she was on her way, she feared Mister

Williams and Leah would think her inconstant and wild as she had assured them she would stay another day. Worse still, she worried that Ben would think the same, although why she felt so, she wasn't sure.

She had seen Edie only once that morning, as the bird took flight into the forest. Certain the falcon's abrupt departure was spurred by shame at her mistress's poor treatment of the doctor, it occurred to Tabby that Edie often displayed more clemency in her nature than her mistress.

Upon learning of her plans to leave so soon, Mister Williams had kindly informed her in detail as to the location of Hill's residence, drawing a map with such a fine and precise hand that Tabby surmised he would have made an excellent surveyor or cartographer. She had examined Kirkcaldie's maps on occasion, drawn with a quadrant, protractor and slide rule, instruments crafted for the specific purpose. Williams's map, sketched freehand, was almost their equal.

But before she made her way to Hill's grand home that lay, according to Mister Williams's calculations, six miles downstream, she hoped to learn the outcome of Achak's journey to Moosehead Lake. *What was my father's response to the news?* Tabby wondered as she strode towards the Green Dragon, anxious, yet with her hopes set high. She hoped the truth would heal him, return him to the man he was – the father who she had known. Then they could rebuild their fractured relationship. Communication with her father had been so tenuous, so exceedingly sparse since the events in New France, that she half feared for his reaction. The ability to predict her father's temperament and moods was lost to her. There was a time when his temper had been as even as a field after harvest. Although she cared for him the best that she was able, Tabby barely recognised him as the father she had so loved.

Riyogi was mopping the floor when she arrived, humming a mournful tune as he did so. The mewling tone of each note amplified her dread and created a dire mood in the sunlit tavern. Breathing in deeply, she took slight comfort in the crisp, unclouded smell of the soap with which he cleaned the floor. Tabby was reluctant to interrupt his toil as he seemed meditative, as though contemplating matters greater than those that lay within the walls of his establishment.

When he noticed her in the doorway, he leant his mop against the bar and bowed his head before walking to her. Removing her hat, she acknowledged him with a similar bow, her hair falling softly against her cheeks.

The gesture was one Riyogi often made – in thanks, in farewell and in welcome – and Tabby found herself involuntarily mimicking it when she was with him. Respect, gratitude and understanding were the primary planes that created the prismatic action, and it amazed Tabby that such a seemingly insignificant motion could convey such great and varied meaning. The idea propelled her, once more, to thoughts of her disastrous final encounter with Ben when she had said too much, and then to her father who had lived so long without speaking. She was eventually led to wonder why people used words at all.

However, the colour and shape of Riyogi's bow today conveyed sympathy. Tabby sensed her belly scroll.

Riyogi took her hands and led her into the empty tavern, signalling her to sit on a three-legged stool at a table that was usually occupied by his clientele. He left for a moment then returned from the kitchen with a tray, bearing a tea pot and two small cups. Steam carried a grassy scent to her nose as he poured.

Despite her urgency to speak with Riyogi that morning, now Tabby had no desire to begin. Yet she did, even before she had taken a sip from the delicately patterned teacup.

'You have news from Achak.' Her words were tinged by a certainty that whatever news Riyogi was about to convey, it was not going to be favourable.

He nodded slowly and sipped gingerly from his cup. 'Achak could not find your father at Moosehead Lake. It appears he is no longer there.'

Tabby's throat constricted so tightly she was unable to speak or swallow. Sensing her distress, Riyogi continued in his usual gentle tone.

'Achak spoke to a man named Mongwau.'

Tabby nodded, indicating she knew of whom he spoke.

'Your father disappeared three days before Achak arrived. He left no indication of his destination.'

As upsetting as this news was, knowing Mongwau had spoken with Achak afforded Tabby a modicum of ease.

'I believe Mongwau was greatly distressed,' Riyogi said. 'As though your father was his responsibility in your absence.'

Tabby remembered her parting words to Mongwau, asking him to watch over her father. She sighed.

'Papa is no-one's responsibility. Not mine, not Mong-wau's. He's a wraith. If a person tried to hold him, their hands would snatch at air.'

Drinking her tea, Tabby mulled over the possible reasons for her father's sudden flight. Why, after living on Sugar Island for almost a decade, had he chosen to flee? And why now, when she was absent? Suddenly, she was struck by the obvious answer.

'Did Mongwau search for his body?'

Riyogi frowned as though the possibility that Ephraim Post had killed himself had struck him, too.

Tabby went on quietly. 'I've always imagined Papa drowning himself in the lake. Weighting his pockets with rocks and stones and just laying down in the water, waiting to be overcome ... In a way, his spirit, his soul, has done that already. Papa gave up on life when Eb was killed. To my mind, it is not unimaginable that he would long to end —'

'His pain,' Riyogi put in, 'his shame.'

'Yes. Exactly. Once and for all.'

'Tabby, your father was not found. Mongwau searched for his body. So did Achak.'

'But that doesn't mean ...'

'No.'

Tabby stared into her tea for a time, ruminating on the events and what they might portend. She nestled the cup gently in her hands like a fledgling. It was a hot morning, but she took reassurance from the warmth the vessel provided. There would be a strange kind of morbid relief in her father taking his life, but to never know for certain would be tortuous. The thought of him untethered, in the world or wilderness alone, was more wretched than the idea that he was dead.

Tabby had comforted a widow once whose husband had hanged himself from the rafters in their kitchen with a length of hemp rope. While she wanted to ease the woman's burden, to tell her that the death of her husband had been an accident, she could not. Tabby *had* sought to find an excuse, a reason ... but there was no space in his death between the noose and his neck for a lie. The truth was hanging in the middle of the kitchen, in the glaring, noontide light of high summer and Tabby could not disguise the brazenness of the facts.

The widow had talked about her husband. He was once a good-humoured and kind soul, the father of five children, she said. She talked into the night about their meeting and marriage, the life they had built together over thirty-five years. Then about his sunny disposition growing dark when the farm had failed and their investments had turned sour, bringing on the baying creditors. Nevertheless, the widow chose to celebrate his life – the sum of it being far greater than his death.

Tabby struggled to do this now. But whether alive or dead, the memory of her father would forever be blemished by one cruel act in which her father played no part. For so many years she had devoted herself to healing the pain of others, but Tabby found her own pain daunting and impossible to confront.

But if Papa is alive, and there is a chance of that, why did he leave in my absence? she mused. Perhaps because had she been there, he knew Tabby would stop him. That spoke of hope in Tabby's mind, that a semblance of their connection remained unbroken.

She gazed at Riyogi across the table.

'How did you and Achak become friends?' she asked, eager for a distraction, even a momentary one.

Riyogi sipped from his cup for some minutes until Tabby believed he was not going to respond. When he finally spoke, after several minutes of deep contemplation, it came as a surprise to her.

'I left Japan when I was seventeen. For more than one hundred years my country had closed its doors to the rest of the world, such was our Emperors' fear and intolerance of Europeans. They were put to death immediately when they landed on Japanese shores. Only the Dutch and Chinese were permitted to trade, and only at one port, in Nagasaki.

Once, not long before my departure, when my tutors were boasting to my father of all that I knew, of all they had taught me, I realised that, apart from in the books from which my tutors drew their lessons, I had never seen a white face. It struck me that, despite my knowledge of Mathematics, the Sciences and Art, my education was severely lacking because of that one small absence. From that moment on, it coloured my entire outlook. However, Japanese people were forbidden to leave the country. If they did, they were not permitted to return.

'My father was a daimyo and close to the shogun through birth.'

Noting Tabby's expression of confusion, Riyogi explained.

'A daimyo is a landowner and the shogun a ruler, like a governor. My father knew of my passion to travel, to leave Japan. But for a daimyo's son to depart would cast humiliation and shame on my father. Even knowing this, I allowed my pride and misinformed enthusiasm to guide my actions. I disguised myself as a peasant and fled to Nagasaki where I bought passage on a Dutch ship headed for Jamaica.

'En route, the ship was overcome by pirates, the captain beheaded and the crew taken away in chains. We were to be sold as slaves. Instead of Jamaica, we landed in Virginia.'

Riyogi shook his head at the memory.

'In Japan, I had power as a daimyo's son, I had a voice. But here, I had nothing. I could not speak English and I had no knowledge of European ways. Realising I was to become a slave, looked on as property, regret over my rashness manifested into a sickness of mind and body. I decided that killing myself was my only option, yet chained as I was, I did not have the means.

'Then one morning, despite my ill health and utter wretchedness, an Indian purchased me. The moment we rode out of Jamestown, he ripped up my bill of sale then threw the pieces to the wind. They flew towards the clouds like terns. That man was Achak. Following that, we travelled together for some time as partners. He taught me English and it soon became apparent that our skills complemented each other.

'Achak has never told me why he chose to do what he did. I often think he saw himself in me.' Riyogi laughed gently. 'However, now that you have met Achak, you must realise the man is as inscrutable as a sphinx.'

'Indeed,' Tabby replied. 'And your father?'

Riyogi shrugged. 'I forsook my family. That is *my* shame. I do not know if my father is alive or dead.' Riyogi cleared his throat. 'And I shall never know.'

Straightening, Tabby placed her cup firmly on the table.

'Then we are alike. Not knowing what happened to our fathers is an affliction we will just have to live with,' she said without emotion. 'In the case of my father, a meaningless crime was committed, a murder for which he was blamed. To find the actual culprit and bring him to justice will be a consolation to me.'

'There is an extremely fine line between justice and revenge,' Riyogi counselled.

'I know this Riyogi. It is not revenge I seek.' Tabby rose from the table. 'Whether my father is alive or dead, I want to set him free. I must.'

Bowing her head to Riyogi, in respect and farewell, Tabby walked to the door and departed the tavern.

18

————

Tabby walked the distance to Hill's home, through the town then along the river to the bend Mister Williams had described. Tabby knew the area as Fiddler's Reach. Appreciating the time the journey provided her, she ordered her thoughts as she walked, mentally indexing the questions she intended to ask the general. She did not wish to distrust the man without reason, yet there was an uncomfortable suspicion congealing in her chest like ice.

Edie joined her halfway along the route, swooping then soaring, skylarking. The cyan sky was mottled by a patchwork of downy clouds that Edie seemed to embroider as she threaded her way among them like a master tapissier. Tabby recognised the house when she reached it. Not as Hill's home, but as one she had passed as she journeyed along the Kennebec in her birchbark canoe. She had wondered who might reside there. *If not a governor,* she had thought, *then surely a government official.*

Mister Williams had described it as a 'manor house'. Now, looking closely at the structure, Tabby considered Williams's description to be quite apt. Positioned close to the Kennebec with a wide balcony surrounded by columns that kept the terrace aloft, the house was far more stately and grand than Mister Williams's own home that, until this moment, was the most stately and grand house Tabby had ever visited. The vast property possessed its own landing that jutted into the river like a defiant child's chin. On it, a Negro stood. He coiled a thick rope over his arm with a degree of care Tabby considered extreme, regardless of the quality of the rope. When Edie flew towards the jetty the man cowered, dropped the rope and instinctively covered his head with his arms.

'Don't be alarmed,' Tabby called as Edie took rest on a thick pylon at the end of the jetty. 'She's quite friendly.'

The man cautiously lowered his arms as Tabby traversed the lawn with a quick step.

'This is Edie,' Tabby said, when she reached him.

He looked towards her, his concerned eyes still circumspect. Yet, when Tabby looked closely, she recognised a soft glimmer of warmth in their depths. The man was young, much younger than his posture and bearing would suggest from afar, Tabby realised as they stood face to face. At first sight, from across the considerable expanse of lawn, Tabby had believed him to be quite aged.

'If it's agreeable, Edie would probably like to rest here for a time. She will not make any fuss.'

The man nodded.

'My name is Tabby Post. Is General John Hill at home?'

He nodded again; his lips clenched tight.

Tabby gazed at him for a moment, but he did not offer to guide her to the house. When he turned his back on her and lowered to retrieve the rope, Tabby took the gesture as indifference to her presence and began her walk across the spring green rise to the house.

It was clear the man was not there by his own will. Tabby did not condone slavery of either Negro or Indian in any form. The knowledge that Hill owned men and women deepened her suspicions and her doubts about the general's integrity grew lush like the summer grass under her feet.

On reaching the house, she found a horse, saddled and waiting for its master, tethered to a post by the balcony. Tabby stroked his neck fondly, taking in its comforting animal scent, wondering who the general's visitor might be. Making her way up the front steps, she pulled the chain of a gleaming brass bell. As she did so, she glimpsed her reflection in its shine. Her face was as misshapen as a gourd.

She was shown into the parlour by an attractive Negro woman, another slave, who asked her to wait for the general as he was currently being attended to by his physician. Tabby's heart plummeted in her chest and, in her panic, she looked around the general's parlour for a place to conceal herself. Within seconds the ridiculousness of the notion struck her, and she regained her composure by ambling the perimeter of the parlour, contemplating the likely conversations she might have with Doctor Benjamin Shute should they meet.

Scanning the bookshelves and peering through the glass doors of the general's gun cabinet, she noted that his library was well considered and the weapons well cared for. A rich burgundy carpet speckled with gold thread lay on the floor. Her deer-skin moccasins, regardless of their suppleness and the shine of the leather, seemed tatty in comparison. As she moved past the window, she glanced at the landing. Edie remained perched on the pylon, dignified and erect as a grenadier. The Negro had disappeared.

To her extreme surprise, when Tabby turned from the window Ben was standing in the doorway, neither in nor out, clearly as mortified as she had been mere moments before. If she had not turned at that exact moment, she was certain the doctor would have made a hasty and silent retreat. Ben cleared his throat and began abruptly.

'The general was shot,' he said.

Seeing Tabby's confusion, he hastily added 'While on campaign some five years ago. In the hip.' He took a step forward into the room as he rolled down his sleeves. 'The ball was removed but the bone was chipped, I think.'

'What is your treatment?' Tabby uttered, keeping her voice as level as possible.

'Twice weekly massages to ease the straining muscles.'

'Has the pain been apparent since the shooting?'

'No. Pain has only just occurred recently, in the past month.' He stepped further into the parlour as he spoke. 'I am using oil of angelica on the area. I believe you spoke to me of its benefits.'

He paused, waiting for Tabby to interject. When she did not, he continued on nervously.

'And lavender for general relaxation. General Hill seems ill at ease ... I've extended the massage to his legs and back. The thought came to mind, you see, that the rest of his muscles might be compensating the lame hip ...'

Ben's words trailed off. He ran his fingers through his hair as if to clear his mind then pointed above him. 'The general should be down shortly, once he is adequately attired ...' He stopped again. Tabby's presence seemed to cause speech to elude him.

Tabby nodded seriously in agreement, although she could not conjure a modicum of harmony with his ministrations. A chipped bone would not cause intermittent pain. More likely, at the time of the injury, the surgeon – if the man who removed the ball was, in fact, a surgeon – had failed to remove all the shot. Now, tiny pellets were shifting, making their way to the surface, looking for release. After a few weeks of pain, the pellets would likely burst through the skin like young seedlings breaking through still earth. After this, he would need the wound washed and bandaged ... However, after the arrogance she had displayed during her last encounter with Ben, Tabby could not find a way to lead the misguided doctor down the correct path. She decided it was better to remain silent.

'It occurred to me,' Ben went on after a moment's deliberation. 'Well, I was wondering ... wondering whether you might like to accompany me to a dissection.'

'A dissection?' Tabby remarked, surprised by such a remarkable invitation.

Mistaking the nature of her inquiry, Ben went on. 'Yes, it is a post-mortem examination of a body in order to discover the cause of –'

'I am familiar with the nature of the procedure,' she smiled.

Now it was Ben's turn to experience shame at his own conceit.

'I apologise. Of course, you would know what a dissection is –'

'But I have never seen one,' Tabby cut in again, to ease his embarrassment. 'I would be pleased to accompany you.'

Ben brightened at this and Tabby noticed his body relax. He placed his bag on the floor. Nestling his hands comfortably into the pockets of his breeches, Ben moved closer to explain.

'I have been invited by my mentor. Women are not usually permitted to attend dissections, but in my correspondence with him recently, I spoke of you and your work, exalting, in fact, your knowledge and expertise. I assured him you would not swoon at the sight of blood or bodily organs.' He laughed to himself at such a ludicrous thought. 'I am confident Doctor William Douglass will be eager to meet you and would be delighted if you attend as his guest. He is an open-minded man and a gifted teacher. I but wait on his response.'

Ben explained that the dissection would take place in Long Reach in a little over a fortnight's time, in the home of a local resident with an interest in Science. The dissection was to be carried out by Douglass and a visiting physician, a former colleague of Douglass's from Bath, England.

'The cadaver, of course, has not yet been chosen, but that should not prove an obstacle. Many citizens have lately become so filled with public-spiritedness that there are no shortage of bodies.'

'I am pleased to hear it,' she said, then blushed at the slight absurdity of her remark.

Ben smiled, easing her embarrassment and the tension between them. Further arrangements were made before the doctor took his leave.

THERE WAS no time to brood over her unexpected meeting with Ben before the general entered the parlour. He was shorter than Tabby had imagined; the tone of his correspondence was rather lofty. Although not haughty, his words were at least elevated beyond the language of a common soldier. Possessing a stocky physique, he seemed as robust as a colt when he marched across the room and took Tabby's hand. There was no hint of a limp. Despite Tabby's misgivings, Ben's treatment must have provided Hill with some relief, if only temporarily.

The general's hair was dusty grey and fell to his shoulder in tight curls that coiled like snakes. The free-flowing nature of it was the only sign of disarray in his attire. Tabby observed the well-cut suit of morning blue, buckled shoes and a cravat that was neatly tied; there was no clue that only moments before he'd lain undressed, face down on a table being pummelled by his physician.

Hill remembered Tabby from their correspondence and immediately began on an impassioned homily regarding the virtues of her father – his courage, his skill and his protective affection for his younger brother. It grieved him, he explained, that Ephraim had allowed himself to become so intoxicated to mistake his brother for a bear.

'I hope the incident has not smeared your relations with him.'

Tabby shuddered at the general's patronising tone. Hill continued, oblivious to her distaste.

'Sadly, Mistress Post, when men are away from home and their loved ones they occasionally indulge, too freely. It is understandable.'

Tabby could not begin to express to this man how the incident, its aftermath and the news that Achak had so recently brought to light had affected her. To suggest her relationship with her father was merely 'smeared' was such a gross understatement. The word implied something that could be cleaned, wiped away without a trace of ever being present, forgotten. Her father was a broken man and all that remained of her relations with him were fragments, slowly being scattered by the four winds to who knew where. The possibility of Tabby one day gathering those splinters and piecing together their bond once more was, at best, paltry. Tabby struggled to compose herself before she responded.

'It is entirely understandable, Sir, and I have seen my

father addled many times. On one occasion, he mistook our closest neighbour– a kindly woman but as ugly as a scarecrow – for my mother. He locked her in an embrace so passionate that I expected the poor woman to shatter. Needless to say, my red-faced father delivered a heartfelt apology the following morning.' Telling the anecdote had a calming effect on her. Despite the circumstance she was now in, Tabby could not help but smile at the memory.

'He drank, but he was not, what I would call, a drinker,' she said, growing serious again. 'Sir, I have been in the presence of more inebriated men than I care to recall. I have been leered at and pawed at and affronted. I have also tended their wounds and injuries when liquor has seen them undone. My experience with those afflicted with drink is vast, I can assure you.'

Tabby paused and watched the general digest her words. She could see by the frown forming on his tanned brow that he found them distasteful.

'Then, Mistress Post,' he began, sternly. 'Why are you here? You clearly need no reassurance of your father's upright character.'

Hill strode to the window, brushing past Tabby, leaving the woody, piquant scent of lavender in his wake. He stared out at the fine summer day, waiting for her to explain. She peered over his shoulder and spied Edie, still perched on the jetty.

'I can accept that my father may have, in a muddled state of drunkenness, become confused.'

Hill turned and glared at her through narrowed, close-set brown eyes.

'But I cannot accept that it took my father three shots to fell what he thought was a bear. He was too good a rifleman. It's a gift you have attested to yourself and heralded in your missives. I have seen my father drop three turkeys from fifty yards after inhaling a quart of whistle-belly. Even boozy, my father's eye was true and his hand steady. He was your sharpshooter, was he not?'

Hill did not answer, although Tabby thought she detected a flicker of something – agitation, irritation – cross his countenance.

'The second fact – for I will call these facts because you have affirmed these yourself – is the knowledge that my uncle was shot three times *in the back*. Now, would I be correct in thinking that you came across many bears during your time in New France, General?'

Hill nodded slowly.

'Have you ever seen a bear turn its back on a man?' Tabby waited for an answer but none came. 'Well, *I* certainly haven't, not ever,' she said.

The general's eyes narrowed again. 'What then, are you suggesting?'

Tabby attempted to keep her tone light as she replied to Hill's question.

'You are aware I am certain of my uncle's lack of wits. He was a senseless individual with a fierce appetite for gambling, attributes that do not keep sound company.'

She smiled briefly, trying to remain composed. Tabby had originally intended to divulge Achak's role in the events she was about to recount but, having met the general, she decided on a different course. She cleared her throat.

'On the night he was killed, I believe my uncle found himself flagrantly in debt, possibly due to the entertainments that the company attended in the town near the camp.'

Hill nodded, contemplating, possibly remembering the events of the evening.

'Having lost the earnings from the campaign that you yourself had only paid the men that afternoon, he returned to the camp and stole my father's wages. So intoxicated was my father that he did not hear his brother rummaging through his belongings. My uncle was accompanied by a man – his creditor, I assume. Eb handed him the pouch containing my father's money. Then, as my uncle walked away, this man, deciding to silence him, shot my uncle in the back.'

Tabby paused, studying the general's reaction. He seemed to be quietly considering her words, nothing more; but then again, she knew him to be a practised dissembler.

'The murderer then placed his gun in my father's hand and ran from the scene.'

Tabby took a small step forward, hoping her next words might incite some form of emotion in the general, something that could shed light on the truth.

'I have heard that this man – this killer – was quite remarkable in appearance and might easily be identified. He is tattooed with an image of the King of Spades.'

Hill's face remained as blank as stone. But when he spoke, his voice had a brittle edge.

'How have you come across this information, Mistress Post? Without witnesses, it is merely hearsay and conjecture.' He paused, softening his tone. 'Naturally, I would like to assist you in your pursuit of the truth. However, before I am able to, I must know how you came across this testimony. Who have you spoken to?'

'I'm afraid, General, that this person has pleaded with me to protect his anonymity. I promised I would.'

Hill snorted, clearly disdainful of promises.

'Then I cannot help you, Mistress Post.'

He strode to the door and held it open for her. It was clear their conversation was over.

'I will send Agatha to see you out,' he muttered by way of farewell.

SHE WAS sorry that Ben was no longer at the house. Now that Tabby had encountered the general, she desired to speak to the doctor about his patient, with the hope of gleaning a clearer portrait of the man. Angelica eased the body, but lavender eased the soul and loosened the tongue. *What did they discuss during the general's treatments?* she wondered. *What might the general have given away during his repose as Ben kneaded his flesh?*

Disappointed by the young doctor's absence, Tabby began her walk to the landing. The tracks of his mare led down the gravel drive. Tabby looked more closely. Horse and rider had departed at a saunter.

The slave she had spoken to on arrival was nowhere in sight. Patient on the pylon, Edie hopped from foot to foot when she saw Tabby approach. The bird was rewarded with an exuberant caress. Tabby was grateful she had such a faithful companion.

'That did not go well, my girl,' Tabby began, shaking her head. 'My head tells me that General Hill is dangerous and that I should leave him to his business. But my heart is crying out for answers.'

Why would Hill want to see my father come to harm? she wondered. Papa had been an asset to Hill's company. At the time of the murder, although the campaign had ended, they still needed to travel back to Maine. *Surely, they would need their sharpshooter,* thought Tabby. She reckoned they would have encountered all manner of hostility – Indians or French soldiers – on the journey home.

Tabby sighed. Before meeting him, it had crossed her mind that Hill might be the King of Spades. When she first laid eyes on him, it struck her that his hair may be loose to cover a tattoo ... Yet even in the blackness of night, Hill would never be mistaken for a reedy man.

'But might he not be *protecting* the King of Spades?' she asked Edie, looking into the falcon's eyes. 'If so, to what end?' Tabby sighed. 'Why am I even bothering to go to these lengths, my girl? It is obvious that Papa does not give a fig. If he did, he would fight, not flee.'

Dejected, Tabby began her walk towards town. Edie took flight, circling overhead, keeping track of her mistress's journey.

19

Kirkcaldie had built his cabin a fifteen-minute walk from the shore, away from the bite of mosquitoes in summer and the sound of shifting ice in winter. At best, he had told Tabby, the noise coming from the ice was a low, blood-curdling moan, as though a woman was trapped beneath it; at worst, it was the crack of a whip. Neither could he tolerate. But to Tabby, those sounds were a comfort, as though the river were making music. At night, when the silence was so heavy it shrouded her like a blanket, Tabby imagined that somewhere beneath the ice, in the swirling, hydrous black, an orchestra played a symphony just for her. When she had confided this folly to Kirkcaldie he had smiled that all-encompassing smile of his, so rarely seen, and said, 'That's the difference between us, isn't it?'

His proximity from the vast liquid thoroughfare would be a hardship to most, but not for Kirkcaldie, who preferred to travel by horse. In spite of – or perhaps because of – her questioning, he had never told her why he spurned the Kennebec. Of course, the other benefit of building so far from the river was that his land had never been kissed by its flooding waters when it thawed. Tabby gazed above the tree-tops as she stepped onto the shore. Smoke funnelled a grey stream into the sky. He was home and, in her mind, she was already in his arms.

Edie waited on a tree stump, eyes fixed, as her mistress hurriedly hauled the canoe onto the bank and secured it to a pine. After retrieving her belongings, which consisted only of her apothecary case, back basket and bow, she set foot into the woods, slinging her quiver over her shoulder. A rough trail, of sorts, was present, created through use rather than intention. As she walked, Tabby was grateful there was still a thin sliver of light in the sky, for roots, rocks and fallen branches were constant but ever-changing hazards. Edie flew high above the treetops to the cabin while Tabby trod the path.

There had been men before Kirkcaldie, but none like him – with scruples as upright as their pricks. Flicking through Kirkcaldie's ledger on one occasion when he was readying his horse, Tabby was impressed with his neat hand and the thoroughness with which he kept his accounts. Surveying, it seemed, was a lucrative but fraught profession. On several occasions, she had tended his scratches and bruises when his camp had been stormed by squatters, fuelled by rage at Governor Dummer's plans to sell parcels of King George's land. They were naught but faint etchings on a body tattooed with scars, but she enjoyed ministering to him, nonetheless. Tabby hoped Cool had not harmed Kirkcaldie seriously; despite Cool's words, she was certain Kirkcaldie would not have given over his compass willingly.

She came out of the woods and into the clearing. She could see his home, sitting on a ridge. Some time ago, the governor had leased 100 acres to his surveyor for the dura-tion of ninety-nine years. Kirkcaldie had never confided the details of the negotiation, except to say he had begun work on the house immediately. Now Tabby noticed a new addition to the property – the beginnings of a wall. It appeared to act as an entranceway, the final touch to the home he had so painstakingly built. It was made of bluestone, no doubt hand-quarried by him in Waterville. It was perfect, the stones fitting together in an intricate puzzle. Tabby imagined a picket gate and a flower bed skirting its edges one day. For a man who was rarely at home, Kirkcaldie took pride in domestic accomplishments.

Lamps burned in the windows and her entire body stirred when she spotted his shadow, moving with purpose behind the glass. Standing two storeys with a steeply pitched slate roof, the sober-coloured dwelling had been meticulously built by Kirkcaldie's own hands. The house looked westward from the eastern side of the river and was grand by Kennebec standards, with a hall and parlour straddling a vast sandstone chimney that stood in the centre like a gently pulsing heart. Wondering, as she often did, why Kirkcaldie needed such a large home, Tabby allowed herself a brief moment of fiction for she had only a short time to spare for idle fantasies.

Relishing the joy she experienced from watching him and anticipating their meeting, she waited longer, her desire eventually mounting to a pitch so immense that the wait became almost as pleasurable as their imminent coupling. She moved closer, with soft, light feet. Kirkcaldie had the hearing of an owl but the Indians who had taught her to hunt had shown her how to move silently through the woods. Cat-like, walking softly on her heels so as to touch less of the ground, she sensed every leaf, stone and pebble through the thin leather of her deer-skin moccasins.

When she reached the window, she lowered slightly and

peeped through the glass. He was at the table making musket balls, pouring molten lead into the mould. Admiring his profile, locked in concentration, and the twitch of the muscles in his forearm as he tilted the ladle, her excitement fast multiplied by the knowledge that Kirkcaldie was oblivious to her presence, now only feet away. It was the closest she had ever come without him noticing. She watched as he made the lamp by which he worked brighter; it had grown dark while she played her game.

Struck by a sound, Tabby raised her eyes to the heavens. It was the tune of Edie's flight from on high. Within seconds she landed with a clang on the slate, momentarily sliding down the roof until her scraping talons found purchase. Tabby shot a glance through the window. Kirkcaldie had disappeared. Dropping her baggage and pressing her back hard against the side of the house, she closed her eyes, listening. But all she could hear was the sound of her own blood, throbbing in her ears. Then she heard the crunch of his feet on gravel. Keeping low, she padded to her right, towards the back of the house where, she presumed, he had just exited. There, a new addition stopped her pursuit, a lean-to that extended the length of the house. Surprised momentarily and confused as to how to proceed, she gasped as an arm fixed around her neck from behind, almost hauling her off her feet.

'That bird will be the death of you,' Kirkcaldie whispered in her ear.

Having not seen each other in nearly five months, their lovemaking that night was unsophisticated but satisfying. Kirkcaldie's appetite proved as fierce as her own, leading

Tabby to assume there were no other women in those times when they did not exist for each other. But it was just an assumption, and Tabby was certain that if Edie could share an opinion, she would say Kirkcaldie was as faithless as fair weather. Tabby wished her friend could speak and articulate her suspicions. There was no denying that Kirkcaldie was a loner who did not easily share his thoughts and feelings; however, he had never given Tabby reason to distrust him.

She examined him now in the dim glow of the waning moon and noticed a cut on his lip, the flesh swollen around it. She wondered if she had bitten him. She touched it lightly with her fingertip and he stirred as though tickled by a feather. It had already scabbed over. The wound was days old, probably a memento from Jeremy Cool. Kirkcaldie opened his eyes and rolled towards her.

Nestling against her, gaining warmth from her body, he asked sleepily, 'Tell me where you've been.'

'Do you want to talk or sleep?' she asked.

Kirkcaldie was not one for light discourse, words to merely fill a silence. To Tabby's ear he was well-practised in conversation, with the ability to match her word for word, but he only seemed to speak when the words mattered. It was a pity. Tabby enjoyed listening to the rich, deep timbre of his voice. And the sound of his laughter dispatched ripples of gladness from her heart to the far reaches of her fingertips and toes.

'I want *you* to talk,' he said, eyes closed.

Yawning, Tabby stretched her legs until they touched the solid foot of the maple-framed bed. She smiled, remembering how much she loved this bed. It was almost three times as wide and lofty as the rush-woven mat she slept on. Lying there, three feet above the ground, protected by four sturdy amber posts, she imagined a queen could not feel more entitled and protected than she did at that moment.

'I journeyed as far as Augusta. I've delivered six babies, one breech, seen to three cases of canker rash and set a broken leg just outside York, where Billy Duttan was thrown off his horse. His foot got caught in the stirrup; Old Artemis dragged him a mile and a half! Then there were teeth pulled and numerous cases of dysentery, gripe, broken breast and worms ... Why, only three miles downriver, I was stopped in my tracks by a man whose big toe was so gripped by gout he howled like a head-lugged bear when I came within a yard of the stricken appendage.' Tabby laughed quietly at the memory. 'But I think I left everyone cleverly.'

She paused for a moment and sighed, her mirth wafting from her with the air she expelled. Kirkcaldie opened his eyes at the noise, reasoning that something troubled her.

'And I met a man named Jeremy Cool.' Tabby reached out and touched Kirkcaldie's lip. 'Is it he who gave you this?'

He nodded then lifted his weight onto his elbow, his dark eyes lighted by alarm. 'How did you two cross paths?'

Tabby briefly related how she met Polly, her visit to the settlement and what Cool had told her about his dealings with the government surveyor. Kirkcaldie immediately bristled when he heard of Cool's account of the meeting.

'Cool raided our camp in the dead of night. He brought his entire settlement, women and children included, with him. They were an army of sorts, all carrying weapons of some description. We had few options, unable as we were to respond in kind for fear of hurting women and children. But there was something amiss with those people, as though they were ghosts. Sleep walking, McPherson suggested. But Horace Peterson was shot in the shoulder by a woman brandishing a musket. They certainly were not asleep.'

'Is Horace alright?' Tabby knew Horace. At five and fifty, he was the oldest of Kirkcaldie's crew. Tabby had delivered his third grandchild just before the thaw.

'The shot went straight through. I cleaned it and stopped the bleeding. It will be a while 'til he can travel with us again, but he will.' Kirkcaldie paused for a moment, deep in thought, before continuing.

'Cool also stole my compass, a horse and most of our supplies. He did not touch the rest of my instruments. The ingrate clearly had no idea how valuable they are.'

'Ingrate? How so?'

'We had come across him a few days before, near Fiddler's Reach. He had been in Augusta to trade, he told us, and was making his way back to his family and brethren when he was fleeced by Indians. Believing him to be a man of God, we gave him food and protection for the night then we parted ways in the morning.'

Tabby thought on this for a moment. Fiddler's Reach.

'The day after the ambush, I returned to the area surrounding Cool's settlement, alone. Tabby, in the past, I have faced squatters who are high on the ropes over their homes being snatched. Even though my profession means I am at odds with them, I can understand their fight, their desire to keep what they have built, what they believe belongs to them. But there was something different about Cool. It was not his *home* he was protecting. There were no livestock or crops, just a few forsaken pigs and a weedy vegetable patch. Then I found what he was protecting. About a mile from his property to the east I came across a poppy field.'

'Opium?' said Tabby, surprised.

Kirkcaldie nodded. 'Acres and acres. Cool is producing it

and, for whatever deranged purpose, keeping his "brethren" woolly with it.'

Tabby frowned and stared at the ceiling, carefully following with her eyes a whorl of dark amber in a broad oak beam. It explained Polly's state of mind when they had first met at the Farnhams's. Listless and distracted, it had been hours before she seemed present.

'Tabby,' he went on gravely, 'I do not want you going near that settlement again, no matter how you think you can help the people there. Any man who'd ply his wife with opium then escort her and his children into harm's way is not a man you want to be acquainted with.'

Tabby knew Kirkcaldie's counsel was wise, but she knew herself well enough to reason she could not leave Polly and her children at Cool's mercy. Since their last meeting, Polly had frequently stolen off with Tabby's thoughts. Intuition told her Polly was in danger and Tabby had devoted many hours to deliberating on solutions to the girl's plight. But there were so many loose threads – Jeremy Cool's violent nature, the four children, a lack of resources and, Tabby feared, a lack of will on Polly's part – that needed to be tied off before any permanent repair might occur ... It frustrated Tabby that at the conclusion of her lengthy musings, all she was left with were more dangling threads. Now this news. *Was it a coincidence*, she wondered, *that Kirkcaldie met Cool near Fiddler's Reach? If not, what has Cool to do with General Hill?*

'What is it that compels you to help people in the way that you do?' Kirkcaldie asked, interrupting her contemplations.

Kirkcaldie's inquiry succeeded in distracting her from her thoughts. The question had never been asked of Tabby before and she did not possess a ready answer. Thinking for a moment, she took in Kirkcaldie's dark features, a countenance that appeared almost sinister due to a slender blade of moonlight severing it from brow to jaw.

'I am none too certain,' she dissembled. The truth was that the memory of something she shouldn't have seen one day long, long ago haunted her still. Something that had changed her life in an instant. It was a tale she had not, as yet, shared with anyone.

'Well, when did it start?' Kirkcaldie altered the question into what he hoped was a more pleasing form.

Tabby thought for a moment. As much as she cared for Kirkcaldie, she chose to share a different part of her history.

'I lived in Wallingford for a time, after my father left for New France. I was employed as a maid by the Ives family. It was a house not unlike this one, with a great hearth, a bath, an attic and a well-ordered cellar where venison and hams were hung to dry and cure. This was the place where we also stacked the jars of fruit we preserved. Apples and pears, mainly, but it seemed like the walls were panelled with gold by the end of bottling season.

That cellar, with its cool earth floor and smells of spice and wood, was my favourite room in the house. There was an enormous amount of bickering and fighting that went on under that shingle roof. Neither of my parents ever had harsh words for the other, you see, so the screech of Goody Ives's voice and the low boom of Mister's sang of discord and hostility, and it made me fretful – made me feel like casting out my breakfast. I suppose it's simply good fortune and even tempers that allow relations between husband and wife to remain harmonious in the course and flow of life, impeded as it is by so many obstacles.' Tabby sighed at the memory. 'Including those who had perished, that couple had produced a total of twelve children, so I can see reasons that they might get nettled by one another.

'Sometimes I'd hide away in the cellar, or I would take myself off to another house on Long High Way and sit in the kitchen, rabbit with the girls while I helped with their chores. It was at the McGillivray's where I sat one high summer afternoon with Solace, my friend, when Goody McGillivray, who was with child at the time, cried out like Satan had reached out a hand to touch her. We were shelling peas in the summer kitchen with our skirts hitched up over our knees, the heat of the day was so burdensome. Mister McGillivray had gone to Falmouth to buy grain so we felt safe in the act, for he had a wandering eye that was oft spoken of among the girls.

'Solace and I ran to the parlour where Goody McGillivray had been at work on a cross stitch only a few minutes before. The child was not expected for another fortnight, but the dam had burst, and the baby was coming. Solace had never seen any woman – human or beast – in travail. She was plunged into a stupor. I sent her to find the midwife. Meanwhile I, who had aided any number of ewes in delivering, helped Goody McGillivray to her chamber and laid her down upon the shakedown. By then Solace had returned with news that the midwife was also in Falmouth, attending to her sister's salt rheum. I instructed Solace to collect as many rags and old linens as she could find. I knew there were burlap sacks in the cellar, so I sent her on her way to collect them. Now my preference is for straw, but there was none of that to be found on Long High Way and the blacksmith's store was at least a half mile away.

'I lifted Goody McGillivray's skirts but there was no sight of the baby. She told me that the urge to push was uncontrollable. Well, I told her to use every ounce of her will to resist that urge until I was ready. I leapt down the stairs to the kitchen and returned with a dish of freshly churned butter. When I plunged my hands deep into the creamy chiffon mound, Solace cried, "Stop! I churned that just this morning."'

Tabby laughed. 'Poor Solace. She was a sweet girl but she had no inkling of what I was intending to use it for.'

Kirkcaldie smiled and pulled her closer.

'I put my hands inside Goody McGillivray, just as I had seen Papa do with our ewes, although his unguent of choice was maize oil. I felt the baby then closed my eyes, attempting to determine what part I was touching. Was it a small round head or a soft plump arse? With the ewes, Papa had told me to picture the youngling in my mind's eye, curled like a flower petal. I could then determine its position. I did so, and then I saw the babe with my hands, imagining it to be as pink as a lonely rose.

'I had to turn him, arse first as he was. There is not much room in there, and he did not want to budge. Eventually, it was as though he realised that I was more stubborn than he and he gave in. Robert James McGillivray slid out into the world and into my hands like July rain off a duck's back feathers.'

Tabby yawned and stretched, reaching her arms behind her head.

'That was the moment I realised it was my calling,' she added, which was true, to a degree. 'That boy would be almost ten. I wonder if he is still as stubborn.'

20

Tabby fell asleep in Kirkcaldie's arms. Safe. Protected. Yet she dreamt.

Maria was in her glade, humming her haunting melodies and dancing among the stones as she anointed them one by one. Gold and violet butterflies frolicked about her head, creating a halo of lively movement and vibrant colour. Sun cast Maria in a glow of heavenly light, her skin rich and buttery, her hair glinting shades of copper and caramel. Tabby stood behind a tree, concealed, admiring the scene of worship.

From the other side of the glade, a man came into view. He wore a crown and carried a small harp. The intensity of the light obscured his face, yet Tabby read danger in the way he moved, a wicked intent. Maria, in her reverie, did not see him. Before Tabby could cry out, the man's harp transformed into a dagger. As he stepped towards Maria, he slashed the blade across her throat; blood spouted from her neck like water from a fountain, pooling vermillion at her feet. When she fell to the ground, the man was no longer there. Then Tabby woke.

The room was dark. Her heart was pounding, her mouth dry. When she turned to face Kirkcaldie, the awareness she was not alone was a comfort.

'I CANNOT PICTURE YOU AS A SERVANT,' Kirkcaldie said as they broke their fast, 'taking orders from those above you.'

Tabby was pleased he had reflected on her story. Pleased also that he perceived her in such an agreeable light.

'I was your servant last night,' she replied, looking over her cup.

He rose and moved towards her, bending and kissing the nape of her neck.

'And I was yours.'

Tabby felt tingles shoot like the keenest arrows through her body. Flushing, she lowered her head so he could not witness her embarrassment.

She avoided speaking of her time at the Williamses' house, concerned she would inadvertently mention Ben. Although there was nothing Tabby wished to conceal, for she was certain a man of Kirkcaldie's vast experience and enlightened character would not be disturbed by a kiss, Tabby remained unsure how to describe her time in Augusta. Her ill-defined feelings towards Ben and her encounters with Maria were aspects of her stay that she was still interpreting herself. What she did wish to speak of with him, however, was the King of Spades.

After she unburdened herself of the tale of her father and reckless uncle once more, a tale she found more harrowing with each retelling, she looked squarely at Kirkcaldie.

'Do you know any man that bears a King of Spades tattoo?'

He shook his head, thinking. After a few moments, clearly bothered by her intentions, he spoke.

'Tabby, what do you hope to gain by finding this man? Revenge is a dark path, one your compassionate nature is not suited to.' He glanced at his hands, intertwined on the table. 'There is a very thin line between Heaven and Hell.'

'It is not revenge I seek, Kirkcaldie, it is justice.'

He looked at her doubtfully.

'Achak is a witness to the crime.'

'An Indian's testimony is worthless.'

'Riyogi can support his claim.'

'An Oriental has even less credibility than an Indian.'

About to remind Kirkcaldie that Riyogi was, in fact, Japanese, she realised a scant detail such as that would make no difference to the small minds of magistrates and juries.

Tabby drummed her fingers on the table in exasperation. 'I will find a way. There is another who knows of this. General John Hill ...'

Kirkcaldie was enraged in an instant. 'That man is a bastard. Do not go near him.'

Tabby drew back, disconcerted. She had never seen Kirkcaldie so riled.

'I met him once at the governor's residence. I had the misfortune to dine with Hill there. He boasted that evening to a table that included ladies that he had cut out the tongue of a slave.'

Tabby's thoughts immediately flew to the young man on the landing. Even though she had tried to engage him in conversation, he had not uttered a word. She recalled now that his mouth had been clenched tight.

'Hill said that, although he had paid more than twenty shillings for the lad, the "lack of a tongue did not hinder hard work or breeding". He then proclaimed that he would happily do it again.'

'And the poor man's crime?' asked Tabby.

'The lad attempted to incite an insurrection among his fellow slaves.'

Kirkcaldie was breathing hard, clearly troubled. He reached across the table and took Tabby's hand.

'You must promise me, Tabby, that you will stay away from Hill.'

Tabby nodded slowly, considering her best course of action.

'And Cool?'

The depth of his concern made her uneasy.

'I promise,' she uttered quietly then watched as the muscles in Kirkcaldie's shoulders relaxed.

'At times, there is no way, Tabby. At times we have to be content that justice itself will find a despicable creature like the King of Spades along a different road. Perhaps you need to be content with simply knowing the truth.'

Tabby thought on these words as she sipped the coffee Kirkcaldie had brewed. It was sharp and bitter on the tongue. It was not chicory coffee or coffee made from corn meal and molasses, it was real coffee he had acquired from a Dutch trader in Brunswick. But in the light of her troubling dream and Kirkcaldie's counsel, the beverage was no less biting.

KIRKCALDIE LIKED to watch her hunt. Although he carried his rifle into the woods, he knew he would not be called to use it. Tabby would just need one arrow to fell a deer. He walked by her side in silence. Occasionally, he would glance her way and see her face altered from its usual tender amiability, locked in concentration as it was. A hardness or seriousness stole over it as she listened and watched for signs of animals, as though all her senses were straining at once to net a clue. The Indians had tutored her well; no dropping, breath sound or scent went unnoticed.

He always insisted they hunt together when she was with him. It was sport enough for Kirkcaldie to watch her. What's more, he enjoyed the peace. The privilege of having company when there was no need to speak, when silence was everything. Being in another's realm was a comfort; allowing her to lead removed a burden from him. Tabby knew the woods intimately, attuned to the subtle smells and sounds of nature that he did not notice. Unless the sound was the slow cock of a rifle or the deliberate crunch of shoes on leaves, Kirkcaldie was deaf and stood astounded at the responsiveness of Tabby's senses.

He remembered that as a child living with his family, he was able to discern with complete accuracy the owner of the foot placed on the ladder that led to the loft where they slept simply by the creak of the timber. Later, when he swung the reaping-hook among the sweep of golden barley, he was able to identify which of his sisters' sweet voices sung to him across the fields from miles away as they toiled at their own burdens. When he had departed his home, not yet a man, he had pressed his mother's kerchief to his nose in times of distress to evoke some solace in his misery. *When*, he wondered, *did I grow so numb?*

Occasionally, Tabby would break his treasured silence when she spied a square of emerald moss on the shaded side of an old, speckled rock or noticed a thicket of a particular plant that would be useful in her healing. She would loosen the moss with her knife or cut snippets of the plant then place her treasures in the turtle-shaped leather pocket she always wore. She would explain in hushed tones how she had learnt of the item's use from the Sisters she'd schooled with, or the midwife in Wallingford, or the Indians at Moosehead Lake. Her voice would be so low that Kirkcaldie needed to stoop to hear her words. Although as a surveyor he made a handsome livelihood from the forest, occupying it for many weeks, sometimes months, dwelling among the wood and leaves, he never felt at home.

There weren't many people with whom Kirkcaldie could tolerate spending significant amounts of time. He had chosen his crew carefully, deciding on men with youth enough to see the hardships they faced – untrodden forest, enraged squatters, Indians and the bereavement that accompanies time away from loved ones – as obstacles to be overcome, but also with experience enough to possess the wherewithal to manage and endure the trials they confronted. Over the years, Kirkcaldie had weeded the arrogant, the agitators, the fools and, most importantly, the jabberers from his crew. What remained was a band of eight trustworthy, intelligent, intrepid and sensible men who, together, possessed all the skills the governor's surveyor required. When he was at his home, away from these men, he appreciated the solitude. Still, Tabby's visits were always welcome. She seemed to have the ability to slot into his life, similar to the way a fine piece of bluestone would slot into the wall he was building.

Tabby raised her hand, an indication they should stop walking. After a few seconds she moved forward alone, her feet rolling from heel to toe over the ground.

They had met two years ago in July. He and his men,

while watering their horses at the river near Hallowell, noticed an Indian canoe coming towards them downstream. They took the pilot for an Indian by the way he was dressed but felt no alarm because it was just one man alone. It wasn't until the canoe was five yards from them that they realised the pilot was a white woman.

Tabby had not stepped from the canoe as a woman might – she had leapt over the side and into the water which splashed her tunic. Her hat had fallen from her head and a cascade of honey spilled onto her shoulders. Unbothered, face flushed from her exertions, she placed the hat back on her head then pulled the boat onto the bank herself, waving Kirkcaldie's offers of assistance affably aside.

Relieving the canoe of its load, she had spoken with the men about their heading, suggesting places they could stop where people might oblige them with food or a roof for the night. Then she noticed McPherson's hand had been cut on the fleshy part of the palm, just below the thumb. He'd done it earlier in the day with a double bit axe as he was chopping through forest. He'd wrapped it in a spotted kerchief he usually wore around his neck.

Did you at least wash the wound before wrapping it in that foul rag?

When your hand rots and drops off, will you be happy living one-handed?

Her words were sharp as a razor but somehow gentle at the same time, her genuine concern blunting their edge. She told McPherson to sit then she opened the black case she carried with her, cleaned the cut with river water, examined it, removed small pieces of dirt with tweezers, dabbed it with a balm then bandaged it tightly in clean cloth.

If I give you clean bandages, will you bother to change the wrapping?

McPherson seemed too frightened to respond, so he just nodded slowly.

By the time she completed her ministrations, it was too late for her to continue on to her original destination, so she had camped with them that night in a small clearing near the river. The men had lines with flies to fish with; high summer was the perfect time for it. They'd been fishing all afternoon. But Tabby had speared more trout in the hour before supper than Kirkcaldie's men had fished combined. The trout were silver and silky, and they watched her gut each one with a jack knife then feed the limp bodies onto sticks for the fire.

That night Kirkcaldie learnt she lived with the Indians. She spoke of it without shame or embarrassment. Although her face was lovely and her arse round and shapely, it was her openness that had attracted him to her and the liberty she demanded from the world. It was then that he met Edie. Tabby had looked at her with love as she fed the bird raw strips of trout.

Laying under the stars, with the woman so near, Kirkcaldie found sleep difficult to find that night. His body stirred as it had not done in many years. He could see the outline of her form in the glow of pluming sparks and then later in the moonlight. Despite his exhaustion after a day of cutting through forest, carrying chains, poles and the circumferentor, Kirkcaldie was as restless as the wind. He closed his eyes, trying to ignore her presence, listening to the grunts and snores of the men around him. After a moment of this, he felt his blanket lift and she slipped under the cover beside him. He hadn't heard her movement over the ground that separated them. Lifting his arm, she nestled close. Her hair smelt of blossoms and he drifted away feeling the warmth of her breath on his neck. Had she sensed he wanted her? Or, he had wondered, was she as lonely as he was?

Now Tabby pointed up ahead. There was a deer, a large handsome stag, foraging near a brook. Watching the animal for a while, she eventually removed an arrow from her quiver and placed it in the bow. She was as straight as a poplar as she lifted it, drew back her arm and released its force. The animal fell to the ground with a loud *thud*. Immediately, Tabby ran to the beast. When she reached it, she fell to her knees, held her hand to its snout and her cheek to its chest, ensuring it was dead. The arrow was perfectly placed in the stag's side, puncturing the animal's lungs and heart, guaranteeing a speedy and painless death. Kirkcaldie handed Tabby his knife. She plunged it into the deer's chest, releasing a river of blood, then she proceeded to cut a rough line down to the beast's hindquarters.

They had never spoken of a life together beyond what they already had. Still, he cared for Tabby, more than he was able to say. The thought of her running afoul of a man like Jeremy Cool or General Hill made him greatly unsettled. And, although he'd had ample opportunities – the strong-willed widow in Winslow and McPherson's spinster sister sprang to mind – he had never strayed from Tabby since that first time with her under the stars.

21

'Do you have a suitor, Tabby?' Leah asked as she nursed Patience. She was sitting in an exquisitely carved rocker that her father had crafted. Tabby looked on from Leah's bed, distracted by the sublime mirroring of shapes – the perfect roundness of Leah's breast reflected in the baby's downy head. The soft, pink light of dusk sidled through the window and touched Patience's head gently.

'Are you promised to anyone?' she clarified when Tabby did not respond immediately.

Tabby smiled at the expression and settled herself against the pillows that gave off Leah's own clean scent, reminding Tabby of rain. Kirkcaldie was not a suitor so she remained mute on that front. There was something thrilling in keeping Kirkcaldie a secret. He was hers alone. What's more, the idea of facing a barrage of questions regarding his 'intentions', as though their togetherness was all his doing, questioned Tabby's sense of independence.

She had spent a week with Kirkcaldie. A blissful week. She intended to spend a further week or so at the Williamses', ensuring mother and baby were well. She and

Ben were leaving for Long Reach in a few days' time. It would have been pointless for her to return to Moosehead Lake or even travel further south towards Portland before the dissection. This is how she justified the atypical sojourn in Augusta to herself. The truth, however, was that Tabby was enjoying being in the company of a family, even if it was not her own.

She obliged Leah with an answer to her question. She felt comfortable both in mind and body resting on Leah's bed. She was a mere breath away from falling asleep.

'Time has passed me by, I fear,' Tabby answered. 'No, that is not right ... remaining unwed is not a situation I *fear*. Circumstances being as they are, I have never lived a wholly conventional life.'

'How so?' asked Leah as she nursed Patience.

'My mother died when I was just seven and my father never viewed me as a daughter to "marry off". My mother had schooled me until the time of her demise and Papa was not equipped to educate me in anything apart from sheep husbandry. He sent me to a convent school in Quebec.'

Leah's eyes rose from the baby's pursed, sucking mouth to Tabby.

'A convent?' Leah asked. 'Are you a Papist?

'I was baptised in the Roman Catholic Church,' Tabby corrected.

Chided, Leah offered a weak smile of apology.

'I lost my mother, too when I was younger ...' She frowned for a moment as though in recollection then lifted Patience onto her shoulder and patted her narrow back gently for a time, humming softly.

'Are you a nun?' Leah finally queried, as though she had been garnering the courage to ask the question.

Laughing at the notion, Tabby shook her head.

'Far from it. I left the convent when I was seventeen. I loved the Sisters and they filled my empty head with knowledge, but I could never have been a nun. I was a novice for a time. A short time. But their sacrifices are the sort I cannot make. I returned to the farm and my father.'

'You do not speak like a novice,' Leah added, raising an eyebrow.

'Six years living among the Kennebec settlers and four years living with Indians has coloured my turn of phrase somewhat, I agree.'

Tabby yawned. Exhausted by her journey that day and feeling the absence of Kirkcaldie acutely, as she always did when the separation was still fresh, Tabby rested her cheek against her hands and closed her eyes. Very soon she was asleep. Images of Hill and Cool began darting to and from the darkest corners of her mind. The urge to catch them was irresistible but in the shadows it was an impossible task. They were too fast, slick like eels among the reeds. Tabby felt certain that the two men were entwined in some way, but then her unconscious mind, distressed at the unknowingness, thrust the men from her dreams. They were replaced with an image of her mother.

She had never seen her mother clothed in a habit, dressed as a Sister, but this is how she was costumed in Tabby's dream. Her mother's beautiful face was framed in white and black by her coif and veil. Tabby could spy not a strand of the chestnut-coloured hair she had so admired as a child.

~

LEAH PLACED her daughter in the crib then crept towards Tabby on the bed, carefully brushing the curtain of hair from her face to reveal creamy, ivory-coloured cheeks. She wagered that the old hat Tabby wore, the one that now sat on the foot of Leah's own bed, shaded her in the heat when she travelled, casting her in shadows so that the pale skin of her face remained untouched by the sun.

If Leah was frank, which she generally chose to be, the young woman appeared a savage. Yet Tabby knew God ... or *had* known him. Examining the array of bright and heavy Indian beads that Tabby wore around her wrists, Leah noticed among them a more delicate strand of sherry-coloured topaz beads. A small, golden crucifix hung from the strand's tail, no bigger than the fingernail of her new-born babe. Leah guessed them to be rosary beads, although she had never seen any before. They were easily lost among the larger, roughly hewn Indian adornments Tabby wore.

Roman Catholics – 'Papists' as Reverend Dent and so many others in Eastham, her parents included, had referred to them – were not tolerated in Massachusetts Colony. Or in any of the thirteen colonies, for that matter. Despite the Act of Toleration some years ago, the group were now even persecuted in Maryland, where the Act was founded – a place where they had once been invited and welcomed. This had been a surprise to Leah; the hatred of Roman Catholics had seemed more ingrained in the north.

Leah, who had forsaken her god, wondered if Tabby had forsaken hers as well. If so, why did she wear the rosary beads? A gift, a keepsake, perhaps from her mother ... Leah was in possession of her own mother's rocking chair and copper curfew, and her mother's wedding band was kept by Maria in her cupboard.

Leah took Tabby's hat and looked at it closely. It was stained and tattered, with broken straw poking out in all directions from the brim and crown. Leah removed her cap then placed Tabby's hat on her own head. It must be years old, as it had taken on Tabby's shape, yet it was comfortable on Leah and shielded her face like an angel's wing.

WHEN TABBY WOKE, she met with Mister Williams in his study. More at ease on the second visit, Tabby sat in the armchair, crossing her legs beneath her as Mister Williams detailed the various investments he had secured for Tabby's funds. There were building projects in Augusta and, on a recent trip to Virginia, he had purchased ten hogsheads of tobacco on her behalf. It was his aim to resell the commodity – for more than twenty-five per cent of its original cost – in Maine, where tobacco was in healthy demand. Tabby approved of all the ventures Mister Williams had sought and felt an unusual sense of satisfaction when he informed her of the amount she had accumulated in so short a time.

To celebrate her gains, Mister Williams opened a bottle of whiskey he had acquired from a farmer, also in Virginia, who transformed his farm's excess barley and corn into liquor; a shrewd practice, much admired by Mister Williams. As they drank, they spoke of Tabby's travels since the time they had last been in one another's company.

Then, taking her second glass, Tabby confided that she went to visit General Hill.

She had not intended to share this information with Mister Williams, fearing it would tarnish his relations with the Committee. However, during the time she had spent with the family, she had discovered Mister Williams to be an intelligent and discerning man and she was in much need of his wise counsel. What's more, the whiskey had sent her tongue flying like a ribbon in the wind. And with the possibility of Ben Shute visiting soon, should he mention their meeting at Fiddler's Reach to Mister Williams, it would appear odd that Tabby had not informed him first.

Williams did not appear surprised by her news.

'What was your reading of the man?' he asked.

Tabby turned the question over in her mind for a moment before she responded.

'I did not like him. I *do not* like him, neither do I trust him. I believe him to be a liar and a savage. I'm certain he was involved in the tragedy that befell my father. Supplying no adequate answers to my inquiries about Papa, he quickly angered when I pressed him.'

Palgrave nodded as though he had predicted Tabby's summation of the man. She went on to relate the story of the young slave made mute by Hill's barbaric hand. When she finished the tale, she blinked hard, attempting to force back her tears. The Sisters of Ursuline had discouraged crying among their charges. Tears 'hindered clear sight and the path to God', they'd said. But now, induced by the whiskey (surely) and the gentle counsel of Mister Williams, there was nothing she could do to stop them, and they flowed unheeded down her cheeks.

Palgrave rose instinctively and moved to her, crouching beside her awkwardly as she sobbed.

'The worst part of the wretched situation is that there is nothing I can do to help him, or my father, for that matter. I am impotent.'

'Sadly, Tabby, the world is full of monsters, men who take pleasure in the pain of others and men who delight in causing that pain. I have met many of them – some who you might expect to have these urges and others ...' Palgrave's thought drifted to Reverend Dent, as greedy a man as he had ever known, despite his religious convictions. 'Matthew expressed it most succinctly in his gospel when he said "Beware of false prophets, which come to you in sheep's clothing, but inwardly they are ravening wolves".'

Tabby looked up and wiped her eyes. 'You know the Bible, Mister Williams.'

'I used to, Tabby.'

'I, too.'

FEELING heady from the whiskey and the weeping, Tabby said goodnight to Mister Williams and made her way up the staircase to Maria's room. She had refused supper, despite the frequent urgings of Leah. Tabby sensed an emptiness at her core, but it was not a hole that food could fill. The feeling seemed to be overtaking her entire body. It felt as hollow as an echo.

She entered the chamber and saw Maria at her easel, sketching. Her arm moved furiously over the paper. Occasionally, she would cease and examine her progress before continuing with the same frenzied movement. Yet all the while, her expression was still, passive. Maria did not look up from the paper or acknowledge Tabby's presence in any way. Even when it grew too dark to see and Tabby lit the candles in the chamber, Maria did not look away from her employment.

From a chair, Tabby watched the shadows made by Maria's fevered movement dance on the wall like dervishes. Before long, the candles filled the room with the honeyed scent of beeswax. Fascinated with the obscure light created by them, Tabby took pleasure in the unusual moment. Although entirely rested from her earlier nap, a fog overcame her that had nothing to do with the whiskey she had imbibed with Mister Williams. The light, combined with the smell of the wax and the scratch of Maria's pencil on paper, produced a strange atmosphere, charged yet not unpleasant.

'May I see your work?' Tabby asked quietly when she heard a clock downstairs strike ten.

Maria looked up then and smiled, her candlelit face a canvas for the flickering shadows. She had been aware of Tabby's presence all along. Maria lowered her hand, an indication that Tabby should come closer.

Comprised of three faces sprouting from the gnarled trunk of a tree, the image was just as tenebrous as Maria's chamber. The likenesses were, Tabby imagined, exact, recognisable – but to Maria only. While Tabby could tell the faces were male, they were obscured by overlying images, one for each man – a hummingbird, a ship and a sheaf of wheat. Air, water, earth ... symbols, Tabby guessed, that Maria used to represent each figure. *Where was fire?* Tabby wondered.

'Who are they, Maria?'

Maria pointed at each in turn. 'My father, the man I love and the man who loved me.'

The features that Tabby could discern were angular, drawn with heavy black lines, some of which Maria had smudged intentionally to create shadows, as though a pall lay upon the portrait – if, indeed, this *was* a portrait Tabby viewed. It felt more like a representation of sorts, but of what, she was unsure. *Could this image, so personal, created with such intent, be a reflection of Maria's soul?* she mused. Tabby focused on the painting, struggling to understand its meaning. She turned to the artist with a questioning look.

'Papa died a year ago,' said Maria, indicating the sheaf of wheat. Then she gestured to the hummingbird. 'Silas, my childhood friend and confidante, killed himself some time past.'

Tabby watched as Maria's gaze moved to the central figure in the portrait.

'And Samuel,' she whispered, lightly touching the ship, 'is coming back to me.'

22

'You see, Mistress Post, even in what you are wearing today, it is difficult for me to view you as a gentlewoman when you are renowned for dressing like a savage.'

'How so?' Tabby asked, looking at directly at Dummer squarely. 'Today I am dressed like a lady,' she said, primly adjusting the sleeves of the bodice she had borrowed from Maria, 'but what does it matter how I costume myself?

'Why do you not dress regularly in the attire fitting a woman of your status and means?'

'Practicality, Sir.'

Dummer glared down at her, clearly unimpressed with her response. She wished to educate him further, but Tabby decided to address the spectators instead. They were far more receptive to her expositions.

'It was Nadie, the wife of Mongwau, who first suggested I wear a tunic. That is to say, she did not suggest it to me in words; at that time, we shared so few. Instead, one day Nadie left a deerskin tunic, beaded at the hemline, and a pair of moccasins in my wigwam when I was absent. The tunic was folded neatly and the moccasins placed on top.

'When I found what she had left me, I sat by the items examining them for at least an hour. The beading was delicate and the stitches at the seams so small I could barely see them. I wondered what Nadie meant by the gesture. You see, I'd seen little kindness in the previous months.

'A week before, when I had been searching in the woods for butterfly weed, I saw Nadie foraging nearby. A sleeping infant in a cradleboard was propped against a spruce. We would catch each other in sly glances but we didn't speak. We were both still unsure in one another's company. I had very little of Nadie's language then, and she knew but a few words of mine. There was no simple or clear means of communication between us. Although my friendship with Mongwau had blossomed immediately, I knew that with Nadie, it needed time and careful tending in order to bloom.

'Nadie was ever wary of me, understandably so. I am sure she questioned why a white woman was suddenly living among her tribe. My father had built a hut on Sugar Island, in the middle of the lake; she must have wondered why I didn't dwell with him. I had read *that* question in her eyes. But my father did not want his daughter near him, so I could not. So I lived nearby.

'After spending what seemed like an age inspecting Nadie's gift, I eventually stepped out of my own clothes and slid the simple garment over my head. Once my arms were in place, the tunic dropped the length of my torso like a plummet down a well. Although tanned until it is as thin as parchment, deerskin is still heavier than cotton, broadcloth or even serge, and the purple and white beading lent the garment added weight. Despite this, it was cool and soft against my skin. Free of the underclothes I usually wore, my body tingled all over as it was kissed by the cool leather.'

There were gasps and laughter from those assembled. Dummer reddened.

'Mistress Post! Will you please be mindful of your turn of phrase?'

'I apologise,' Tabby said, remembering her audience. 'I slipped my feet into the moccasins and the deerskin wrapped around them like it was my own. In the winter, Nadie made me a warmer dress that I pulled on like a robe. It reminded me of the banyan that I had seen my former employer Mister Ives wear. However, the dress wrapped around my body like a swaddle and secured with a belt which tied at the back. Attached to this was a small bag in the shape of a turtle, intended for collecting medicinal herbs. Nadie was thoughtful like a sister might be, if I had ever had one.

'Without undergarments and with my legs visible to just below the knee, I was, at first, apprehensive to step outside the protection of my wigwam. Then I remembered I was among women who dressed like this every day. Men wore even less. In the summer, just a loincloth, no bigger than a dish clout, concealed their plug tails.'

Dummer sighed in exasperation then shot Tabby a sharp look. Shrugging, unrepentant, Tabby continued.

'The breeze off the lake immediately touched the skin of my legs and I felt goose bumps prickle my skin – an odd sensation for one so used to wearing layers of petticoats and skirts. I stood there for a moment, unsure of what to do next, feeling as though the entire clan's eyes were on me. But no-one cast a glance in my direction. Then I saw Nadie, crouched by the water cleaning fish. I approached her.

'*Wlioni*,' I said. By then, I had gained enough knowledge of the language to say 'thank you'.

'Nadie rose and looked me up and down, quite critically,

I thought, then smiled, clearly pleased with her handiwork.

'At twilight, when Mongwau returned, he came to my wigwam. He told me that a little while back, Nadie had seen me in the wood, foraging. Even though the woods were damp and cool, she noticed I seemed hot and that my skirt kept getting snagged on branches and twigs. She thought the fabric seemed heavy and awkward. That was why she made me the tunic.

'"The beads have meaning, too, *Mekwi*," he said. Mongwau sometimes called me by this name. I had often heard men call my father by the same epithet. It means 'red'. "The beads mark you as a member of this clan."

'I sensed the sting of tears behind my eyes. Although my father was near, he no longer looked at me as family, and there was no-one else. Mongwau's words moved me. Fearing speech, because my voice would surely break, I took a deep breath but remained silent.

'Sensing my emotion, Mongwau informed me with a grin, "Nadie said, if you were going to live with us, you should dress like us." I could tell by his expression of awe that Mongwau clearly admired his wife's decisive action.

'"And you should eat with us, too," Mongwau decided. He reached for my hand and hauled me to my feet gracelessly. I rubbed my eyes with the heels of my hand. It was my habit to eat alone, usually a simple meal of broth or fish. It had been an age since I had broken bread with anyone, let alone among a family.

'After that evening I never ate alone among the Penobscot again. I love Mongwau as I would a brother. And Nadie, now that I know more of her language, has become my friend and sister. I am grateful to be accepted as part of their clan, to be considered as part of their family. But Ephraim Post will always be my father.'

23

Tabby awoke alongside Maria in her generous bed. It was the day of the dissection. Ben was arriving at eight o'clock. Despite the rest, Tabby remained weary. Images of Cool and Hill and her mother had intruded on her slumber like comets sent from both Heaven and Hell. Then there was Maria's painting, still present by the window, haunting, the meaning of which Tabby was still struggling to comprehend. As she leant over the washbowl and splashed her face with water, tiredness wreathed her in fog and she longed to crawl into bed beside Maria again, close her eyes and hope for a more peaceful rest.

Maria did not stir while Tabby dressed. Her satiny hair was draped over the pillow like silk and the gentle, early sunlight caught the tips of her lashes as though dusting them with gold. Tabby wondered briefly why the Samuel in Maria's portrait had abandoned such a creature. *Is it her strangeness, her difference to others?* mused Tabby, as she tied the laces of the shoes she had borrowed from her bedfellow.

Although Ben had not spoken of it directly, Tabby sensed it would be inappropriate to attend Doctor

Douglass's dissection in her tunic, beads and moccasins. And she imagined that Ben would think it unchivalrous to ask her to don more conventional attire. With this in mind, from Leah she obtained the garments befitting such an occasion: stays, shift, and a bodice and skirt of teal blue. Leah's feet, however, were smaller than Tabby's own.

Maria awoke as Tabby was examining her hair in the looking glass, despairing at the sight of her unruly locks.

'Where are you going dressed up in my sister's clothes?'

'Ben is escorting me to Long Reach,' Tabby said. 'It's a trip I've made many times before without the protection of a male escort; however, Ben insisted.'

Maria raised an eyebrow.

'He cited "hostile Indians, robbers and gangs of runaway slaves" as just a few examples of the many dangers I might face en route. He's impossible to say "no" to.'

She raised the mirror to catch Maria in its reflection.

'We are to view a dissection.'

Maria was not fazed by the information. Instead, she stretched out her slender body like a cat, threw off the bedclothes, slid from the bed and padded over to Tabby in her bare feet.

'Then I shall fix your hair in a style suitable for a dissection,' she said, straight-faced.

She set to work immediately with an ivory-backed hairbrush and comb retrieved from her exuberant cupboard. Apart from her mother, whose manner and habits Tabby had difficulty remembering, no woman had ever devoted such concentration and energy to Tabby's contentment. Tabby enjoyed the sensation of Maria's fingers in her hair and against her scalp. Her skin tingled and she closed her eyes. The wave of tiredness she had only just overcome minutes before now returned, enveloping her once more as Maria separated the hair into equal sections, braided each with nimble fingers then brought the three together in an elaborate loaf-like knot at the back of Tabby's head. Pinning it securely, she then carefully drew out thin pieces of hair from around Tabby's face that, once loose, instantly kinked like springs. These framed her features delicately, lending them a femininity to which Tabby was not accustomed. Observing her reflection in the looking glass, Tabby was quite astounded at the transformation.

When she was a child at the convent her hair had been secured in a thick braid at the base of her neck and her head covered by a crisp, white linen cap that tied under her chin. For ten years, her appearance did not alter. She grew taller, her face thinned and the colour of her eyes darkened, yet the braid and the cap endured.

Each morning, while the Sisters were at the Breviary and after the students had washed and dressed, the girls would stand in a ring that looped around their barn-like dormitory and braid one another's hair. This taught the students the values of trust and communal responsibility. Each braid was perfectly balanced and tight like rope and tied at the end with a thin black ribbon. It was a fashion that Tabby begrudgingly adhered to in womanhood. Not having had a mother or sister to instruct her on such matters, Tabby was limited in regard to womanly ways.

When she rose from the stool, Maria embraced her, holding her for a long time. Tabby sensed her heat as though she was standing too close to a hearth.

'What is it between we two?' Maria asked as she drew away, gazing into Tabby's eyes.

Tabby thought for a moment, needing to supply an answer, as much to satisfy her own mind as Maria's. Her friend wandered back to the bed contemplating the question as well.

'I'm really not sure. We have similar interests, I suppose,' Tabby said, gesturing to Maria's cupboard then to her black apothecary case in the corner of the chamber.

Maria's smooth brow furrowed as she lay back against her pillows. 'It's more than that.'

'Our ages? Our ... spinsterhood?' Tabby smiled, plucking answers like apples, attempting to find one appetising enough for Maria.

'Perchance,' Maria contemplated, unconvinced. Then a notion took her, and an arch smile curled her wide mouth. 'You may not be a spinster for too much longer if Doctor Benjamin Shute has his way.'

Tabby narrowed her eyes then gathered her belongings before leaving the chamber and Maria.

BEN WAS grateful that Palgrave had been kind enough to lend them a gig for the journey to Long Reach. As he sat next to Tabby on the narrow seat, he was unsurprised to feel nervous at her proximity. Her skirts pressing against his thigh, and the thought of what lay beneath, created an image of which he could not rid himself.

Since the kiss they shared in the woods, he found himself distracted by her constantly – the taste of her lips and the weight of her breast in his hand. He had always considered himself to have an abundance of self-discipline and mental fortitude. However, since that day, both seemed to be depleting rapidly.

Ben did not notice when Tabby entered the parlour. He was preoccupied cooing and ahing at Patience who lay peacefully in her father's arms. But when he did, he reddened.

'You have a way with children, Ben,' Tabby said gliding towards the group, noting his embarrassment. 'It is a recommended quality for a doctor. Both boys and girls will protest any treatment if they don't take to you.' She immediately joined Ben in his antics.

As they played with the baby, Ben noted the colour of her dress and how it appeared to bring out the colour of her hair and intelligent eyes all at once. Dressed as she was, Tabby appeared refined, genteel and the equal of any person she might meet in Long Reach. Donned in her usual garb, Ben felt these qualities were more difficult to recognise. *Then again, perhaps that is her purpose*, he thought.

THE JOURNEY to Long Reach began in silence. He was at a loss as what to say for fear of stammering or blundering into territory where he had been forbidden. Instead, he concentrated on the rhythm of the horse's gait, hoping the sound might hone his muddled thoughts into something resembling a sensical comment. He recalled their conversation in Palgrave's parlour before they had departed. Tabby possessed many wonderful qualities as a healer and as a woman; to Ben's thinking, she could be anything she wished. *Why then*, he mused, *does she live among savages and travel the length and breadth of Maine alone?* He puzzled on this question until Tabby finally broke the silence, turning her pretty face towards him.

'Maria and I have grown quite fond of one another. We were attempting to reason why this morning but none of the possibilities seemed adequate.'

It was an unusual observation with which to begin a conversation. He wondered if there was an agenda in the tone of her remark.

'You are both extremely unique women,' he responded. 'Perchance, that lies at the foundation of the bond that has developed between you. Like souls are often drawn close.'

'Unique, that is true,' she agreed. Now she had opened discussion, Tabby shifted and rested her weight on her hip in order to face him. Her hand brushed his thigh in an inadvertent gesture, and Ben's eyes widened as though a lightning bolt had shot through him. He shifted slightly and hurried the horses along.

'A few nights past, Maria was sketching in her chamber. It was a portrait of three men. She explained that they were her father, a friend who took his own life, and her love. She insisted the latter, a man called Samuel, would come back to her. I was intrigued, and desperately longed to know more about her past, but I felt that I was in no position to inquire.'

'Why so?'

'Maria's focus on her work came near to reverie, as though she had been transported from her chamber to another place entirely.'

Although Ben 'desperately longed' to please Tabby with insight into Maria's nature, he was barely more versed in her history than she. However, he confided all he had been told. The family moved from Wellfleet when Leah's father had died, leaving Palgrave with a handsome enough sum to invest in the blossoming settlement of Augusta. Maria had never been married and Abby, a former slave who had been given her freedom, visited often from her home in Wellfleet. Leah refused the employment of maids and servants, despite her husband's protestations.

'Some would say that Maria is bedevilled,' Tabby said.

Her tone was cynical. 'Then again, I have been called the same and much worse.'

Ben turned to her, alarmed, saddened that all her good works had led people to this conclusion. At that moment Ben desired nothing more than to be the one responsible for altering and colouring her jaded outlook.

Then Tabby heaved a sigh and gazed towards the heavens, hoping, he suspected, to catch a glimpse of Edie.

IT WAS difficult to know the age of the dead woman. Tabby looked at her hard, waiting for the proceedings to begin. Without the mask of life, age was impossible to discern. Apart from the deceased, Tabby was the sole female in the room. Her presence at the dissection garnered a number of glares from Maine's scientific and medical fraternity, all of whom were male. As shoulders touched and jostled, she allowed the disapproval to wash over her and, once Douglass's scalpel penetrated flesh, her attendance at the dissection seem to fade like a passing breath.

The room where they gathered was an ordinary parlour in the home of a local shipwright, Daniel Cooper. Cooper possessed a keen interest in matters scientific, from 'the position of the stars in the heavens to the germination of seedlings in the earth', as Tabby was informed by Ben. The curtains shielding the windows were lace and Tabby noticed a number of recently polished brass candlesticks adorned the maple hutch that stood behind Douglass, giving the scene the impression of a priest standing before an altar. Public dissections weren't strictly legal, Ben had said, but Maine society, including the magistrates and lawyers, possessed such a hunger for scientific knowledge that the authorities tended to turn a blind eye. It heartened Tabby to know that men could be so enlightened.

The body rested on a large oak table that was covered in linens. *The witness to many family suppers*, Tabby thought, for the scent of roast mutton still hung in the air. The body was also draped in fabric, with only a small window revealing the space below the breast. Tabby was impressed and surprised that Douglass had taken the trouble to preserve the woman's dignity in death. She was pleased Ben had been so fortunate to have such a considerate mentor. The doctor's instruments were laid out neatly on the table as well – a scalpel, a small hand saw and a pair of large, robust scissors. Tabby's eye was drawn to the scalpel, larger than her own but just as keen. She purposefully returned her attention to the body of the woman.

Doctor Douglass was a tall man with a head covered in thick silver hair that was tied at the base of his neck. He wore a heavy leather apron, like a blacksmith, and stood high above the poor woman's supine body. He appeared more the tradesman than the physician. Broad of chest with muscled forearms, Douglass dwarfed the deceased. He made his preliminary incision beneath the woman's breasts then began to speak.

'This is Dorothy Smithers, aged thirty, from Long Reach. Unmarried, childless and from a Puritan family, she did much, I am told, to aid those in the Long Reach community less fortunate than herself. For many years she nursed her ailing brother Jacob before he died of the same disease. It is not unreasonable to think that it was likely her goodwill that led to her death at so young an age, and still her altruism lives on. A mere sixteen hours before she died, as she rested in the embrace of her mother and younger sister, Dorothy expressed an earnest desire that her viscera might be anatomically inspected for the benefit of those who may be afflicted with like disorders. We are fortunate that her family granted her dying wish.'

Douglass's voice was the voice of any ordinary man, neither educated nor polished. But it was warm and sincere, without the uniformness that characterised the well-bred British accent that she was expecting from one so highly accomplished and qualified in his field.

'The disorder she spoke of was pulmonary phthisis – consumption.'

Unexpectedly, Ben clutched her hand. Tabby looked at him but his eyes were fixed on the proceedings. His expression gave nothing away.

Douglass laboured – and it was *labour* – to cut through layers of pink flesh that looked no different to the flesh of any other animal: spongy, yielding readily under the blade of his scalpel. His assistant Doctor Fletcher used clouts to dab at the small amount of fluid that seeped from the wound onto the skin.

'I am not here today to discover the cause of Dorothy Smithers's death,' Douglass went on without raising his eyes from the body, seemingly voicing his thoughts rather than speaking to the audience. The physician seemed lost in the deepening layers of Dorothy's flesh, unaware of the onlookers who ringed the table where he worked. 'That we know. It is to honour her wishes and seek to gather greater knowledge and understanding about the disease so someone might devise a remedy, or better yet, discover a means of prevention.

'I am told by Dorothy's grieving mother that for more than two years her daughter had been plagued by a hacking cough that worsened each day. The sputum she expelled was often bloody. She was also listless, short of breath and without appetite. Dorothy was feverous and suffered night sweats. Her daughter wasted away until she was a mere husk. Based on those symptoms, there is not an iota of doubt in my mind that Dorothy was overcome with what John Bunyan termed the "Captain of all these men of death".'

Tabby had attended many consumptive patients, or 'lungers' as they were known among the Kennebec settlers. As she watched Douglass, she considered what relief she might have prescribed to Dorothy Smithers. *Perhaps a pipe of thornapple and coltsfoot*, she thought, *to ease the cough and the inflammation.* She knew that fresh air and mild exercise, if the patient was able, also seemed to have positive benefits. Yet all these treatments combined only to draw out life, not rid the person of the illness entirely. Millicent Ferguson had seemed cured after just a fortnight of Tabby administering such medicines, by Christmas she had succumbed again and come St Valentine's Day, Millicent knew there was no point to her pinning bay leaves to her pillow. She was in the ground two weeks before Easter.

When Douglass had completed this first stage of the procedure, he placed the scalpel on the table and picked up the scissors. He eyed the incision for a moment before plunging them into the cavity.

'He is cutting through the sternum,' Ben whispered, 'in order to access the entire pulmonary system.' Although Tabby had never used that exact phraseology herself, she was able to fathom the doctor's process.

'Dorothy was once promised to a young man, who also lived in Long Reach,' Douglass said as he cut through the bone. 'Before they were to be wed, he courageously, foolishly joined the Queen's forces in the war against the

French. He did not return. Devastated by the loss, Dorothy Smithers never thought of marriage again.'

Finished with the scissors, Douglass placed them next to the body and with his hands separated the chest. It opened like a clamshell and the audience took a step towards the body in curiosity as though peering down a well. Douglass took a step back, making room for a gentleman who clearly had no stomach for dissections. As Douglass watched him hurry from the room, he placed his blood-coated hands on his hips. Then he looked at the body like an artist might view an unfinished portrait. Exhaling, his large hand grasped the scalpel once more. A final brushstroke was needed.

He approached the body, took another moment of pause, then delicately removed Dorothy Smithers's lungs, placing both in a porcelain dish.

WHEN DOUGLASS COMPLETED the dissection by stitching Dorothy's chest closed, a number of the men approached him with awe. Tabby held back, observing Douglass's handi-work. The stitches were neat and uniform; she appreciated the additional minutes he took to close the wound so tidily.

As he did so, without reason or cause, Tabby had remembered the chimneypiece her mother had stitched. It had rested on the wall above the hearth. Tabby had no inkling of when her mother had stitched it; her mother never shared with her daughter the story of the fine embroi-dery. It was simply there. Its origin and presence were never questioned.

Her mother's stitches were so intensely accurate, unwa-vering in their precision that the scene it depicted, from only a short distance away, appeared as though it had been created with an artist's brush. And the scene? What a scene it was! The foreground depicted a village, with narrow lanes and roads that foxes and hounds traversed. The background was pastoral with rolling emerald hills, a sparkling lake and fields that stretched to the horizon. They were dotted with barley, wheat and corn. Birds of all varieties clung to branches and roamed the sky, wings outstretched. Against this, women, and only women, toiled at all description of industry – a gentlewoman sewed a sampler, a Negro woman toiled at a stream with a washing board, and another woman, of no particular birth, harvested barley, a basket slung over her shoulder.

Each time Tabby had raised her eyes above the hearth she would come upon a new, undiscovered treasure in the design. But her favourite detail was that of a woman with a gentle face tending to a child in a bed. Tabby recalled that the woman wore a headscarf and the child's cheeks were as red as hot coal.

She wondered now where that chimneypiece had found a home. Whose hearth was it gracing at that moment? Whose imagination was it capturing? Who was it rousing? Before her father departed for New France and she for Wallingford, they had sold their flock to their nearest neighbours in New Haven, the Devoys. These good people had promised to watch over their home, ensuring no squatters or the like took up residence. Tabby and her father had closed up the cabin and she had covered the furniture with bed linens. That was ten years ago.

Later, when her father reappeared in Wallingford then just as suddenly disappeared, Tabby had written to the Devoys. She had been matter of fact in her correspondence and wrote of the difficulties father and daughter had come to face, giving them licence to sell the farm and all that was in it. Tabby had written that they should consider the proceeds payment for watching over the property for so long. But she had never received a reply to her letter, despite leaving the town clerk's office in Hallowell as an address.

At the time, in the fraught moments of searching for her father, Tabby had not given the real value of her mother's chimneypiece a thought. But standing in Daniel Cooper's parlour beside Dorothy Smithers's body, it was all she could think of. Then her mind turned to her mother's rosary beads, left behind with her other belongings in Maria's chamber. She had those at least.

As the spectators approached Douglass, they were ushered to another room by Doctor Fletcher. In the doorway, Douglass turned. Easily able to see above the heads of those who surrounded him, Douglas indicated to Ben with a nod and a quick raise of his eyebrows that he and Tabby should wait behind.

Once the room was entirely vacated of all but Tabby and Ben, they approached Dorothy's body. Tabby looked at her grey face, brushing back a lock of chestnut hair that curtained her brow. She looked as if she were resting.

'She was a handsome woman,' Tabby said, gazing hard at her fine features, the high cheekbones and celestial nose.

Ben had only released Tabby's hand when the party had begun to trickle from the parlour, but the ghost of his touch lingered on her skin.

He nodded, moving closer, joining Tabby in her contemplations.

'Doctor Douglass treated her well, do you not agree?' said Tabby. 'He portrayed her as a woman, a daughter and a sister. He painted her with compassion.'

They were silent as they gazed at the woman's face.

'Perchance, he limned her too well,' said Ben.

Tabby looked up to see his brow furrowed in concern. 'You appear troubled. What is it?'

Ben sighed. 'I hope I did not offend you by taking your hand today. I assure you my action was entirely involuntary.'

'You did not offend me,' she said, hoping to reassure him.

They met one another's gaze across the body. Tabby searched his face for a hint of meaning.

Ben rested his hands on the table. He looked down again at Dorothy, the young woman whose compassion had led to her own demise. He kept his eyes on her face as he spoke.

'Do you ever worry, Tabby,' he began slowly as though mining for each word, 'that your kindness, your philanthropy – your selflessness – will be your undoing?'

Tabby frowned.

'Your desire, your need to help others – the sick, the abused, those excluded from society – not only puts your physical and emotional health at risk but, I fear, could also lead you into the paths of dangerous people who do not share your unselfish ways.'

She contemplated her response. Everything he spoke was true. Men such as Cool and Hill were dangerous, and she believed even Achak was self-serving at heart, but how could she explain her calling? Arguments for her choices far outweighed those against. There were practical considerations, such as earning a living and supporting herself because if she did not, she would be destitute. Then there were esoteric motives. These were difficult to contend because Tabby did not fully grasp them herself. Besides, healing in all its many guises was at her core. It was her very essence.

'Ben, I do not see myself as any less opportunistic than

others. Healing is an entirely selfish act on my behalf. Helping to birth a babe reminds me of my place in the world. Bandaging a wound makes more sense than anything else in my life. Taking away pain from another is entirely natural. I was born to do this – there is no other path for me.'

He looked up to face her. Tabby walked over to him and took his hands in her own.

'Surely, you of all people understand this,' she said.

He nodded slowly then sighed again. 'I do.'

'WOULD you like to do the honours, Mistress Post?'

Tabby looked at Doctor Douglass, who was holding his scalpel aloft in her direction then down at Dorothy Smithers's lungs. Douglass, Shute and Tabby had moved to Daniel Cooper's kitchen and the organs lay on a white cloth in the middle of the table, a macabre centrepiece. The left lung was smaller than the right, Douglass explained, as it shared its space with the heart. An 'accommodating bedfellow' he called the scarred and withered organ. Ben handed Tabby a fresh, crisp apron and she slipped it over her head, tying the garment at the back. Tabby then unbuttoned the sleeves of her dress at the wrist, careful not to tear the minute, tortoiseshell buttons from the soft fabric, unaccustomed as she was to delicate garments. She rolled the sleeves to her elbows.

She took the scalpel and turned the instrument over in her fingers for a moment. Douglass's scalpel did not fit her hand as comfortably as did her own, neither did it seem as sharp. However, having never used her own blade, it was difficult to draw a true comparison.

'Slice the lung vertically,' Douglass instructed. 'All the way through to the table. Lay it open like a book.'

Tabby held the organ between her fingers, pressing on it gently. It had the tactility of a plump shad's belly, a fish she had gutted many times, and this thought gave her confidence to lay the scalpel into the organ. Following Douglass's careful directions, she spread the two halves of Dorothy Smithers's right lung on the table.

The three leant in closer and examined the organ.

'What can we read from this?' Douglass asked.

Tabby could see the lung had been diminished by disease, but she could not articulate how as she had nothing to compare it to apart from the pink, glowing variety she had removed from animals. She examined it closely, noting a cheese-like substance scattered throughout. Looking closer as Douglass probed the organ, Tabby noted hollows, pockets in the lung, seemingly eaten away. She wondered if it was by the illness. Since she had been tending to consumptive patients, Tabby had imagined the illness, 'pulmonary phthisis' as Douglass called it, as a weakness in the patient. Not that they were weak people, lacking fortitude, but somewhere, she believed, an inherent weakness lay. Now, seeing this, she believed the disorder itself was something living, like a persistent weevil eating tunnels through a bag of grain. However, in the lung, blood eventually seeps in through the cavities made by the disease. Finally, the afflicted drown in their own blood.

Her heart ached at this realisation. Now she had seen inside a human body, where the organs lay, she was able to imagine it happening.

'Are you well, Mistress Post?' Douglass asked, noting the colour drain from her face. 'Are you feeling faint?'

She shook her head, taking a minute to compose herself. Once she had, she voiced her theory to the two doctors.

Douglass grinned in satisfaction. 'You are quite right, Mistress Post. That is my view, in a nutshell.'

'Doctor Douglass believes that pulmonary phthisis is infectious, not hereditary,' said Ben. 'It passes between people in a sneeze or, more likely, a cough. You are quite right in saying that it is a living thing. It is a living organism.'

'But where is it?' Tabby asked, pointing to the cross section. 'Has it concealed itself in another organ? Why is it not present in the lung?'

'It is.' Douglass stated. 'I believe this here,' he indicated the cheese-like matter, 'is the disease at its later stages.' The doctor probed the flesh some more. 'And see here?' Tabby leant in closer. 'This is what phthisis looks like in the first stages.'

She moved closer to examine multiple small mustard-coloured warts resembling millet seeds.

'Doctor Manget of Geneva has named this stage "military tuberculosis".'

'Like an army, it is deadly and practically unstoppable,' Ben added.

Tabby lifted her gaze and looked at the doctors calmly.

'Then you need to recruit a more formidable regiment, Doctor Douglass.'

24

The return journey to Augusta was undertaken predominantly in silence. It troubled Ben that he had vexed her so soundly, hurt her so profoundly. In his disappointment, he had said too much; words issued from his tongue that he had no stomach for now. Yet out they had spat like poison from the fangs of a serpent. Finding the courage to glance in her direction after more than an hour into the journey, he was stricken to discover her typically mild and amiable countenance still in possession of the stone-cold hardness that had overcome it beside Daniel Cooper's hearth in Long Reach.

Neither Ben nor Tabby had prior knowledge of Doctor Douglass's intentions, yet Ben could not but feel wounded. His pride was inflicted with a short, sharp jab when, as he was preparing the lungs of Dorothy Smithers for preservation, Douglass asked Tabby to work with him at his practice in Long Reach.

However, the initial pain of being overlooked soon transformed into joy and Ben's mind swarmed with possibilities. To imagine Tabby, lodging in comfortable rooms in Long

Reach, working by Douglass's side, away from danger, was an immense comfort. They would likely encounter each other frequently and, once a more conventional path had been mapped for her, he thought she may come to accept him as a partner in work and life. He had imagined all this in an instant.

'So many of my female patients would appreciate a woman's touch,' Douglass said. 'And you would be immensely helpful in my research into this dreadful disease.'

He indicated the organs that had been submerged in a jar of alcohol.

'You have a sharp eye for detail and a natural inkling towards pathology. I understand you are self-taught in the field?' he asked Tabby.

He screwed the lid onto the jar tightly with his large hand then placed it on the table, taking another hard look at the organs as though a scar, pock or blemish may have been overlooked.

Tabby took a moment to consider the question before she responded. Ben could see she was flattered by the proposition. He imagined that even though he had never seen her seek them out, she welcomed approval and praise when it did come her way.

'I had some tutoring when I was in the care of the Ursuline Sisters. The order is dedicated to caring for the sick and the needy, as well as to the education of young girls.'

Ben shot her a look of caution. Douglass had an open mind, but Ben feared he might share the Colonies' prejudice towards Roman Catholics and revoke his proposition. In the time they spent together when Ben was a student, they had never discussed religion. Ben studied Douglass's guarded expression, waiting for him to respond, attempting to decipher what might be the nature of his thoughts.

'The knowledge they shared was a solid grounding,' Tabby continued. 'How to bandage a wound and splint a break, how to bring down a fever and stitch a wound were just the fundamentals. Most importantly, the Sisters taught me how to show compassion. It's one thing to feel, but quite another to put it into practice.'

'The Ursuline Sisters of Quebec, yes?' Douglass asked.

Tabby nodded.

'They have indeed succeeded in their mission with you, Mistress Post,' Douglass smiled. He leant his long arms against the table. Douglass appreciated her candour and was not fazed by her admission.

'What is your answer? Will you tarry in Long Reach and assist me in *my* mission?'

Without a second's more contemplation, Tabby said, 'I fear that I cannot. I have a mission of my own I must attend to before I can rest. But it has been an honour to assist you this day, Doctor Douglass.'

Douglass accepted the refusal gracefully, said his farewells, then departed. Ben, however, stood astounded at Tabby's decision. He watched as she calmly fixed a pin in her hair that had come loose. When she had asked coolly when they might be leaving for Augusta, Ben's astonishment rose to red hot anger. How could she be so indifferent to Douglass's offer? he puzzled. How could she be so oblivious to the opportunities the doctor's offer would afford her?

Needing to give vent to his frustration, Ben thumped his hand hard on the table. She jerked at the noise.

'Whatever is the matter?'

That utterance was a spur. The barrier had been released.

'Whatever is the matter?' he repeated, flabbergasted. 'You have declined a position with Doctor William Douglass, a position that most physicians the world over, including myself, would covet.'

'Are you jealous?' she replied, her colour rising.

'Of course, I'm jealous,' he responded, struggling to keep an even tone. 'But my annoyance runs deeper than my own rebuffing by Doctor Douglass. I sympathise with your situation, Tabby, but I am left dumbfounded. You live like a savage, place yourself in danger at every opportunity and decline proposals, reasonable proposals ... such as Douglass's. Tabby, your choices will lead to your ruin.'

Her eyes narrowed and, even though Ben knew he had gone too far already, he continued towards the precipice propelled by fear that he might lose her.

'Judging by the direction your life has taken, you clearly need counsel to prevent the dire end it continues towards.'

When she did not respond, he foolishly went on.

'I voiced my honest feelings to you some weeks ago in Augusta and I believe, although you may not love me now, there is a seed of attraction – one that you cannot deny – which, with careful nurturing, will blossom into affection. You need not give up your work ... in fact, I am sure we could work together, as partners, until it was time to begin a family. The life you lead is so fraught; a woman should not venture into the wilderness alone, in a canoe unassisted along the river ...'

Tabby remained silent. Her lack of response infuriated him further. He continued speaking, uttering the words of which he would soon be so ashamed.

'Considering your past, your family and your reputation, I cannot imagine that you will ever receive a more agreeable proposal. You need me, Tabby.'

Rising, her chest heaved – in fury, Ben was to momentarily discover – yet she fixed him in her steady gaze.

'I would not have you, Doctor Shute, in a month of Sundays.' The words wounded him like a volley of arrows.

'Do you expect me to be flattered by your proposal? You have grievously insulted my family, myself and the choices I have made. You know nothing of sacrifices. You believe forgoing a husband, a home and a warm hearth are the sacrifices I have made? Well, I have sacrificed nothing! I have only gained from my endeavours. For you to forsake wealth and comfort means little when you still possess the sway of a good name and the opportunities that name has offered you. You wear your elbow patches like medals of honour, but yours are not true sacrifices.'

She moved around the table towards him. They stood toe to toe, so close he could discern flecks of shimmering, fiery gold in her clear, blue eyes.

'I do not need you, or any man for that matter. And to smooth your crumpled ego, consider it my "savagery" which compelled our encounter in the forest, born simply from lust and nothing more – certainly not attraction.'

Marching from the room, every essence of her bristled with wild fury. She slammed the door, leaving the scene behind her.

He had underestimated Tabby's strength and deep-rooted independence. Ben crumpled into a chair, her words resounding like Heaven's thunder in his head. All her assessments were true, except for the last. Ben was certain her kiss sprang from the wellspring of affection, not lust. Placing his face in his hands, he counted his crimes and cursed his own stupidity and tempestuousness. Then he soon realised that his cruel censure was not only rooted in arrogance and disappointment but also in his keenest instinct – to protect the woman he loves.

Ben gathered his belongings and departed the home of Daniel Cooper. Tabby was waiting in the gig, straight-backed and noble. The storm of her rage had subsided to a rigid stillness, but Ben could discern from her clenched jaw and steely countenance that she was striving to contain her emotions. Even Edie's presence, who perched on the dash-board, failed to soften her and Ben was certain at any moment that the bird would be commanded by her mistress to peck his eyes out. When he picked up the reins, Tabby spoke. His heart lifted instantly.

'If I was in possession of my canoe, I would not be sharing this gig with you.'

His spirits dropped like a wounded bird. Unable to speak, he clicked his tongue – *tchic-tchik* – inciting the horses to move.

THEY ARRIVED in Augusta at dusk. The journey passed entirely in silence and lent Ben ample opportunity to reflect on his poor behaviour. Tabby had exposed him. Now, ashamed and repentant, he was determined to repair the damage he had inflicted. As he brought the gig along the Williamses' drive, he glanced at her again and the low, amber rays of the sun cast her in a fiery glow. Ben wondered if this infernal hue mirrored her temperament. He brought the horses to a halt and, pre-empting her hasty quitting of his company, touched her arm. As he did so, he sensed her muscles tense.

'I implore you to forgive me, Tabby,' he said quietly. 'My remarks were rash and fuelled only by my ignorance. I have not been so well tutored in the gentle art of compassion as you have. I require a gift I do not possess: the ability to view a situation from another's point of view. My own family's model was of indifference when confronted with another's woes.

'I do not understand your choices but that is for me to remedy. In truth, I know very little about you but, in my arrogance, I have assumed too much and all of it misguided. Whatever choices you have made are your own and if you would deign to share with me, now or in the future, all that has passed in your life, I would be honoured to listen.'

They sat in the gig for a time, silent, each meditating on the day and the events that had passed.

'My actions in the forest on the day Patience was born were not triggered by savagery.' She paused. 'In truth, I was lonely.'

She turned to him and he could see tears glistening on her pale cheeks.

'It occurred to me on the journey here that perhaps I *have* sacrificed more than I care to admit in my desire to help others.'

Jumping from the gig, she took the stairs to the door two at a time, leaving in her wake the lingering scent of her torment. Edie flew from the gig and into the dusty violet of the sky.

25

———

'Have you ever been called a witch, Mistress Post?' Dummer queried.

Tabby laughed. The glorious, silvery sound resonated in the high, vaulted ceilings of the courthouse.

'Of course, Sir, I warrant there is not one woman in the colonies who has not been called such.'

Dummer cleared his throat. It was not the response he had expected. 'Do such claims not concern you?'

Tabby shook her head, smiling wearily. She knew the subject of witchcraft would arise sooner or later.

'Any woman with power is slandered a witch, Sir. Given I have the power of healing, I have heard it more than most. However, it is a common allegation, too common in my opinion. Why, any woman that challenges a man, even her own husband, has had her reputation smeared in this way.

'Although it's more than thirty years since those terrible events in Salem, not all remain mindful of the consequences the cry of 'witch' has among unhappy, bitter people. However, even Reverend Mather has admitted his errors in judgement on this matter. And, Sir, to my mind, no person –

man or woman – possesses the magics to curse or bewitch others or control the forces of nature ... or fly through the air with the wind.'

The spectators laughed.

'And the Devil's Book ... Poppycock.'

'Is it your testimony that you are not a witch?'

'Witches, as small-minded people imagine them, do not exist. They are fiction, the stuff of fairytales.'

Tabby paused, thinking carefully on her next words.

'I have heard of white women – European women – who consider themselves pagans. They worship nature and conjure what some might call "white magic". The sun, the moon and the stars are their gods ... and the sea. But I am not one of those women.

'There are people, male and female, who have learnt to make tonics and poultices in order to ease the suffering of others. They can discern what ails those who suffer by a touch of their patient's skin, or the sound of their heartbeat. For reasons of which I am unaware, I have been gifted in this way. It is an undeniable fact.'

'Mistress Post, the only undeniable fact I am aware of at present is that you are gifted at mincing words,' Dummer put in.

'Sir,' said Tabby, lifting her chin, 'I am *not* mincing words. I have sworn an oath to tell the truth and that is what I have done each day during this trial. However, I will not label myself a witch in this courtroom.

'What's more, if I actually were a witch – the type of witch that *you* believe exists – would it not have made more sense to kill a man with a curse rather than an arrow?'

26

Maria's room was empty when Tabby entered. She pulled back the curtain and watched as Ben turned the horses towards the stables. Sighing, she removed her bonnet and kicked off the shoes she had borrowed. She stretched out her toes. Exhausted and restless all at once, Tabby went downstairs in search of company. She found the family in the kitchen, finishing their supper. Baby Patience was by Leah's side in her crib, the mother rocking the infant gently. They welcomed her with a place at the table and the children immediately began all at once on a tangled string of questions regarding the dissection. Caleb was the most incessant, seeming to be more aware of human anatomy than Tabby was herself.

The clash with Ben and the subsequent détente had snatched away any trace of hunger. But as soon as the scents of the kitchen reached her nose, she found herself starving. Elizabeth offered her a generous plate of partridge baked in a pie with turnips and Tabby furiously devoured it while responding to the children's queries.

'And what was the poor woman's affliction?' Maria finally asked.

'Consumption,' Tabby responded. 'Through such dissections, Doctor Douglass is hoping to develop a remedy for the disease or, if not a remedy, then he seeks to gain greater knowledge in order to assist in the prevention of the disease.'

'Prevention?' Caleb inquired.

'Well, consumption is more prevalent in the overcrowded areas of cities than in the countryside, so he believes the disease is not an inherent weakness in the lungs. More likely, it is *contagious*,' she emphasised the word as she knew Caleb valued unfamiliar vocabulary. 'He believes it is spread among people through the air when they cough or sneeze.'

'Fascinating,' the boy replied.

Tabby smiled. 'But I imagine you are all quite safe here, surrounded by space and fresh, clean air as you are.'

It calmed her to discuss her recent learnings with the family. It is what she had hoped to do with Ben on the return journey to Augusta.

When Patience began to whimper, Leah removed her from the crib, untied her bodice and placed the baby to her breast. Tabby looked on, admiring the soft, downy roundness of the baby's head.

Palgrave inquired after Ben. He was seeing to the horses, Tabby informed him. Palgrave nodded, but asked no more. Tabby's attention returned to Leah who, beatific, Madonna-like, gazed adoringly at the baby on her breast. As Sarah and Elizabeth began to clear the table, Leah took the opportunity to move Patience to her right breast. When the baby took hold, Leah winced, drawing in breath. Instinctively, Tabby's eye fell to the source of Leah's discomfort. From her position at the table, Tabby was able to examine the profile of the breast, unobscured. A lump the size of a walnut was evident beneath the skin, just above the crown of the baby's head. Troubled, yet concerned her observations would be noticed, Tabby lifted her gaze after just a few seconds only to discover Leah's eyes on her.

TABBY ROUNDED the house towards the summer kitchen in search of Edie. As she passed by the parlour window, she heard the voices of Palgrave and Ben, their silhouettes flickering by candlelight on the walls. She stopped beneath the window, listening as Ben recounted the dissection. He spoke avidly, using the language of Science, well-suited to a physician. Tobacco smoke stole through the open window. The smell reminded Tabby of her father, so she breathed in deeply. Waiting for a moment in the dark, very soon she heard the sweep of wings above her. In an instant, Edie was clutching tightly to her arm. Nuzzling, as was their way of greeting, the pair took in one another's presence. When Edie began to wail, Tabby rushed from her position so close to the house.

'Shhhhh, you will wake the entire family, Edie! Baby Patience is fast asleep,' Tabby whispered, attempting to stifle her laughter at the bird's obvious distress regarding her attire. 'I smell different and I look different, but I am still me.'

Edie quieted when she heard the familiar sound of Tabby's voice. 'It has been a strange day, my friend, a confounding mix of the marvellous and direful. And, it pleases me none to tell you, that I'm afraid the day will end on a bleak note.'

When she had looked into Leah's eyes from the other side of the table, she was instantly certain that Leah was aware of the lump and its implications.

To Tabby's mind, the swelling was too large to be an abscess brought on by broken breast. She had seen tumours before – some that seemed to resemble Leah's own swelling. She frowned, contemplating the consequences as she stroked Edie's cool mantle. She remembered Sarah Farnham, the last case of broken breast she had treated. By comparison, Leah had no fever and the baby was nursing happily.

Tabby needed to speak with Leah. And, more importantly, she needed to examine her more closely.

'If it is a tumour, her life is threatened, Edie. The lump will need to be removed.' Tabby had never performed such a surgery before and groaned at such an abominable prospect.

'I wonder if Ben is more acquainted with such a procedure ... or perhaps Doctor Douglass.'

Her thoughts turned to the scalpel, as yet unused, in her own possession. She lived in fear of cutting through living flesh. 'I don't know if I could do it, Edie.'

The bird's head bobbed beside Tabby's, seemingly in agreement. She smiled, aware this was Edie's means to see around her, scanning the distance behind Tabby, checking for danger.

'But I am getting ahead of myself.' She took a comforting breath, taking in Edie's nutty scent. Edie's feathers were cool after flying high in the night.

She recalled a time at the convent when she had assisted in the amputation of a leg. She was just thirteen at the time. A man by the name of des Grosseillers, a *coureur de bois,* was mistaken for an Indian by a settler. Unaware des Grosseillers was approaching their home to trade furs for wine, the farmer shot him in the leg, shattering the bone. Des Grosseillers was bought to the convent by his assailant who, once he realised his mistake, was overcome with remorse.

All those sinister fears that apprehended her now – anxiety, sickness, dread – had not paralysed her then. As she sat with the man, she watched Sister Angela slice through his flesh, heard his muffled screams of agony as Sister sawed through bone, and smelt the blood and the scent of fatty beef frying in a pan when the wound was eventually cauterised. Worst of all, she had felt his breath against her cheek while she whispered prayers of comfort and peace into his ear.

Tabby began to whisper to Edie now, reliving that moment.

'Que mon âme se glorifie en l'Eternel!

Que les malheureux écoutent et se réjouissent!

Exaltez avec moi l'Eternel! Célébrons tous son nom!

'Oh, Edie, I *am* growing morose in my old age ...'

Tabby ceased their discussion, hearing footsteps on the gravel.

'I do not agree.'

It was Ben, heading back to the stable to sleep. He was holding a woollen blanket under one arm.

'Owing to my studies, these days my Latin surpasses my French, but I believe I recognised Psalm 34 ...'

Edie took flight. Tabby and Ben watched her rise like a feathered Mercury into the stars.

Tabby nodded then Ben finished the prayer she had begun.

'I sought the Lord, and he heard me,

and delivered me from all my fears.

They looked unto him, and were lightened;

and their faces were not ashamed.

'They are beautiful words, penned by King David when he was living among the Philistines.'

Tabby had forgotten that. She issued a heavy sigh.

'You do seem rather forlorn,' Ben observed with concern. 'I hope it has nothing to do with my foolishness at Long Reach. Tabby, I feel wretched ...'

She shook her head. Tabby indicated to Ben that they should move away from the house. He followed her as she walked into the dark. Tabby feared that Leah and Palgrave might hear their conversation.

'Have you any experience assessing cancer of the breast?'

Ben thought for a moment, thrown a little by the unexpected nature of Tabby's question.

'There was one woman who came to Doctor Douglass when I was a student,' he said. 'Douglass excised the lump in her breast successfully, although I do not know the woman's eventual outcome.'

'What do you mean?' Tabby responded, perturbed.

'Unless all the cancer is removed successfully – and this is difficult to discern – the disease can return. The only absolute means of ridding the disease from the body is a complete breast amputation. Why do you ask, Tabby? Is there something wrong?' Ben's heart quickened at the thought that Tabby may herself be in danger of the disease.

'During supper I noticed a swelling on Leah's breast. It is not broken breast as she has no fever. What's more, the baby feeds contentedly. I fear it is a tumour.'

Tabby heard Ben's sharp intake of breath. She knew how much Palgrave and Leah meant to him; he seemed closer to them than to his own family.

'Then we must act, as soon as possible. I have books on

the subject if you would like to read them. Wiseman's *Eight Chirurgical Treatises* is particularly informative ...'

Tabby turned suddenly, her eyes fixing on Ben's. There was something in them he could not quite discern, something he had not witnessed in her before. If it had been any other woman – any other person – he would have judged it to be fear.

'I will examine Leah in the morning, if she is agreeable,' she said. Then she turned and walked towards the house.

THERE WAS EXTREMELY little that Tabby failed to notice, Leah noted as she tipped the dough from the bowl and onto the floured table. She was in the summer kitchen alone, except for Patience who lay on a quilt on the ground near where Leah worked. She privately called the act of kneading the soft, pliable dough her 'thinking chore'.

In less than a fortnight the swelling in her breast had doubled in size to the point where it was clearly visible. Leah was certain the swelling was not due to her daughter's birth or the feeding of her. It felt different to anything else she had bodily experienced. Taking comfort from the familiar smell of the yeast and the zephyr-like coos coming from Patience's sweet, rose-pink lips, Leah pushed and folded the dough with increasing intensity as she contemplated the possibilities. But her life had been so insular – the tiny enclaves of Eastham then Wellfleet, expanding only recently to Augusta – that no reasonable possibilities came to mind. Her experience with her breasts had always been simple, definite – they gave pleasure and they gave life. But now that distinction had become blurred. They appeared also to be the potential source of pain and death, she was certain, judging from the expression on Tabby's face during supper.

'Your bread will be as tough as the Devil's nagnails if you keep kneading like that,' Tabby said from the doorway.

Leah stopped, smiled uneasily then wiped her top lip of the perspiration that had gathered there during her exertions. She cleaned the flour from her hands with her apron.

'Where would you like to examine me?'

Tabby moved towards her, relieved that Leah understood.

'Wherever you prefer.'

'Here,' Leah replied firmly, untying her apron.

Tabby directed her to sit then Leah began unlacing her bodice. Once done, she untied her shift and dropped it from her shoulder. Tabby knelt beside her and looked closely at the swelling for a moment. It was inflamed, shining marbled pink through the skin. Tabby placed her hand gently over the bulge; it was hot to touch. Prodding more firmly for just a few seconds, Leah grimaced in pain. Tabby rested back on her haunches, cupping her hands in her lap as she considered the situation.

Leah retied her shift and relaced her bodice. She turned to Tabby, raising an eyebrow.

'I believe the swelling is a cancerous tumour, Leah.'

'I have never heard of such an ailment.'

'I've only seen one other, in the neck of a man from Pullman's Crossing. But Ben has more experience in this matter, as does Doctor Douglass. His wealth of knowledge goes far beyond that of either mine or Ben's. Would you allow him to examine you? Or at least Ben?'

Patience began to whimper. Leah rose and went to her daughter. Lifting her from the quilt, she rocked her gently as she spoke.

'If this lump is a tumour, what is the cure?

'There is no cure, save removing the lump in surgery. For greater certainty, the removal of the entire breast is recommended.'

Leah nodded, seeming calm, still rocking her baby in her arms.

'Otherwise?'

'You will die.'

Leah held Patience more closely to her chest and kissed her silky forehead.

'This is not the first time I have faced death, Tabby,' she said, inhaling deeply, seemingly rising to the challenge.

'Perhaps you should discuss the matter with your husband?' Tabby suggested.

In the past, Leah had confronted far greater decisions than this on her own, decisions where the stakes were far more perilous. When it came down to life or death, then or now, there was no doubt in her mind – she always chose life.

Following a second examination by Ben, it was agreed that the safest course of action was to remove the breast. Leah refused to bother Doctor Douglass by calling him from Boston, more than a day's ride away, claiming he had 'patients suffering and in far greater pain' than she. Leah was also reluctant to procure the services of a nurse for Patience during the period of her recovery, campaigning to delay the surgery until Patience had been weaned. Given the haste with which the lump was growing, Tabby advised against this course of action. Eventually, Leah acquiesced.

Initially, it had been Polly Cool who sprung to Tabby's mind as a likely wet nurse. Having her in Augusta with her children might allow Tabby time enough to pluck her from her husband's wretched grasp. However, after careful consideration, Tabby feared introducing the likes of Jeremy Cool into the Williamses' house. What's more, the image of Polly and her children armed, crazed by opium, at Kirkcaldie's camp haunted her still. Ben secured the services of a nurse in Augusta, a kindly woman. Her husband was a client of Mister Williams. They had one child, a babe of five months.

As practicalities were ensured, Tabby grew increasingly confident that Leah's decision to amputate the breast was the correct one. However, her composure was thrown into disarray once more when Leah insisted that Tabby carry out the surgery. Despite her terror at the prospect, Tabby could not refuse her patient. 'You are the only person I trust to hold the blade,' Leah had said. 'You're a woman, the only person who is able to fathom the true meaning of what is about to occur.'

Tabby stayed on in Augusta for a further week, readying herself.

For six days and nights, Tabby and Ben worked together all day and long into the evening. The young doctor had gathered as many books on the subject as he was able; Tabby figured the only means of allaying her demons was through preparation. Reading Ben's medical tomes from cover to cover, compiling notes, comparing procedures and discussing the operation, always discussing, both fortified and composed her. Ben stayed on in the stable so they could work together, their earlier discomfort forgotten.

During this time, Palgrave sequestered himself from his roles as father and provider, concerning himself only with Leah. With Maria and Elizabeth to run the household, the couple spent hours together, walking, reading or merely talking. The glances that passed between them, although fleeting, were weighed heavy with both love and terror. It occurred to Tabby that she had never witnessed this kind of emotion between a man and woman before, the kind of feeling that seemed too encumbering for either of them to bear singularly and so they came together – each supporting the other, sharing the other's burden.

On the seventh evening, the evening before the surgery, it was agreed that all the knowledge that was to be gleaned had been and that both – surgeon and assistant – would benefit most greatly from rest. Maria departed the house at dusk with a linen bag strung across her shoulder, taking to the forest without saying a word. Tabby assumed she was heading to her glade. Hopefully, whatever ritual or ceremony she was about to embark upon would aid both patient and healer.

Retiring after supper, Tabby lay in bed on her own, tired but agitated, unable to find rest, let alone sleep. When she heard the lantern clock on the landing chime eleven, she swept back the covers and crept out the door. The house was dark, save for a thin channel of dim light flickering beneath Leah and Palgrave's door. Padding down the stairs in bare feet, Tabby believed she was heading outside in search of Edie. But when the cool serenity of the evening breeze touched her, she turned towards the stable.

BEN HEARD the door creak but he was dreaming and refused to be drawn from his blissful imaginings. Tabby had come to him in his dreams, wearing only her shift. The fabric was so fine and white that he could see the shape of her body, sketched by the moonlight. She knelt beside him in the hay, her hair untamed and caping her shoulders, the ends falling lightly onto his chest like vines. The scent of it – white lilac – overcame the smell of hay and manure. Ben reached out and wove his fingers among those locks, losing sight of his hand as he pulled her towards himself. Her hair was silken to the touch, and as bountiful as April rains.

Each sensation was so real that he resisted opening his

eyes, fearing the moment would end. Then he heard her speak his name.

In an instant he was awake.

Tabby was beside him, his hand in her hair. She was framed by the moonlight.

'Am I dreaming?' he asked, sitting up.

'No,' she replied.

Ben gazed at her, drinking in the site of her hair raining down her shoulders like autumn leaves. She took his other hand, then drew closer, sitting astride him.

'I don't understand. Why now?' he asked, perplexed and enchanted in equal measure.

Tabby took Ben's face in her hands and kissed him. The sensation was more than he could bear. When their lips parted, he looked at her, searching for answers.

'Talk to me.'

She shook her head and kissed him again.

WITH HER FACE resting against his chest, Ben could feel Tabby's eyelashes flicker, as soft as feathers against his skin, as her eyes opened from a brief sleep. He pressed her more tightly to him. She responded by nestling her curves into the nooks and crevices of his body. *We fit together perfectly*, he thought with a sigh. Although he knew what they faced in the morning, he did not want to sleep, for slumber would only bring dawn closer. Instead, he tried to recall his earlier pleasure before it faded with the stars. Imagining their coupling many times in the weeks since he had met Tabby, a considerable part of him hoped what had just passed had been a dream. Then, night after night, she would return to him. But he both revelled and quailed in the certainty that it was real.

The experience had not been the one he had imagined and dreamt of night after night. His night-time imaginings were based on his very meagre experience with women. But to have a woman open herself to him fully, shed her skin and he do the same, was somehow purifying. It was a sacrament of sorts. Yet the hunger he felt for her now, the desperation, was an urge of the basest, most animal kind and far from holy. At that moment, he would kill any person who attempted to come between them. He was astonished that when she had come to him, he could sense her hunger, too. When she had cried out in pleasure, he was momentarily stunned that her urges were as his own.

'You asked me why,' she whispered in the dark. Ben kissed her forehead, longing to keep her by his side always, shuddering at the thought that it would never be possible to restrict Tabby's independence.

'When I was a child, only seven, my mother went into travail with my brother. In my memory, she was labouring for days. A midwife was present. I do not recall who the woman was, but she was not familiar to me. My father stayed with me and we listened together as my mother screamed and cried out in pain. Then I would hear her praying, her voice drenched in anguish. Neither of us were permitted to see her. I wanted to help, go to her, if only to offer comfort, but they kept me away. All I could do was pray that God would deliver her from the agony she was suffering.

'Eventually, a man arrived at the door. He was hard-faced, as grave as a judge. I believed my prayers had been answered, that he had been sent to cure her and bring the babe into the world. But when I looked to my father for reassurance, for a sign of hope in his eyes, I saw only despair. My father, knowing what was to come, departed the house hastily. Left alone, I crept to my mother's door.

All was quiet as I approached. The door had been left ajar. I took this for a good thing as I could hear that my mother was finally silent. My spirits lifted for the first time in days. But when I peered through the crack, I saw the grave-faced man's hands inside my mother, fiercely hacking at something. I could see blood, so much blood, spilling onto the crisp, white sheets of my mother's bed.'

Ben was filled with dismay by Tabby's words. 'A barber surgeon?'

'Yes. My mother lay deathly still, staring up at the oak beams of the ceiling. I reckon now, looking back at that evening, my mother had placed herself in a sort of trance for she was praying softly. I would not have known this save I noticed her lips moving and, listening more closely, I heard the Lord's Prayer. She must have repeated it ten or twelve times before the surgeon was finished with her. My poor brother Joel was brought into this world carved into pieces. My mother had removed a part of herself, her soul, I suppose, from the abomination she was living through.

'It was when the Sisters at the convent delivered a babe that was breech that I had realised what must have occurred and I wept for my mother again. The Sisters would have saved Joel's life. They would have saved my mother's, too. My mother's midwife lacked the skills to turn the baby, so Joel had died, desperate to be brought into the world but with nobody to help him. My mother followed her son to Heaven eight days later, when she succumbed to childbed fever.'

Ben nodded solemnly.

'Some years ago, I purchased a scalpel,' Tabby confided.

'However, the violence of that memory has prevented me from ever using it.' She sighed as though attempting to free herself of a thousand fears. 'Yet tomorrow, I must.'

She paused for a moment. He watched her staring into the darkness.

'In truth, I feel as though no-one on the earth exists apart from me.'

Ben tightened his arms, securing her in his embrace.

'Tabby, you are not alone,' he whispered, stroking her hair.

LEAH DREW the curtains closed and turned to Palgrave.

'Tabby,' she said. 'Heading towards the stable like a lost soul.'

'You believe she has found her mate, then?' Palgrave asked, wryly.

'I hope so. She has so much to offer a man but she cherishes her freedom. I don't think she realises she can have both – her independence and a mate.'

Palgrave stretched out his long legs beneath the covers. 'I have decided to send my apologies to the governor.'

Leah glanced at him, concerned.

'Two days is too soon to leave you ... Besides, the meeting will soon be reduced to nothing more than a melee, a common brawl. Granted it will be fought with words and not fists, but I fear nought will be achieved in a setting with so many opposing interests.'

'Then it's all-important you attend to speak reason,' insisted Leah. 'And to keep the peace.'

Palgrave frowned, resolute, unconvinced. Leah would need to work harder to persuade him.

'It is a certainty that my condition will not alter from you worrying at my bedside, but you might bring much change if you attend the meeting.'

Palgrave's desire to move slowly in regard to clearing land and selling it off, in order to preserve the forests and relations with the Indians, was a unique view among the Committee. Most often Palgrave was certain his arguments fell on deaf ears, however, Leah knew Palgrave would need to at least try to change opinion.

Leah walked to Palgrave's side and slid into bed beside him.

'I will give your counsel some thought,' he eventually said before they both fell silent. The millstone of the morning suddenly crushed the exchange.

During the week, Leah had grappled with her own uncertainty about the future. She had not been a vain child. Neither had she grown into a vain woman. However, the idea of losing a breast had nurtured unknown insecurities.

'When I have healed,' she said hesitantly, 'will you still want to gaze on me?'

Palgrave frowned in confusion.

'Unclothed.'

Palgrave took her hand. 'You're a beautiful woman, Leah, there is no denying that.' He swallowed hard, attempting to hold back his turmoil. 'But your beauty is greater than your appearance.'

It was all he said. It was all he could say.

But it was enough.

They held hands, aware of what was coming but terrified any utterance would shatter the harmony that had grown and billowed around them like a protective haze in the past week. Yet Leah could not avoid it any longer. There had been so much left unsaid since Palgrave's return eight years ago. In the intervening years, she had been plagued by her crimes. She grew more certain each day that, until she shared them with Palgrave, she and her husband could never be whole again.

When they had wed, Reverend Dent, the man she had later blackmailed and killed, had joined them, had made them one. She believed this although even then, before his son had defiled Maria, before he had shunned her father and her family, she had held the minister in low regard. But her faith had her believe he had been elected by God so the gravity of his words at their wedding had crystallised in Leah's mind.

But since Palgrave's return from Nassau, it had never seemed to her that she and Palgrave had been completely reunited. Their relationship was forever fractured, and the fissure only seemed to grow wider as the years passed. She was sure they could only be mended with the truth. Keenly aware that she might die in the morn, Leah was compelled to confront all her sins before the sun rose.

'It was I who killed Reverend Dent,' she said plainly.

Palgrave turned to her. She could see him considering her confession, wrestling with the implications.

'It was a fire, was it not?'

'Yes. One that I lit.'

'Because he had you whipped?'

Leah thought back to the early hours of that morning eight years ago. Silently entering the minister's chamber, she and Abby had set the sleeping Dent's curtains and bedding alight then fled through the forest, their hearts racing, the blood pounding in their ears. Recalling the full moon that illuminated their path, she now questioned her actions for the first time. She wondered if it *had* been revenge she had sought for the humiliation Dent had heaped upon her.

Eight years ago, when Palgrave returned and she had tallied Dent's injustices, described the destruction the minister had wrought in the months of Palgrave's absence, Palgrave had concluded, 'It's a good thing that he is dead. He can harm us no more.' Despite his ignorance of her role in Dent's death, Palgrave had hit upon her only motivation. At the time, abandoned, impoverished and ostracised by her community, she could think of no other means of stopping him.

'Because he had me whipped and so much more. Dent would not have stopped until we were all destroyed – my father, Maria, us and our children. He allowed Maria's baby, his own grandson, to be buried in a field where the cows grazed. What sort of a person ...' She took a deep breath.

Palgrave moved closer. Leah composed herself before she continued.

'I have longed in my heart to tell you the truth but I could not for fear you would see me differently, as a woman capable of murder.'

He wrapped his arms around her then and drew her to him.

'Oh, Leah,' he said, with a lightness of tone she had not expected. 'How could I ever see you as anything but the marvellous creature that you are? You are the woman who saved me all those years ago. You are the woman who saved our family when I was gone. There's nothing that could tarnish you in my eyes.'

Palgrave felt her body relax in his arms and he held her even tighter. He could not bear to lose this woman and the thought of the pain and the possibilities that awaited them were tearing at his soul like a lion, shredding his spirit. Until that moment he had not realised the enormity of everything they had kept from each other. They rested in each other's arms, in silence. A million vivid memories flickered like fireflies across his mind – the Sunday morning when he had first looked upon Leah Hallett at meeting and believed for an instant he was in the presence of an angel; the way his spirit had lifted immediately at the sight of her that winter's afternoon when she had called on him in his despair, offering her kindness; the sight of her again, after his many months away, on the seashore in Wellfleet. Walking towards her then, with the glaring sunlight glinting off the sea, she had been obscured until he was just a few feet away from her. But when her form and her lovely face were clear, his heart was suddenly nourished, even though he had been unaware he had been starving.

'We two are so similar,' he murmured. 'It's as though we believed the naysayers who scorned us when we wed, citing our differences – our age and upbringing, our means.'

Leah stirred and lifted her face. 'We should have had more faith in our love.'

'I too have avoided telling you the truth about the past. I did not ply my trade as a silversmith in Nassau.' Palgrave paused. He was not as adept as Leah at plain speaking, he was not as courageous. Noting his hesitation, she lifted her face and kissed him softly on the lips. The touch of her, the familiar smell of her hair and sweet taste of her lips was reassurance enough for him to continue.

'I killed men ... many men. Together with Sam and our crew, I sailed the oceans, terrorising merchant ships and slave ships. We ruled the seas for a time. Leah, we were pirates in Nassau.'

It took Leah some time to react. 'I suspected. I had heard once, just in passing, that a dark-haired pirate from the West Country constantly thwarted the British navy's schemes to capture him. My imagination immediately turned to Bellamy, of course. And of you, his friend.'

Palgrave nodded before continuing.

'The shipwreck near Wellfleet ... it was Sam's ship, the *Whydah*. On board were thousands of pounds of gold and silver ... such riches. Lying somewhere on the ocean floor below the cliffs of Eastham is a substantial fortune.' Palgrave shook his head, considering all that had been lost. It was not for the treasure, but for his friends that he mourned.

'From my share of my own ship's bounty, I fenced what I was able and only took what I could carry in my saddlebags. I was aware there would be a price on my head. When I farewelled my crew, the rest of our haul was divided among them.'

Leah did not say a word in response. She did not sigh or groan at the loss of Bellamy, his ship and his riches. Instead she thought on what had just been gained.

MARIA SAT among the stones in the glade. Unlike the sunny morning when Tabby had spied her, this night the space she so cherished was lit by candles and torches. As she rose, moving gently into the centre of the circle, her pale, slender arms reached to the heavens as though they were guided by forces unseen. Eyes closed, her body was a ribbon coloured goldenrod by the candlelight and the moonlight combined. As her movements increased in speed, circling, dipping, her shadow swept beside her and behind her – as if it were a separate entity and not the night's reflection of her form. Had anyone seen her, they may have thought she was fevered; yet her state of mind was utterly calm.

Then she stopped. Closing her eyes, she listened. Crickets. An owl. The Kennebec in the distance.

Something else.

Her eyes opened at once. 'I know you are there.'

Maria stared hard into the blackened trees.

'Show yourself.'

28

As the sun rose, Tabby readied herself. Now the day had finally arrived, her dread had vanished. Even so, she did not want to ponder its whereabouts too long for fear it would observe her searching and decide to return.

She was certain that voicing her apprehension to Ben the night before had played a role in her calm demeanour this morning, as did the physical release they shared. Washing her face, braiding her hair in a tight, thick plait, her mind returned to her mother. Tabby had not readied Leah for the pain that was to come. She had not done so because it was impossible. Recalling the dreadful vision of her brother's birth, she took comfort in realising her mother had most certainly removed herself from the barber surgeon's vicious, unfeeling hands in some way, whether that was by seeking comfort in God or simply in the rhythmic pulsing of the words she had prayed.

When Tabby ventured downstairs to the kitchen, Ben was already seated. He was breaking his fast alone with a large steaming bowl of porage. Tabby found him leaning over his bowl, staring into its contents, seemingly lost in thought for he did not hear her enter the room. When she pulled a stool from the table, he raised his eyes and offered her a warm smile.

'Good morning,' he said.

'Good morning,' she returned.

Rising, he gestured to the pot on the hearth.

Tabby shook her head. 'I do not think I can stomach one morsel this morning until my unfortunate task is complete.'

'*Our* unfortunate task,' he corrected.

'Our,' she acknowledged.

Tabby took comfort in watching Ben eat.

EAGER TO BEGIN, Tabby rose in search of Leah the moment Ben's spoon scraped against the pewter of the bowl. She found her in her chamber. Palgrave stood by her side wringing his hands as though they were clouts, grave in the knowledge of what they must do, of what was to come. Maria, who had returned in the early morning, had removed the children from the house at Tabby's request. Tabby worried one of them would hear or see something they should not, and Leah, not wanting to alarm them, had chosen to keep the fact of the surgery secret. The group had departed with their fishing lines. As cheerfully as she could muster, Maria had advised her charges it had been an age since they had caught their own supper.

Tabby approached Leah as Ben began to ready the chamber. He stripped the bed of all of its linens and replaced them with a clean white cloth that he tucked under the mattress tightly. He fitted a second over it then placed a stack of small clouts on the low table he had moved from its usual spot by the window. Here, he also laid out the instruments Tabby was to use, including her own scalpel.

'The pain will be great, Leah,' Tabby advised. 'Greater, I imagine, than anything you have experienced before.' Leah nodded solemnly.

'I was whipped a long time ago, Tabby,' she said. 'Twelve strokes on my bare back. I fainted. It shamed me at the time but now I believe it was a blessing.'

'That is understandable.'

'Do you think the pain will be as terrible?'

'Perhaps. Probably. But your husband is here to hold you, for you must stay very still. If you faint, I will continue.' Tabby paused for a moment as she contemplated how to word her next thought. 'I have seen some patients transgress their pain through prayer.'

Leah frowned, concerned.

'It's as though they're able to rise above the physical sensations.'

'With the help of God?' Leah asked.

Tabby shrugged. 'They are convinced it is so'

Leah shook her head. 'I have not believed in many years, Tabby. I cannot turn to God now. It would be a coward's act.'

Account of the Breast Operation drawn up by Doctor Benjamin Shute

Monday, July 16th, 1725

Augusta, Maine

Yesterday, at seven o'clock in the morning, Leah Williams underwent the removal of a Cancerous Tumour. It was the size of a Child's Fist and had developed in the right Breast, adherent to the Pectoralis Major Muscle. The Operation was performed by

Mistress Tabitha Post, a Midwife and Healer and assisted by myself, Doctor Benjamin Shute. The Operation was exceptionally painful but was tolerated with immense Courage by the Patient who refused a Tincture of Laudanum and Wine to mute the Pain. In my Opinion, no Case of such a serious Operation has offered greater Hope of Success.

The Scirrhus showed the beginning of Cancerous Degeneration in its Centre. However, all the Root was removed and the Breast Bone scraped clean of all Matter. The Wound was then stitched and dressed. Mistress Post kept a steady Hand and an intense Focus during the Operation which concluded after one and one-half Hours.

Within an hour of the Operation's Conclusion, the Patient underwent a series of violent, intermittent Spasms which did not diminish until well after Midnight. Administration of calming Antispasmodic Potions prepared by Mistress Post and the Patient's Sister, Mistress Maria Hallett, served to reduce and eventually dissipate the aforementioned Spasms.

From two to three in the Morning, the Patient experienced some moments of agitated Sleep and Headache, and Attacks of Nausea and Vomiting made her quite Tired and Weak. These Events, which Mistress Post had indicated would necessarily end the Spasms, were followed by Calm and two Hours of peaceful Sleep.

By ten o'clock, the Patient was awake and surprised by the Wellbeing she experienced. Mistress Post found her without Fever and the Pain close to non-existent in the Wound. I believe this to be due to the herbal medications administered by Mistress Post and Mistress Hallett. The precise Ligature of the Arteries by Mistress Post had also prevented even the ordinary Transudation of Blood through the Dressing, further ensuring the patient's Comfort.

We prescribe boiled Rice Pudding and Meat Jelly to be given as Sustenance during the Day. To drink, alternate doses of Chicken Broth and Barley Water, gummed and acidified with Lemon, are recommended. In the evenings, the Patient is to be administered with a Potion of Linseed and Poppy Head to ease discomfort as required.

The chamber had been kept dark, so Ben wrote by the light of a single candle. Palgrave had not wanted to attend the meeting, but Ben had encouraged him to leave. He would only be absent for a day; Leah's condition was stable and Palgrave could do no good worrying away in his study.

Ben laid down his quill when he felt her hand on his shoulder. He had not heard her enter the room. She was as light-footed as a hare and the scent of her potions – rosemary and lemon balm – followed in her wake. Tabby squeezed the space between his neck and shoulder gently, too fleetingly. First, she walked to the window and opened it slightly, allowing fresh air and the sounds of life to enter the room. Then she moved to Leah who was peaceful, her angelic countenance betraying no sign of what she had so recently endured. She was silent throughout the ordeal, her eyes focused on only her husband's. Leah had transcended the experience, although it was not through prayer, Tabby realised. Lifting the covers so as not to wake the resting patient, Tabby examined the dressing for signs of blood or pus then placed her hand against Leah's forehead. Moving towards the door she indicated with a crooked finger that Ben should join her on the landing.

When they were outside the room, she turned to face him. Cupping his jaw in her hand, she examined his face closely.

'You are exhausted. Go and sleep. You have been watching over her since the surgery. You must rest or you will be useless if and when you are needed. There are other people in Augusta who might fall ill.'

'But with Palgrave gone –'

'He will return by sunset. Leah has Maria to watch over her in the meantime. She will fetch you, if you are needed.'

Ben did not like the connotation behind her instructions.

'Are you leaving?'

She nodded. 'A child is deathly ill with scarlet fever in Vassalboro. It will only take the day. From the message, I understand that there is very little I will be able to do except make the poor girl comfortable.'

'I should come with you ...' While Ben had vowed to himself to respect Tabby's independence, he still found that, at times, he could not keep his chivalry in check.

'No, Ben. You must remain here in case Leah becomes fevered. Maria will help you with the potions.'

Before he could protest, she kissed him lightly on the lips. The fleeting, feathery sensation brought to his mind the flutter of an angel's wings. Then she grinned, ran down the stairs and disappeared like a sprite.

29

Palgrave entered the room and scanned the gathering, seeking out Governor Dummer. Although both Leah and Ben had insisted he attend, he had no interest in being there. He wanted to be by Leah's side, he wanted to be with her when she woke. Since the surgery, she had drifted in and out of sleep. It was the body's way of healing, Tabby advised. Coming so close to losing her again, combined with the truths they had revealed on the eve of her surgery, had only served to strengthen their connection.

The Committee had burgeoned significantly since the last meeting, he noted. Now that Dummer had successfully pushed back the Indians, an increasing number of men were demanding the right to have a say in how those lands were used. Palgrave eyed them carefully, aware that none of their interests would be matching. For the future, he foresaw only discord and argument.

There was a time, not long past, where he had relished the company of men. On deck or below, coming together to vote on a course of action afforded a unity between them that he had not experienced since. There would be music and banter, and the certain knowledge that all of those present were equal, and, therefore, had an equal voice. What's more, although often unspoken, there was a common goal among them. Despite the petty rivalries, squabbles and hardships, Bellamy had never allowed his crew to lose sight of their dream: freedom. Wasn't true freedom the dream of all men? he had often argued.

Although his friend had died, Palgrave had achieved that dream – in his honour, he supposed. With wealth enough to live as he pleased, he had assured that he and his family would have to answer to no man again. However, at that moment, among *these* men, in the stuffy, smoky confines of the Augusta town hall, Palgrave was feeling decidedly trapped.

Taking Leah's advice, Palgrave had planned to be the voice of reason, the voice of conciliation at the meeting. He had witnessed bravery before, with Bellamy. Thanks to his friend, even Palgrave had faced his darkest fears and overcome them. He recalled the first incursion with Captain Jennings. How terrified he was to face another man – one to one, eye to eye – when he had boarded the *Gaviota*. Then his mind drifted to the *Whydah* survivors in the courthouse in Boston.

Palgrave had travelled there to free Bellamy. Discovering he wasn't among them, he had hoped to free the others. But they had refused. Inspired by Bellamy's own bravery, they preferred to face the noose with courage in their hearts. However, Leah's bravery surpassed all he had seen. When Tabby had placed her scalpel against his wife's flesh, he believed he would faint. Leah had pressed his hand to her lips in a silent missive telling him that, like all the challenges they had overcome, they would overcome this, too.

He searched the room for the governor. To Palgrave's

eye, he was nowhere in sight. *Perhaps some concessions might be granted to the Indians,* he mused, *compromises that might ward off future war* ... To be mindful and respectful of the forest would mean the wellbeing of their forebears would be secured. His mind wandered to Tabby, who had adopted many Indian ways and habits, and then to Ade from the *Bathsheba*, the African who was rescued from slavery. Despite the colour of his skin and his divergent tongue, he had become Palgrave's trusted friend. At this point, Edward Teach strayed into his thoughts. Shaking his head in wonder, Palgrave considered the pirate who, despite his brutal end, attained his freedom by following no rules imparted by man or God.

However, looking at the faces around him now, Palgrave began to doubt his best intentions. These men in their powdered wigs and satin waistcoats did not know the meaning of freedom, he realised. They obeyed a set of rules, none of which were of their own devising. *Was it worth leaving Leah to come here?* he wondered.

After checking his timepiece, Palgrave felt the weight of a hand on his shoulder. Turning, he saw that it was Governor Dummer. He nodded in greeting then turned his eyes to the man at Dummer's side.

It took a few seconds for Palgrave to recognise him. It was a strange sensation, as though he were dreaming. The face before him and the expression on it were as familiar as his own, yet, all at once, it was as though the man were a stranger. Remembering the moment later, Palgrave was heartily embarrassed and ashamed he had not recognised his friend immediately.

Bellamy. Sam.

Bellamy was clean-shaven, and his dark hair had been lightened, silvered at the temples by time. It was pulled back neatly at the neck. But it was the same man. There was humour in his dark eyes and something else. Caution. Palgrave swallowed, instantly remembering the same gaze, shot towards him a hundred times, asking Palgrave to comprehend what could not be spoken.

He opened his mouth in utterance but no words came. He felt his face drain of blood. Mouth dry, heart pounding at a furious rhythm, he stood there motionless, unable to communicate any of all that he was feeling.

'Are you feeling well, Mister Williams?' Dummer inquired, a look of concern spread across his features. 'You're as white as a sheet. Come, sit down.'

Palgrave nodded, waving aside all assistance. He cleared his throat and, as quickly as possible, composed himself.

'Quite well. Please excuse me, Governor. I was awake for most of the night. My wife has been ill.'

'I am sorry to hear it,' Dummer responded.

'As am I,' remarked Bellamy.

Reminded of his companion's presence, Dummer said, 'Mister Williams, I would like to present my surveyor, Mister Kirkcaldie.'

Palgrave lifted his arm and Bellamy took his hand. Although their hands were fixed tight in a firm press for longer than was acceptable, it was not enough. Palgrave recalled their final embrace upon the *Whydah*, the smell of salt on his skin and the feel of his whiskered cheek against his own. He wanted to embrace him again. He wanted to know that it was Bellamy, flesh and bone.

'Mister Williams.'

Bellamy nodded.

'It is a pleasure to meet you.'

It was the same voice, an octave deeper than he recalled, but still as thick and sweet as honeycomb.

'Mister Kirk ... caldie,' Palgrave returned, unsure. The name sat oddly on his tongue. 'A pleasure.'

The three men stood for a few moments more, discussing the upcoming meeting – nothing more than banal, inoffensive statements – but Palgrave did not hear a word, nor did he remember later what he had said. He could not take his gaze from Bellamy.

'Excuse me, Governor,' Bellamy finally interrupted, noting his old friend's uncanny manner. 'There are many more men in this room who desire your ear, I am sure. Please ...' He gestured to the room, giving the governor freedom to take his leave.

When he did, Bellamy took Palgrave by the elbow and led him hastily through the crowd then outdoors and behind the building to the muddied embankment of the Kennebec.

Once in the open air, Palgrave immediately bent forward, resting his hands on his knees, sucking in air in great mouthfuls. Bellamy patted him on the back, laughing.

'You look like you have seen a ghost.'

'I believed I had,' said Palgrave, straightening.

The pair laughed, the humour just shared between them seemingly so familiar yet it gradually waned and for some time neither man spoke. Looking over the river, they glanced at each other occasionally, surreptitiously, as though each were concerned that either of them could disappear in an instant.

Eventually, Palgrave fixed his gaze on Bellamy, unashamedly. Taking the inquisitive cast of his friend's eyes as leave to speak, Bellamy began to describe the storm that saw the *Whydah* destroyed against the cliffs of Eastham eight years before.

'There was nothing left to do but leap into the spume. At

least then, I thought, we might have a chance of being swept to the safety of a beach or into a crag. But to be frank, I did not hold out hope.'

'We?' Palgrave queried.

'John and I.'

Palgrave's face brightened immediately.

'John is alive? He is well?'

Bellamy nodded, smiling. 'Very well. He is studying at Harvard University. He has hopes of being a lawyer one day. Can you believe the boy who dreamt of nothing else than captaining his own ship wants to champion the King's law?'

'It is not surprising,' Palgrave muttered, recalling the violence and injustice of Tamesine's death, murdered on the eve of her marriage to Bellamy. Palgrave was heartened her son had survived.

Bellamy's grin waned as he recalled that terrible morning in Nassau.

The men grew pensive in memoriam for a moment until Palgrave finally cried out in amazement.

'Good God, man! For all these years. If I had only known ...'

The myriad of vast, lost opportunities swarmed in Palgrave's mind like mayflies. To have had his friend with him during those lost years – Bellamy, perhaps reconciled with Maria ... together with John, they could have been a family ...

'Whether by chance or by the hand of a power greater than God himself, a wave seemed to cup John and I, carrying us high above the turmoil and placing us both in a shallow cave, but deep enough to provide shelter until the storm broke. At dawn we climbed to the top of the cliff which was not more than ten or fifteen yards above us. Aware authorities would be searching for us, we stopped in

Eastham for but a few moments in order to drink from a horse's trough. In that moment, I spied John Julian and Mister Quintor heading into the tavern. My heart lifted at the sight of them, but I could not tarry. Later, I discovered they, and seven more of my crew, were apprehended in that same tavern not an hour after we had seen them.'

Palgrave nodded sombrely, remembering the storm and his thoughts at the time. He had been sure there was no ship built or man alive who could weather that storm. Not even the *Whydah* and Samuel Bellamy.

'John and I headed inland in order to avoid capture. Since you had departed Virginia a day before me, I was confident you would have outrun the storm, but I could not risk seeking you out. There was a price on my head. Black Sam was the man the authorities wanted and I could not risk placing you in harm's way.'

Palgrave sat down heavily on the riverbank, unaware or without concern of the quaggy ground beneath him. He would have faced one thousand trials with Bellamy by his side. Bellamy allowed him a moment to contemplate all that he had revealed before continuing.

'For many years, John and I travelled, living among woodsman. Prize-fighting was my means of survival.'

Palgrave's thoughts darted fondly to the blistering summer's day in Eastham nine years before when Bellamy had bested Judah Doane at quarterstaff, winning himself a handsome sum.

'Soon, I had netted enough coin to begin building a home for us. I had become "Kirkcaldie" by then and made myself known to Governor Shute. To my mind, I had journeyed every inch of the eastern interior and, with my knowledge of navigation, I was certain I could be of use as a surveyor. As partial payment, I negotiated a prize piece of land, on a ridge outside Hallowell.'

'But such a gamble! Shute was responsible for sending Quintor and the others to the gallows!'

'It was four years on,' Bellamy explained. 'Black Sam was long forgotten, I figured. And what better place to hide than right under their noses?'

Palgrave shook his head in wonder.

'You always enjoyed a high stakes gambit, my friend,' he said. 'Why did you not seek me out before this?'

'Who knew if and when someone might recognise me? Although our separation has grieved me greatly these years past – there have been many times I was in need of your wise counsel – I could not put you in harm's way. That was one risk I was not willing to take.'

'Then why now? Although I am joyous, rapturous at the sight of you, why have you decided to show your hand now?'

Bellamy crouched beside his friend.

'Maria. I was riding to Augusta in search of a friend. I cannot explain the occurrence, but I found Maria in a glade or ... Maria found me,' he confided in a low voice. 'She's changed. I know not how, but she has something about her I can neither explain nor fathom.'

'You are not the only person among us to have altered during these past nine years.'

'And Leah?' Bellamy's brow furrowed. 'You remarked she is ill?'

Before Palgrave could respond, he was interrupted by a cry.

'Thanks heavens I found you,' Ben called, running towards them. 'It's Tabby. She has departed. Gone to Harper's Creek. She received a letter from General Hill asking her to meet him there ...'

'Tabby Post?' Bellamy exclaimed, rising. 'And you let her leave?'

Palgrave turned to his friend in confusion, but there wasn't time to discover Bellamy's connection to Tabby.

'Sir, I do not believe I have had the pleasure ...' Ben began, clearly affronted by the stranger's tone and obvious concern for the woman he loved.

'My name is Kirkcaldie and I am well acquainted with Tabby Post, as I am with General Hill and Jeremy Cool. Tabby will be skinned alive and much worse by the likes of those two.'

Ben's colour drained away in an instant.

'She told me she was heading to Vassalboro ... a case of scarlet fever ...' Ben said, distress clouding his features. 'But I found a note she had left for me on my pallet. She must realise she's in danger or she wouldn't have written the message ... But who is Jeremy Cool?'

'A scoundrel, a black-hearted scoundrel who Tabby swore she wouldn't go near again,' Bellamy said, unable to keep the anger from his voice.

'Hill is expected here tonight,' said Palgrave to Bellamy.

'Then it is definitely a trap ...'

'Kirkcaldie, you must stay here,' Palgrave instructed. 'It will raise suspicions if you were to disappear suddenly.'

He squeezed his friend's shoulder and turned to Ben, who appeared overcome with concern and dismay.

'Ben, Leah needs you. Go back to the house at once. I will go to Vassalboro and bring Tabby home.'

30

Tabby realised it had been some weeks since she had stepped into her canoe. The muscles in her arms and shoulders began to ache as they recalled the act of paddling, the enormity and exertion of the movement. Likewise, for the first time in what seemed like an age, Tabby remembered what it was to be alone. Since she departed Moosehead Lake, besides those ailing, she had been in the company of so many with whom she had formed strong attachments – Riyogi, Kirkcaldie, Ben and the Williams family, even Achak – that she struggled to remember her silent, solitary world and be at peace with it. But, she reasoned, she had chosen this life. *As one makes one's bed, so one finds it,* she reminded herself as she set her sights on the river ahead.

Edie travelled with her for the entire time it took Tabby to reach Vassalboro half a day later, only leaving her perch on the bow of the canoe to hunt. Edie was wary and watchful, her head turning as though on pivots at each rustle from the shore or ripplet of water. Although the danger went unspoken, Edie knew. How, Tabby could not reason, but she figured animals possessed senses that were different to those of man or woman. Kirkcaldie had once marvelled at her own senses, remarking she was a deer, a wolf and an owl combined. She hoped his summation was true, for she would need the qualities of all three animals for her to survive a confrontation with Cool and Hill.

En route, Tabby struggled with her decision to leave the Williamses' home when she did, and on her own. But she could not discuss her apprehension with Edie. She was certain the bird would disapprove of her decision to meet General Hill at Cool's settlement. 'Leave well enough alone,' Edie would rebuke if she could speak.

Stopping in on Maurice Heathcote on her way to Harper's Creek, Tabby inquired after the Cools. Heathcote had seen neither hide nor hair of the family since Tabby departed with Polly and the children in his wagon all those weeks before. Neither had Hill ventured into the township.

She took some minutes to steel herself before she departed Heathcote's tavern, uncertain what she would find when she arrived at Harper's Creek. Standing outside, as the foot traffic of Vassalboro parted around her, she produced Hill's letter for what was possibly the one hundredth time and read it again. The missive was guarded and she did not trust the words that were written so elaborately on the page; the swirling loops on the Ts and Ps, and the snail-shell labyrinth of his Ss made her doubt his claims even more. Tabby knew the letter contained nothing but lies, but what angered her each time she ran her eyes over Hill's serpentine script was the condescension of its tone.

Dear Mistress Post,

I hope this Correspondence finds you well. I am pleased to write that a Morsel of News has come my way regarding your father, Ephraim.

Following our Meeting at Fiddler's Reach, your heartfelt Words regarding your Plight and that of your Father resonated with me for many Days. I apologise if, at that time, you took my Manner for abrupt; however, the Idea that I might have done something further to aid your Father (if, in fact, he was not the Killer) prompted me to embark upon many hours of Reflective Contemplation, after which I realised I had been ignorant.

In an attempt to ease my Mind of Culpability, I recently hired the Services of an Indian who was once in my employ. A shrewder and more furtive Scout I have never encountered. This Indian, who goes by the name of Achak, knew your Father for some time before the dreadful Incident we discussed at length when you visited Fiddler's Reach. After several Weeks of tracking and inquiry, Achak located your Father in the small Settlement of Harper's Creek. He is doing Business with a Settler named Jeremy Cool.

Achak could not discern the Nature of their Business completely, but he surmises your Father is moving Goods, Barrels and Crates and the like, for Cool. The Contents of the Barrels and Crates Achak could not determine for Fear of being discovered by Cool.

However, Harper's Creek is where your Father can be found. Moreover, I feel Jeremy Cool might hold the Answers for which you have been searching. I am acutely aware of the Urgency you feel regarding your Father's Wellbeing and there is no Doubt in my Mind that, on reading this Missive, you will depart for Harper's Creek immediately. However, Achak suspects Cool is dangerous (he has seen any number of Rifles and Pistols in Cool's possession), therefore I feel it is my Duty as a Soldier in the Queen's Army to travel to Harper's Creek myself in order to assist you. I am departing Fiddler's Reach immediately. I trust I will meet you at this place forthwith.

Yours Sincerely,

General John Hill

Tabby folded the letter and placed it carefully in her pocket then attempted to recall all the various, many-coloured threads that she needed to bring together in order to weave a coherent tale, a narrative as clear and precise as her mother's chimneypiece. Tabby was certain Achak would not have aided Hill in an investigation, if in fact there was one – and Tabby was certain there was not. Likewise, Tabby trusted that her father, despite his wretched state, would not engage with the likes of Cool. The truth was that Tabby did not believe her father *capable* of engaging in anything, considering his unbalanced state of mind.

After reading Hill's letter, Tabby's suspicion of a connection between Hill and Cool was all but confirmed. She suspected both had played a role in her uncle's murder, and now the idea that Cool could be the King of Spades circled and circled in her mind. Tabby knew she would be walking into a trap but the compulsion to travel to Harper's Creek to discover the truth was overwhelming, regardless of what her good sense was shouting at her as loud and clear as a church bell on Sunday.

During her moments of contemplation, she realised her breathing had quickened and a sweat had broken out on her brow. Steadying herself, moving into the shade of a chestnut tree only a few feet from Heathcote's tavern, she attempted to still her mind by dissecting the reasons for her altered humour. She was angry, to be certain. Hill believed she was an oaf, too stupid or unworldly to recognise the deception that hung on his every word like a disease. Her pride had been wounded. A small price to pay, she figured, for getting to the bottom of her uncle's murder.

If she was able to rid her mind of the patronising tone of the letter, the fury it awakened could work to her advantage in the end, she reasoned. Based on what Kirkcaldie had told her when they were last together, she would likely be outnumbered when she arrived at Harper's Creek. But she was skilled with a bow and as stealthy and fast as a cat. She was also quick-witted, a quality both Hill and Cool considered her to be lacking.

There was hope, she concluded in the end. But there was also terror so thick and brutal that it blanketed all the favourable thoughts that had sparked in her mind, beating them out like a brush fire.

WHEN THEY REACHED the path through the forest that led to Cool's settlement, Edie departed, flying high above the tree-tops. She would not go far, Tabby trusted, hoped. For the third time since she had left Vassalboro, she secured her bow across her shoulders and checked her quiver for its contents – six arrows – gaining a modicum of comfort as her fingers located the feathered fletching.

It was midday, Tabby guessed, when she lifted her eyes to the sky, hoping she might spy Edie in the distance. Despite the noontide sun, the woods were cool, cold even, with the treetop canopy acting as a parasol. Tabby felt herself shiver as she moved deeper into the forest. She hoped the cause was the increasing shade and not her mounting anxiety.

When she finally stepped into the clearing of Cool's settlement, she was immediately struck by sunlight, yet its warmth seemed to elude her.

All was quiet save the pigs who still snorted and rooted in the undergrowth beneath the cabins' windows. The area still reeked and there was no sign that a pit had been dug.

Tabby was disappointed her counsel had been ignored, although she was positive at the time of offering it that it would be. She was constantly surprised by the ineptitude of others and their inability to help themselves. Hopelessness was often borne from lack of intelligence, will or opportunity, but on Cool's part it was occasioned by sheer meanness.

Edging closer to Cool's cabin, the one she had seen the children enter on her previous visit, Tabby looked behind and around her. When she was in the middle of the clearing, the cabin door opened and Polly stepped out. She nursed a rifle in her thin, pale arms. Polly was wan and distant, as she had first appeared to Tabby when they had met at the Farnhams's, as though existing only in the narrow space between wake and sleep. She seemed as white and fragile as a snowflake. As far as Tabby could see, Polly was alone, but it was impossible to discern anything behind her through the skewed, blackened doorway.

'I am pleased to see you again, Polly,' Tabby said, struggling to keep her voice level. 'How are the children?' Tabby stepped closer and noticed a bruise, as ripe and purple as a damson around her eye. Polly raised the rifle slowly.

'Did Mister Cool give you that, Polly?' Tabby inquired, calmly, gesturing towards the girl's face. 'I have some comfrey ointment that will help.' Tabby placed her hand in her pocket. Polly cocked the rifle, nestling the butt in the hollow of her shoulder.

'He found the seeds you had me eating. Beat me black and blue.'

Tabby withdrew her hand from her pocket and licked her lips, nodding.

'Is your husband at home today?' Tabby asked, attempting to ignore the rifle aimed at her head. 'I came here today because I have heard he might be the bearer of information that I seek.' She took a breath. 'Perchance, you might know if General John Hill has arrived.'

Polly shook her head back and forth just once. She read warning in the girl's eyes and a single drop of hope fell on Tabby. Just one, but it felt like a waterfall. Polly was on her side.

Then Jeremy Cool emerged from behind his wife, out of the darkness of the cabin. There was a pistol clutched in his veiny hand.

'Good day to you, Mistress Post,' he said with a smile that was stiff and cruel. 'To what do we owe the pleasure?'

Tabby's eyes scanned the surrounds. Very gradually, more of Cool's disciples began emerging from their cabins, all of them chalky white with a faraway look to them. All armed, Tabby noted, every one of them. She wondered where they had procured the guns but then realised that it must be the trade Cool had been carrying with the Indians: opium for guns.

There was not a child in sight. While Tabby was grateful for this, there was also a palpable sense of foreboding that rode along with it. *What had Cool done with the children?* she wondered.

Tabby swallowed. She cleared her throat slightly before she spoke.

'I received a letter from General Hill, Mister Cool,' Tabby began. 'He believes you might have knowledge of how my uncle was killed.'

Cool took a step towards her. The urge to take a step back was powerful but Tabby stood her ground. There was a curious expression on his face that Tabby could not readily interpret. It was pleasure, she concluded after a moment. Cool was enjoying this confrontation. He had been waiting for it; she recognised the truth of this easily in his glaucous eyes.

'It was I who killed your uncle.'

Tabby was momentarily disorientated. It was what she had hoped to hear, but the words had not come from Cool. The voice came from behind her. It was a familiar voice, one that Tabby had not expected to hear in this place. The resonant, rounded tones struck a note of discord in Cool's environment like a note played off key. Tabby turned.

Achak stepped out of the woods.

For a moment Tabby could not draw breath. Her chest seized. Her throat followed suit and a dozen thoughts stammered and echoed in her mind. Achak. Riyogi had described him as being mercenary, once, long ago. But he had also saved Riyogi. He had spoken with such warmth and affection about her father. She had trusted every word that he had spoken.

'What? How?' she finally managed to utter in her confusion.

Cool sniggered derisively at her surprise.

Achak walked towards her. Tabby examined his form. What was once attractive and compelling now sickened her. Despite his physical stature and blood-borne authority, in Tabby's eyes he was just as repulsive as Cool.

'It is as I told you when we met.' He calmly remarked. His voice seemed to echo in the silence of the open clearing. 'But only up to a point.'

Tabby glared at him through narrow eyes. Her composure was returning as he moved closer. At the same time her fear was mounting. If fleeing was an option at that moment, she surely would have run. But she knew she could not outrun Achak, neither could she hide from him in the forest. He was an Indian, an expert tracker and he had not taken his eyes off her. For his part, Achak was aware of her skill with a bow and the fact that Edie was always near. He was not going to risk Tabby calling for her.

'Tell me the truth,' she said.

'The evening your uncle was killed, I was watching from the cover of the trees from the opposite side of the camp. When your uncle returned from the town after losing his money to Cool, it is the truth that he stole from his brother and handed Mister Cool your father's earnings. Cool turned to leave. It might have ended there, and I believed it would. To my mind, Ephraim would wake in the morning and he would chastise his brother, harshly. But all that would be lost would be money.

'What I had not expected was your uncle's courage. When Cool was almost safe under the cover of darkness, Ebenezer removed his knife from his belt and ran for Cool in a rage, intent on, if not murder, then retrieval of the funds. In that instant, I felt a surge of respect for Ebenezer Post. However, I stepped out of the trees and raised my rifle. Sadly, I was never a dead shot like your father. My weapon of choice is a throwing knife. I shot your uncle in the back three times before I was sure he was dead.'

Tabby looked from Achak to Cool, barely comprehending the words that had just spilled so easily and calmly from the Indian's mouth. Although she wanted to weep, fall to her knees and sob with the injustice of it, she stood firm.

'Why not Cool? Why didn't you kill *him*?' Tabby cried in shock. 'He is the thief! My uncle, for the first time in his life, was trying to make amends ...'

'Hill paid my salary. Cool was his middleman in the general's dealings with the Indians, French and English. I had to protect him.'

'He should have killed your father, too,' Cool added,

directing a curt nod in Achak's direction. 'If I had known what a meddlesome, irksome daughter he had, I surely would have put a shot in his head as well.'

Tabby threw a look of disgust at Cool. 'And the King of Spades?' Tabby asked Achak. She needed to know the depths of her gullibility.

'Cool was travelling with the troupe of performers Hill's men went to see that night. Cool was a jack-of-all-trades – a card sharp, musician, fortune teller. He even took stints, on occasion, as Captain Conjurer, the Tattooed Man'

Cool laughed at Tabby's puzzled look.

'The tattoos were painted onto his skin, Mistress Post,' Achak explained. 'They were not permanent. One of them was the King of Spades.'

Tabby shook her head in disbelief. She had been chasing a phantom.

'I did not think you would persist in your quest,' continued Achak. 'I have never met a woman, any individual in fact, who is as tenacious as you.'

Tabby sighed in exasperation. Tenacious she might be, but she had also been a dunderhead and she was momentarily embarrassed. *Why hadn't I thought of it? That the tattoo could have been a mere costume?* she wondered. *Yet how could I have known...*

And Achak. She had trusted him. At least now she knew the truth. Despite Achak's revelation of his involvement in her father's misery, despite all the pain and suffering Eb's rash, thoughtless actions had caused, Tabby gained some consolation from Achak's account of her uncle's bravery at the last.

'Did you travel to Moosehead Lake, Achak?' Tabby asked, defeated. She was expecting, even hoping, for a reply in the negative. 'Tell me the truth.'

He nodded solemnly. 'I did. That was not a lie. Your father was not to be found.'

Tabby's mind was fast unravelling. Pounded by the revelations, she could not consider the outcome of this meeting. To discover her uncle's killer had been her crusade since Matthew Hawkins had first spoken to her of Achak all those months ago and, whatever the consequences of her visit to Harper's Creek today, she still yearned for all the answers. Her mind in turmoil, she did not notice Cool until he took another step forward.

'You were Hill's go-between, his middleman ...' she said slowly, addressing Cool. 'You sold British guns to the French and the Indians, and vice versa, on his behalf. And Achak was paid to protect you.' Summarising the events aloud helped her to untangle the threads.

'Hill knew about this, didn't he? And yet he allowed my father to believe he was the killer, making up the story about the bear,'

'If I had known your father was a sharpshooter,' said Cool, 'I would have advised the general against such a tale. He knew of your father's talents so I can only credit panic with the flimsiness of his lie.'

Then Tabby remembered: Achak knew, too. She turned to the Indian who stood grimly beside Cool. Why had he not revealed the fact that Ephraim Post was a dead shot to Cool? Achak's values had been corrupted by Europeans years ago, but perhaps a shred of morality still clung like a drowning man to his native core. Had he purposefully left a thread untied, in the hope someone might find the truth?

Once she had woven the entire narrative in her mind, Tabby was surprised by the outrage that instantly rose in her like a pillar of fire.

'The devastation the two of you have caused is *colossal*,'

Tabby rebuked, flashing her eyes at Cool and Achak. 'Do either of you feel any remorse? Are you so stone-hearted?'

Achak lowered his eyes to the ground but Cool remained unrepentant. Tabby scanned the faces of his disciples, the enormity of Cool's crimes dawning on her like a light through the dark tatters of a nightmare. Although he had not pulled the trigger that night long ago, it was his actions, more than Achak's, that fuelled her ire.

'And you keep these poor people stupefied by the opium they are harvesting for you,' she said, gesturing to the others. 'Where are the children?' Tabby demanded.

Cool's mouth curled into a sly smile.

'They are working. Only their delicate fingers can squeeze the pods just so,' he pinched two fingers together less than an inch from Tabby's face. 'The opium drips from the pod like mother's milk.'

His words reeked of conceit and Tabby's belly swirled with bile. She turned to face Achak, hoping to find a shimmer of support in his dark eyes, but he was gone. He had vanished, phantom-like, into the trees. Spinning her body away from Cool to scan the surrounds, seeking out the Indian, her heart stopped when she felt the cold metal of Cool's gun against her temple. The scent of black powder filled her nostrils.

'I took you for a fool like your uncle, Mistress Post, or a do-gooder, too engaged with correcting all the superficial ills in the world that you were apt to look past the real ones. But you are neither and I stand corrected. And by the set of your jaw and the hate glistening in your pretty blue eyes, I doubt you will be silenced by threats of violence or offers of cash.

'But I admire your fire and I'd pay good money to see some more of it.' He wrapped his arm around her throat and lowered his voice. 'I have imagined that red hair of yours falling onto my chest. And I have imagined wrapping it around your neck like a rope, slowly tightening it until your eyes bulge and burst.' He plunged his nose into her hair and inhaled deeply.

Tabby had received worse threats but not from any man as vilely loathsome as Jeremy Cool. He would follow through on them, of that she was certain. Every urge in her insisted she look towards the sky for Edie. At the same time, every instinct screamed for her not to. Although it sickened her to do so, she turned slowly and fixed her gaze on Cool. His pale green eyes were marble.

'Mister Cool. Drop your pistol and let Tabby leave. No good will come of hurting her. She is widely known and her absence will be noticed.'

Cool spun towards Polly, clearly stunned by such a forthright voice coming from his wife's small mouth.

'You will not touch a hair on her head.'

Cool began to move towards his wife. Although Polly now had her rifle trained on her husband, Cool lifted his arm and pointed the pistol at Tabby. Before she could react, she heard Edie's familiar cry and the beat of her wings. Cool lifted his eyes towards the sound. Tear-shaped, the bird had begun her dive. Her intent was clear. In an instant, Cool redirected his aim and squinted against the sun. Tabby cried out to Edie to turn. Cool fired.

Like a flame blown out, life vanished in an instant. Edie plummeted to the ground and into the dirt.

Incandescent with fury, Tabby released a loud, monstrous groan then her rage exploded, consuming every ounce of her reason. She plucked an arrow from her quiver and set it in her bow in one seamless movement. She released the shaft before Cool had taken his eyes from his kill.

The arrow spiked his thin neck. Blood spilled from the wound in a torrent. It took a few seconds before he reacted, until he was alerted by a noise – it was the blood splashing on his boots and pooling at his feet. He fell to the ground.

Unable to move, Tabby stood with the bow in hand gulping air like it was water.

A moment later, she felt a hand on her shoulder. Startled, she turned. It was Mister Williams. She fell, like a mass of dead flesh, into his arms.

31

BOSTON
AUGUST 1725

'As soon as I was able, I rushed to Cool first, before Edie, even though my every instinct would have it otherwise. Despite my hatred of the wretch, I attempted to help him for no other person at the settlement hurried to his aid. But the blood was flowing fast from the wound and there was little I could do. I stared into those cold eyes of his as he gurgled through the blood in his throat. He was stunned, I believe, that I had done it.

'To be truthful, Sir, I was stunned myself. It was the sound Edie's body made when she fell onto the earth that triggered me: a dull *plod*. It was the sound of death and it set my spleen afire. I know that actions have consequences; if the consequence for mine is death then so be it. Cool had evil in him, he had terrorised a dozen people, raped and beaten his wife ... His crimes were countless. So, after an exceedingly and unexpectedly lengthy duration, when the final flicker of light was snuffed out in that man, I was glad of it.

'Over the years, on the Kennebec, I have been at the side of twenty-seven people as they lay dying, attempting to comfort their body as well as their soul. Yet there has been no other single instance that I can recall where I felt so satisfied with the job that Death had done.

'That is a reprehensible admission, Mistress Post,' Dummer commented.

Tabby nodded. 'At the beginning of this trial, Sir, you asked me how I accounted for my actions on July 16th of this year and I could not offer you a response. I still cannot. However, I have asked myself, if my fury had not blinded me, would I have drawn my bow? I have puzzled it over in my mind in the weeks since that day and the answer eludes me still.

'Cool's shot had struck Edie in her breast. I could barely see the wound through the speckled feathers. She was dead. I nursed her for an age as the loss settled in my chest like a brume. I was heartsick; I still am. And, as far as I know, there is no ready cure for that. Each time I recall the moment of her death it is as though my heart is being stepped on all over again.

'I cried and cried and, although I wiped my eyes, the tears would not cease. I cried so much that I thought my insides were going to burst out of my mouth. A cloud came across the world then and hushed the babel that my actions had ignited. I sat in the dirt; my arms heavy with Edie, stuck. She saved my life by sacrificing hers. How does a soul reconcile that? I had taken the life of Jeremy Cool but that was no recompense for the losses I have endured – not for my dearest friend, my uncle or for my father, who is gone in all manner of ways.

'As I sat holding Edie close to me, Mister Williams familiarised himself with the settlement. He informed me of this later as I was in no state for discourse at the time. He found the children in a cabin, huddled in the dim light squeezing the pods delicately, just as Cool had described. Mister Williams burned the poppy field and at least fifty blocks of opium he found in crates that had been buried in order to conceal them. The smoke billowed and blossomed above me like a great grey wreath. Not a soul tried to stop him.

'When I thought about this later, I concluded that the field had been a gaol of sorts for those poor people. Cool's death gave them their freedom. In the past, what had struck me about Cool's settlement was the silence. But as I sat in the dirt with Edie hugged to my breast watching Cool's ash blooms drift into the heavens, I began to hear the sounds of life. Polly was organising her few possessions and the children as they prepared to depart that godforsaken place, and there was movement and discussion. Life.

'Sir, to my mind, only good can come out of the death of a man like Jeremy Cool. As for Edie, nothing good has come from hers. My heart still aches for her every day, every minute. A dirge plays in my head constantly. The outcome of this trial matters little to me but I need the truth to be out.'

Dummer observed Tabby as she explained her position. He placed the tips of his fingers together in thought for several minutes before finally speaking.

'Mistress Post,' began Dummer. 'You admit to the murder and you admit to experiencing no regret following the incident. In fact, you admit to feeling a definite sense of satisfaction.'

'That is correct, Sir. You have heard Mister Palgrave Williams, Doctor William Douglass, Polly Cool and more than a handful of people speak to my good character. If you asked it of me, I could supply a hundred more people to attest to my honest and virtuous nature. What's more, I turned myself in, after travelling to Moosehead Lake to bestow on Edie a proper Indian burial –'

'However,' interrupted Dummer, 'the fact remains that you killed Jeremy Cool.'

'Yes,' confirmed Tabby. 'I won't deny it. And if I could go back in time to alter my actions, I can't say in all honesty that I wouldn't do the same.'

32

Kirkcaldie had watched the proceedings for the five days they endured, desperate to free her. Palgrave, who had been by his side for two of those days, possessed a similar urgency and was eager to execute a plan he had conceived. He knew the courthouse intimately, Palgrave confided. Eight years before, he had been consumed by the notion of freeing his friend had he stood among the condemned. He had considered his options at length.

'There is a door to the right, behind the court table. It leads into a storeroom where the prisoners are held,' he explained furtively. 'There is a further door, beyond the one leading to the outside.'

His scheme involved a distraction in the courtroom instigated by Palgrave, so, while the fracas was quieted, Kirkcaldie would have opportunity to sweep Tabby to freedom. While Palgrave's strategy was not ill-conceived – Kirkcaldie had similar ideas – he had sent him back to his home in Augusta immediately. If Palgrave was recognised as an accomplice, the loss of his friend's freedom would be too much for Kirkcaldie to bear.

Knowing Governor Dummer and General Hill were acquaintances – perchance more than acquaintances – Tabby had not mentioned all that she knew about the general during her testimony. Her words had been heartfelt and noble, so noble that Kirkcaldie was certain they would get her killed.

Tabby had testified that Cool had murdered her uncle. Cool's wife, a mealy-mouthed girl who Kirkcaldie remembered from the raid, had corroborated Tabby's story. But he knew the truth. *Why was Tabby protecting Achak?* he wondered. Kirkcaldie had asked her during a recess in the proceedings. Shrugging, Tabby had merely shaken her head. She had spoken of goodness and hope and hardships ... Loyalties were at play which Kirkcaldie did not comprehend and, although experience had taught him not to trust, he trusted Tabby in this. Loyalty was difficult to account for and often as beclouded as the winter sky.

However, the cold, hard, glaring fact remained that, despite her good works and her honourable character, in the court's eyes, Tabby was a woman who had slain a man in cold blood. It mattered not a jot that the man himself was a killer and worse.

Tabby was brave and, if need be, she would walk to the gibbet courageously. *But what good would that do the world?* Kirkcaldie asked himself.

After the killings, Tabby had returned to Augusta with Palgrave. Unable to part with Edie, she had kept her dear friend, secured tight in an Indian swaddle, with her on the journey; heartbroken, Tabby was, nevertheless, determined to bury Edie at Moosehead Lake. It was with this in mind that she allowed Palgrave to place Edie in his icehouse, until Tabby's tears ebbed enough to allow her to travel.

A few days later, when she had insisted on returning to

Moosehead Lake despite the Williamses' concern, Palgrave had advised her to remain there for a time, throughout winter and fall, perhaps recommencing her work the following spring. If Kirkcaldie's experience had proved anything it was that even the worst evils could be forgotten like waves on the sea. Eight years ago, Kirkcaldie had been the most wanted man in the colonies; now he was the governor's surveyor. But Tabby had refused. It was not confidence in the outcome of the trial that prompted her actions, it was her conscience.

For the fortnight Tabby was at Moosehead, Kirkcaldie remained at his home, completing his wall. He could not recall being as focused for some time, so utterly determined was he to finish the task. It was as though Tabby's life depended on it.

In the building of that wall, working with his hands had cleared his mind and he was able to construct the foundations of a plan of his own. The first thing he had done was to ask Palgrave to be discreet – the more people who knew Samuel Bellamy was alive, the greater the chance of his identity being discovered. Even Leah could not know.

Maria had vowed to keep his secret, too, however, there was a cost to her silence. It had taken him by surprise, but he had reasoned that it was perhaps not excessive, given what she had endured in the many years of his absence.

However, he could still not explain their encounter in the woods. *How was I drawn to that glade?* he asked himself time and time again. Waking that night, he had thought he had heard the call of a woman. Lying in the darkness, he waited, anxious, tense until he heard the sound a second time. When he did not, he presumed that it was merely the wind howling as it roamed among the pines. But when he settled, he could not find sleep. What possessed him to then leave his bed, saddle his horse and ride into the woods, he could not discern.

He rode for hours before finding himself approaching Augusta. The thought came to him as he neared the town that he was riding towards Tabby. But when he entered the glade, he saw someone else.

Maria.

It was as if she had been waiting for him. The shock halted his journey.

They spoke at length. She told him of the trials she had endured after he departed Eastham. She told him of Silas and of the child she had lost, the child who had come into the world inside a gaol cell.

Kirkcaldie listened but did not offer comfort. He could discern from her sober tone and the precision with which she related events that she was past consolation. Their meeting, her story and the events of that night demonstrated to him that she was much changed from the girl he had known in Eastham.

In the weeks since then, Kirkcaldie had brooded on the idea that it was his departure that had occasioned her altered humour. He struggled to convince himself otherwise – their affection had been so fleeting. Yet he *had* made promises.

Then there was Tabby. He knew not what lengths he would go to for this woman to whom no promises had been made. *Would I risk my hard-won freedom?* he wondered.

On the day he finished the wall, he had wiped his brow and stood back to reflect on its construction. If Tabby was convicted and sentenced to hang, he would save her. He had decided as much in the moment he laid the final piece of bluestone in its place. The authorities would never suspect the governor's surveyor of snatching her and concealing her.

Kirkcaldie felt sure that after a period, they could begin again, together.

Before acting on his decision, there was John to consider. Kirkcaldie wrote a note, sealed it with wax and propped it on the mantelpiece above the hearth for the boy to find, although he was a boy no more. He was now a young man, a scholar. A man of Law. He was proud of John; he was his mother's son – shrewd, resourceful, wise.

Now, as he sat in the court room, Kircaldie could feel the weight of the last puzzle piece in his hands, its jutting angles and soothing curves. His plan was to wait until she was being transported to the gaol. One woman alone would warrant just one guard, surely. Still, he could manage two or three if they were the typical breed of red coat – pot-bellied or scrawny, helpless in a brawl.

Kirkcaldie's contemplation was interrupted after less than forty minutes when Dummer and the magistrates returned to the room. He placed his watch in his pocket, doubtful such short deliberations would lead to a positive outcome.

Tabby rose and bowed her head, acknowledging the presence of the officials.

The governor waited for the crowd to silence. Men shifted along the pews to their seats or jostled for a standing place. Dummer cleared his throat.

'It is the decision of the court that Mistress Tabitha Post be pardoned of the crime of the murder of Mister Jeremy Cool.'

Simultaneously, the onlookers gasped. Chatter threatened to drown out the remainder of Dummer's verdict. Tabby looked the governor's way in astonishment. She watched him as he waited, rigid-faced, for several minutes for the murmurs in the courtroom to cease.

'Mistress Post was aware of Jeremy Cool's violent nature. Therefore, with ample reason, she was in fear for her own life and the wellbeing of the children who lived on the property. The court is in agreement that she did not act maliciously or for gain. Mistress Post, under English law, has the right to protect herself from injury and harm. We feel that Mistress Post acted within the boundaries of the law. Therefore, she is pardoned.'

Kirkcaldie kept his eyes on Tabby throughout the verdict. Her chest heaved in relief and he could see the blood drain from her face.

'You are free to leave, Mistress Post,' announced Dummer.

Fearing Tabby might faint, the moment Dummer concluded Kirkcaldie shouldered his way through the audience who, stunned themselves, were milling about like ants. When he reached her, he took her hand. It was as cold as clay.

'I was certain I would hang,' she said slowly.

Kirkcaldie nodded.

'I had prepared myself. For a long time, I have considered myself in tune with life and death. There is a harmony between these two states. I felt I was ready to enter the latter having gained so immensely from the former.'

He reached his arm around her and lifted her to her feet, knowing what she was experiencing, the shock of it. Kirkcaldie had prepared himself for certain death many times. It was an odd sensation to be living when you had convinced yourself you would be no more; an odd mingling of release and distress that events had not adhered to the plan.

'I have seen plenty of death,' she went on, strangely calm now. 'But over the years I have thought little of my own.

Even when Jeremy Cool held a gun to my head, I had not really thought about dying.'

Kirkcaldie drew her closer, attempting to closet her from the spectators but she looked only at him.

'Watching Jeremy Cool die showed me that death can be long and slow and painful.' Tabby blinked up at him. She appeared to be in a trance-like state. 'Tell truth, by the time his eyes went dull, I was bored by it.'

He tried to hush her, hoping no-one would hear, and guided her to the back door of the courthouse. It was the door to the storeroom that Palgrave had located as a means of escape.

'I had never thought my end would come from hanging ... Falling through the ice, perhaps, or ... In those minutes when Dummer and the magistrates were deciding my fate, I had not thought of God at all. I tried to think of Him. But I could not.'

Successfully ushering her out of the courtroom, Kirk-caldie closed the door and took her in his arms, squeezing her, relishing the sensation of her.

'Why?' she whispered. 'The verdict seemed so certain. Why, Kirkcaldie?'

'It is just as Dummer explained. You were merely defending yourself in the face of an individual you knew to be capable of great brutality.'

She shook her head. To her, it made no sense. Why would the governor and his cronies burden the colony with the effort and expense of a trial? Why wear a mask of unbending, rigid rule if they had resolved to pardon her? Tabby had not pleaded self-defence at any time. Her motives were born from white-hot fury. To this she had confessed. Dummer's mortification at her candour, only moments before his final verdict, indicated to her – and, she had supposed, to all – that she would hang.

'I will take you back to the Williamses' house, Tabby. You can tarry there for a day or two, until you are feeling entirely yourself.'

Kirkcaldie opened the door onto a narrow alley, but then took a step back.

They were not alone. Ben was waiting there.

Kirkcaldie stared, unsure what to do, as the young doctor removed his hat.

33

———

The three remained silent for a moment. Fall was beginning to show its face in the amber leaves eddying around their feet. Tabby shivered.

'Kirkcaldie,' Ben said finally, offering a slight bow.

'Doctor,' Kirkcaldie replied. 'We are leaving for Augusta. Mister Williams and his wife are keen to care for Tabby's needs for as long as is required. Would you care to join us? I am conscious of the failing light and it is quite a long journey.'

'Thank you for the offer, Mister Kirkcaldie, but I fear I must decline. I am about to embark on rather a long journey myself.'

Tabby looked at him, confused

'If you would permit me just a few moments alone with Mistress Post, I would be forever grateful.'

Kirkcaldie nodded then turned to Tabby. 'I have a gig and horses waiting at the smithy's around the corner. I will meet you there when you are ready.' Then he took his leave.

'Journey?' Tabby inquired immediately when Kirkcaldie was out of sight.

Clearly nervous, Ben fingered the brim of his hat. He licked his lips before he spoke.

'I am joining Governor Dummer's forces in New France. I must be in Quebec by Thursday. I have scant time for farewells.'

'What do you mean? As a doctor?'

'No, as a soldier. A lieutenant, in fact.' He smiled, an uncomfortable grimace that answered all her questions.

She breathed in, her eyes fixing on a flurry of chestnut-coloured leaves.

'You negotiated my pardon,' she said, looking at him. Although her mind was working quickly, she spoke slowly. 'Your name ... Your father ...' She frowned in concentration. 'You asked your father to use his influence with Dummer and in return you granted his only ambition for his son; you agreed to join the army.'

Ben reached for her, but she swatted his hand away in annoyance.

'I will not have it! I will not allow it!'

She stormed a few paces along the alleyway and screamed in frustration, her torment mirrored in the whirlpool of fallen leaves. It was as though she was one of them, suddenly unstuck, displaced, caught in a force over which she had no control.

'But you must, darling Tabby. It was settled early this morning.'

He went to her, gently touching her hair.

'I could not bear to see you imprisoned. And the thought of you hanging ...' He took a deep breath. 'To sacrifice medicine is such a meagre price for your life.'

Once her anger quelled, tears pooled in her eyes then soon began falling over her pale cheeks in a soft, flowing stream. He wiped each droplet away gently as though her skin were the finest parchment.

'To ask you to follow me, to be my wife, would be futile, for I know that you would not. It is gratification enough that you are shedding these tears for me. But I live in hope that one day, in the future, you might love me.'

Now that she had calmed, she had no words. No-one – no *person* – had sacrificed so much for her. How could she live with the burden? The gallows would have been preferable.

Ben embraced her, hoping to drink in the feel of her, the musky scent of her before he departed. He kissed her forehead lightly then, with a fortifying sigh, walked away.

Tabby watched his route along the alleyway. She touched her forehead, still tingling from his kiss, wishing that the press of his lips would remain there forever. When he reached the crossroad, he fixed his hat on his head, turned the corner and was gone.

Kirkcaldie prepared the horses and the gig. He paid the blacksmith then sat waiting for Tabby, checking his pocket watch every few minutes. After a half hour, a time he considered adequate for a farewell, he returned to the alleyway where he had left Tabby with Benjamin Shute.

As he turned the corner, he froze.

There was no-one in sight.

AFTERWORD

When I wrote *The Hummingbird and the Sea*, it was intended as a standalone novel. You see, historians believe Samuel Bellamy did die when the *Whydah* was wrecked off the Cape Cod coast in 1717. However, even when I first learnt of the existence of the pirate "Black Sam" Bellamy (see *The Hummingbird and the Sea* afterword) and his fate, I wondered: *If his body was never found, can anyone be certain that he actually died? What if Sam Bellamy simply remained dead to the world forever?* These musings led me, after four years, to consider a sequel.

That's when the idea of *The Falconer* was born. Now, when I read the book, *The Falconer* is so clearly Tabby's story. But the original first chapter described Sam and John building a new life for themselves in the colony.

One day, as I was writing, I stopped to research a natural remedy John was concocting to heal one of Bellamy's many wounds. This is when I came across the story of Martha Ballard, a midwife (in the 18th century the term 'midwife' meant healer, too) who worked along the Kennebec River in Maine between 1785 and 1812. I went on to read historian,

Laurel Thatcher Ulrich's *The Midwife's Tale*, a work of non-fiction that blends Ballard's colourful diary entries with Ulrich's commentary. Martha Ballard though, is nothing like Tabby Post except for the fact that she travelled the river in a canoe, dedicated to providing settlers with excellent medical care.

Tabby Post took shape in my mind as a fiercely independent, white midwife and healer who lives with the Indians from whom she draws much of her healing know-how. Bellamy was pushed to the background and into hiding - just the way he likes it! However, that original first chapter was not to be wasted. It now features in Book 3, *The Lark's Call*.

Many of the townships Tabby visited along the Kennebec River, as she was seeing to the pregnant, ill and needy, may not be seen on a map today. If they existed at all, they might have been in a different location in 1725. In fact, there were very few townships named on maps of the time! As a result, if you are a reader from Maine and surrounds, you might find some discrepancies. I've taken some creative licence, inventing names for certain locations Tabby visits for the benefit of the storyline.

ACKNOWLEDGMENTS

Thank you so much for reading Tabby's story. I hope you found her journey engaging, moving and inspiring. I wish there were more women like Tabby Post in the world today.

As always, I would like to give great thanks to my editor, Sylvia Balog, who I am so fortunate to have found, and my proofreader and friend, Jo Egan. And finally, my husband Chris, whose enduring support, encouragement and IT problem-solving skills I could not do without.

ALSO BY JENNY BOND

HISTORICAL FICTION AVAILABLE AT
WWW.JENNYBONDBOOKS.COM

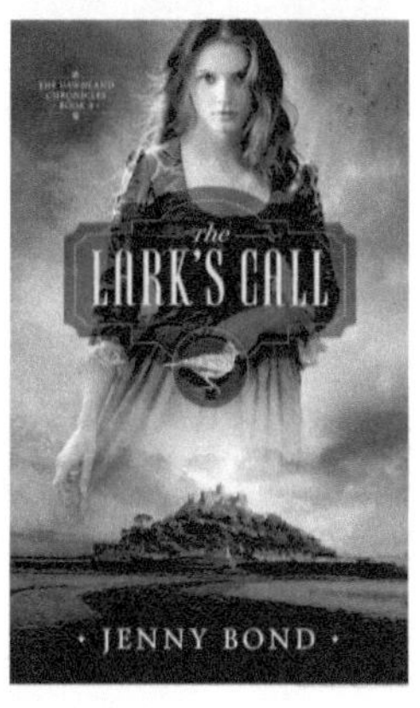

A compelling novel of intrigue, love, loss and redemption that spanned a lifetime ... inspired by true events
JENNY BOND
Perfect North

THE PRESIDENT'S LUNCH
Will a chance encounter change her life forever?
JENNY BOND

ALSO BY JENNY BOND

CONTEMPORARY FICTION AVAILABLE AT
WWW.JENNYBONDBOOKS.COM

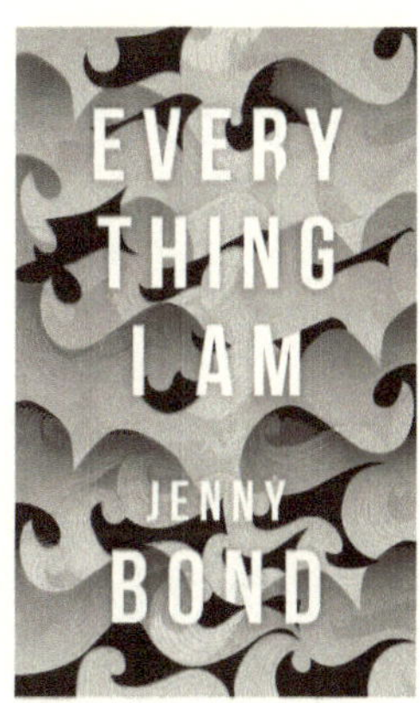

ENJOYED THE FALCONER?

T hanks for reading *The Falconer*. If you enjoyed the story, share a review where you bought the book, on Goodreads, or contact me at jennybondbooks.com and share your thoughts.

FREE SHORT STORY
THE FALCONER

Get a free copy of *Lake Champlain* when you sign up for my newsletter via this link: https://BookHip.com/JVZVRKX

You'll also be notified of giveaways and new releases and receive updates of my author journey

FLY FURTHER INTO THE WORLD OF THE FALCONER

Check out my Pinterest board for the novel - images that provided inspiration and information during the writing process.

~

Listen to the Spotify playlist of the novel. Music, past and present, aimed to reflect the themes and atmosphere of the story.

~

To access either of the above, on the relevant platform search 'jennybondbooks'.

SAMPLE CHAPTER BOOK 3

THE LARK'S CALL

When Tamesine reached the top of the carn, she was breathless. Her chest ached and her face still rippled with the force of her father's slap. Drawing in deep breaths, she wiped the tears and perspiration away with the flat of her hands. She looked at them, noticing a rosy tinge to the palette of her palms. Blood. Sitting on a rock overlooking Penzance and St Michael's Mount, she buried her head in her apron. Although she wanted to, needed to, it was impossible to stem the flow of tears that followed.

Tamesine tolerated the beatings because she had to, because her mother had tolerated them for years. Even at fifteen, she knew her father was not angry with her or her mother. He had been tied to a lugger – never his own – since he was a boy. Other fisherman in Madron loved the sea and life on a boat. Cleaning pilchards at the bay, Tamesine had heard these men regale in the life, sharing tales and memories as they mended driftnets. Her father was never one to join them, preferring to retreat to the alehouse as soon as his work was done. She often wondered what life he had dreamt for when he had been a young, soft-skinned boy.

Now his hands were chafed, his face gnawed to rags by wind, salt and rain.

She tolerated her father's anger because she understood the limits of his life and recognised his frustration – they mirrored her own. And they were choking. Tamesine looked at her blood-tinged hands, her heart saddening at the sight of them; they were already pink and raw from years of hard labour.

Few gifts were in her possession. All the village spoke of her beauty and she knew she was clever, learning numbers and letters at the knee of her granny when not yet five. But unless she married well, which was unlikely due to her humble family, her future was bleak. In her fantasies, Tamesine had been swept off her feet any number of times by the handsome son of the noble family who lived on St Michael's Mount. But these were just imaginings. Coal or fish were her choices. One day, she would be as angry as her father.

After a time, her tears stopped. Rising, she drew a bolstering breath and fixed her shawl around her shoulders. It was June but the wind blowing across the carn from Mount's Bay was as cold as a dog's nose.

She turned in a circle, taking in the bay and the seemingly endless moor, and noticed her sister striding towards her. Eseld's gait was unmistakeable. Not yet ten years old, she was already as tall as her older sister. Tamesine admired her gracefulness and poise. Eseld was the other reason Tamesine tolerated her father's furies; he had never laid a hand on the girl and Tamesine feared if she protested at her own mistreatment, fought back in any way, he might turn on her precious sister.

Eseld said nothing when she approached, but Tamesine noticed she was holding a cap. Tamesine's hand went to her head. In her bitter sorrow, she had not noticed hers had been lost on her frenzied journey up the carn, probably plucked from her head by the mossy branch of a hawthorn tree. Eseld kept the cap clutched in her reedy fingers and slid her long slender arms around her sister's waist as if they were elegant ribbons. The pair embraced for some time before Eseld passed her the cap. Then she stood back and examined Tamesine's face.

'It's not noticeable,' she said, her voice small against the wind. 'Was there blood?'

'A little.'

Eseld nodded, concerned but unsurprised.

Tamesine's thick auburn hair blew like banners in the wind.

'It is wild,' Eseld laughed at the sight. The sound lifted Tamesine's spirits. 'As wild as the breeze that blows it.'

Tamesine secured her cap then took her sister's hand.

'*Meur ras*,' she said, smiling, wincing. Her lip stung. It was only the fisherman and their families who spoke Cornish now. Even Tamesine and Eseld were speaking it less often to each other.

'You are most welcome, m'lady,' Eseld replied, offering her sister a low, courtly bow. It was a game they often played to cheer their spirits – 'm'lady and m'lord'. Although their father did not approve, they felt there was no harm in pretending.

'I have been sent to seek you out,' Eseld continued in a cultured voice. 'A third rate ship of the line has laid anchor in Penzance harbour. The captain has requested permission to come ashore.'

'Is that so?' Tamesine replied lifting her chin haughtily and rubbing her hand theatrically across it, contemplating the appeal.

'As high sheriff, you are the only person in the land who can grant his request.'

'Escort me to the ... what is this ship's name, m'lord?' Tamesine inquired, looking down her nose with distaste.

'The *Greyhound*, m'lady,' Eseld answered with a slight bow.

'Then pray escort me to the *Greyhound* ...'

With a small flourish, Eseld offered her arm. Tamesine accepted it with a gracious nod before continuing.

'... and we shall see if this captain is worthy of stepping foot onto our blessed shore.'

Eseld bowed again then the two made their way through the soft, lush heather towards to the harbour.

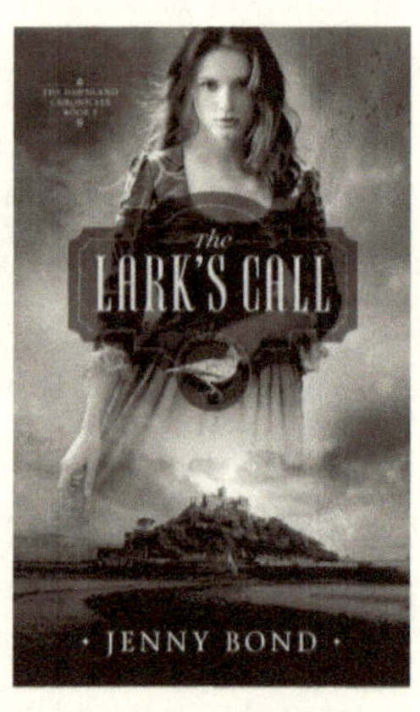

Available at www.jennybondbooks.com

ABOUT THE AUTHOR

I'm an author of contemporary fiction, historical fiction and non-fiction. I have published my books in Australia, New Zealand, USA and Europe.

I'm also an English teacher and I've been lucky enough to introduce the love of language to many students around the world.

I guess this also planted the seed of an idea that I should give writing a go, myself

Sydney, Australia, is where I was born and raised, but prior to my reinvention as a writer (which had something to do with a friendly argument with my husband!), I held the position of Head of English at Eaton House The Manor in London's Clapham Common. I also taught English and Drama for eight years at a selective high school in Sydney, and for five years at a private girls' college in Canberra.

Whether I've been at home, living and working in another country, or travelling for the sake of adventure, I have never spent a single day without a book by my side. This meant slipping from the act of reading into the act of writing didn't actually seem that much of a change.

I've long been a fan of great historical fiction writers such as Hilary Mantel, but I also spend quality time with books by authors from other genres, such as Margaret Atwood, Kate Atkinson, Tim Winton, Ian McEwan, Jane Austen, John Irving and E. Annie Proulx.

When I'm not writing, I enjoy keeping fit and love to

travel. I live in Canberra, Australia with my husband, two sons, and a lively Staffordshire Bull Terrier named Mick.

I enjoy running, swimming and yoga daily, as I believe staying active is an integral component of a happy writing life. You can visit me at www.jennybondbooks.com.au.

Jenny